A 'Killer Pick'
by the Independent Mystery Booksellers Assoc.

"One of the most intriguing and original ideas for a mystery novel I've read all year!"
— Zoë Sharp, author of the Charlie Fox crime thriller series

"Troy Cook's debut novel is a rarity. From such an auspicious start, one can only imagine how good he may become. Did someone say Edgar?"
— I Love a Mystery

"The twists and laughs keep coming in this highly entertaining debut. A Pick of the Week."
— Sarah Weinman, Confessions of an Idiosyncratic Mind

"A wild west romp of a novel."
— Maggie Mason, Deadly Pleasures

"A fun book from a talented author. And if you can't find it in your bookstore, check the 'self help' section."
— Crimespree Magazine

"Racy fun, peopled with strange and wonderful characters."
— Mystery Scene Magazine

"A cracking good read. Cook can write crackling good dialogue and tell a damn good yarn. I took it on a long train journey and resented having to get off at my stop as I was enjoying the book so much. Take this to the beach with you, or just recline in your front room with it and enjoy the crazy, switchback ride.
— Reviewing the Evidence

"Will keep you turning the pages. This is no ordinary mystery."
— ForeWord Magazine

"A gem."
— Ind. Mystery Booksellers

"Well written, clever, and laugh (
— Stacy Alesi, Bookbitch.cc

"You'll find yourself cheering. . .a high speed adrenaline filled crime caper novel of the 1st degree. Exceedingly delightful. . .a resplendent job of weaving delightfully droll bits of humor throughout the story. A terrific debut."
— Spinetingler Magazine

"In this hilarious debut, Troy Cook proves himself worthy to join the likes of such masters of the comic thriller as Carl Hiaasen and Lawrence Shames."
— I Love A Mystery Bookstore

"A fabulous first novel. Based on a cleverly cynical premise, from the first page to the last the story never bogs down."
— Gumshoe Review

"This is great crime noir, bleached by the Arizona sun."
— Mysterious Galaxy Books

"A delightful concoction."
— Harriet Klausner, reviewer

"A fast and funny romp through the criminal world."
— Sleuth of Baker Street Bookstore

"Light-hearted, fast-moving fare—a good summer read."
— Mystery Morgue

"This is a mystery, not a how-to book."
— Bookreporter

"Cook writes with a director's eye, each scene choreographed for optimal effect. A cast of painfully funny characters weaves throughout the story... a remarkable fresh spin on the Bonnie and Clyde-style that was a pleasure to read."
— Futures Mystery Anthology Magazine

"Humor with mystery is a difficult balancing act, a feat for even the most seasoned writer; nonetheless, Cook manages to cleverly pull it off."
— Book Pleasures

47 Rules
of
Highly Effective
Bank Robbers

47 RULES
OF
HIGHLY EFFECTIVE
BANK ROBBERS

TROY COOK

CAPITAL CRIME PRESS

Second printing November 2006.

Published in the United States by Capital Crime Press, Fort Collins, Colorado

Capital Crime Press is a registered trademark

Library of Congress Catalog Card Number: 2005938853
ISBN-13: 978-0-9776276-6-0
ISBN-10: 0-9776276-6-7

www.capitalcrimepress.com

Thanks go to Lori, Jeff, Su, Ellen, Marjorie, Ed, and Bob for their help with the writing and editing process.

Special thanks to Mom and Dad—for raising me—and for their help with the whole writing experience.

And a very special thanks to Cheryl and Ian. Without their love and support, none of this would be possible.

This book is dedicated to my brother,
in loving memory.

Thanks for making us laugh.

CHAPTER 1

At the tender age of nine, Tara Evans was one of the youngest bank robbers in history. At least, that's what they said on TV. But they also called her the "Crying Bandit," and she didn't care for that at all. She'd tried *really* hard not to cry.

She snuck a glance at her daddy as he drove the car. He didn't like the nickname. And he definitely didn't like it when she cried.

At a bump in the road, her gaze drifted to the seat between them. She frowned—her Barbie doll sat right next to her daddy's gun. *That's not good.* She snatched the doll away, rescuing it from the creepy thing.

Daddy stopped the car in front of the Federal Savings and Loan and tossed a Lone Ranger mask and hat onto her lap. "Time to get ready," he said.

"Okay, Daddy."

He gave her a glare. "Now what have I told you?"

Tara put her hand over her mouth. He hated to be called Daddy! Ever since Mama died. And it wasn't good to make him angry. "I'm sorry...Wyatt. It's hard to remember."

Wyatt grinned. "No problem, sugar. Just do your best. And hide that thick mop. This is it."

Oh, boy. Here we go again. She shoved her long, dark hair under the hat. It didn't want to fit but she finally managed.

Putting on the mask, she glanced in the visor mirror and giggled. The mask was way too large for her tiny face.

Through the eyeholes, she watched her daddy...Wyatt... stretch pantyhose over his face and slide a clip into his gun. He grabbed the Barbie from her and pulled a couple of Ken dolls from under the seat. One Ken wore a police uniform. The other was scuffed up and had a beard drawn on its face with a marker.

"Now remember," he said. "The guard will be to the left."

Tara watched with great concentration as Wyatt walked Scruffy Ken and Barbie over toward Guard Ken. Then she frowned. "Why doesn't Barbie have a mask on, like me?"

Wyatt grumbled, then pulled a marker from his pocket. He drew a mask on Barbie's face. "Is that better?"

Tara clapped and bobbed her head in agreement.

"You keep your gun pointed straight at him and say anything you want. The crazier the better." He walked Scruffy Ken away from the other two dolls. "Now I'm going to the teller to grab the money. If the guard makes a move, you yell out for me, okay?"

He took Scruffy Ken and Barbie and hopped them across the front seat, then tossed them into the back. Tara giggled.

"Questions?" he asked.

"Yeah, how come they don't make a Bank Robber Barbie?" Tara said.

Wyatt's lower lip quivered and his eyes closed to a squint. "Now don't get me started! You might as well ask why they make her with a female form of impossible proportions. It just ain't natural!"

He grabbed a revolver from the glove compartment and swung open the cylinder. "It's that damn Corporate America! They're trying to warp your fragile little mind." He spun the revolver's chambers, clicked it shut, and handed her the gun.

It was so heavy! Wyatt continued preaching but she ignored him, staring at the gun in her hand. She didn't think she could do this! The last time had been a disaster, or close enough.

She looked at her daddy. His attention was elsewhere,

but on his burly arm a familiar tattoo stared back at her. And below the bug-eyed skull it said "SCHIZO." That was his nickname—that or Preacher, on account of how much he went on and on about his favorite topics.

Wyatt paused and gazed at her with a puzzled expression. He leaned over and lightly slapped her across the face—a love tap. "Wake up, girl. What's the matter with you? This here's important stuff, so pay attention."

Tara hesitated. "This isn't gonna work. Nobody will ever think I could shoot somebody."

He raised the pantyhose to his forehead. She smiled, because he looked kind of like a floppy-eared bunny—if bunnies weighed two-fifty and had major five-o'clock shadow.

"They *will* take you seriously if you do as I say. The crazier you are, the more respect you get. This is one of life's lessons here, so remember it. All right?"

Tara nodded.

He sighed and took hold of her shoulders. "I'm doing this for you, baby. I'm trying to teach you a trade…something that will bring you wealth and happiness."

Tara smiled. "I'm sorry, Wyatt. I'll do better this time."

He grinned and said, "That's my girl. I know you'll make me proud."

Wyatt pulled the pantyhose over his face and slipped a duffel bag over his shoulder, then cracked open the car door. He stopped, leaned real close and grabbed her chin. She could feel his hot breath.

"Now I don't want to see a single tear. I don't care what happens in there. You don't cry! That was embarrassing last time."

Tara nodded and they both got out of the car. *I can do this,* she thought.

She followed him up the steps and toward the door, gun at the ready, but paused as she caught her reflection in the plate-glass window. The mask was too big, but overall she thought she looked pretty. The gun made her look kind of grown-up, too. Sophisticated, maybe. She wasn't quite sure what that word meant, but it sounded right.

And Wyatt *wanted* her to be more grown-up. He'd said so just the other day. It was probably why he didn't want her shedding any more tears. She was pretty sure that grown-ups never cried. At least, not that she'd ever seen.

"Don't stand there gawking," Wyatt said. He pointed two fingers toward his eyes. "Stay focused or we could be in a world of hurt. You know what I mean?"

Tara cocked her head to the side, confused.

"I mean there'd be trouble. The kind of trouble where I could get hurt or the two of us could get caught. And if that happens they'll take you away from me and you'll never get to see me again."

Tara leapt into his arms and gave him a big squeeze. "I'll do a good job, I promise. I don't ever want them to take you away." She gave him a kiss on his pantyhose-covered face.

Wyatt kissed her back, put her on the ground, and pulled his gun out. "All right. Now don't ever get in the way of my gun hand, in case I have to draw it quickly. We're gonna have to come up with some rules after this one."

He yanked open the door. "Let's go."

Wyatt stormed into the bank, brandishing his gun. "Everyone down on your knees and get your hands where I can see them. This here's a robbery."

He grabbed the lone, elderly security guard and pushed the gun into his nostril. "You give my son here any problems and there'll be hell to pay. I guarantee it."

The man nodded slowly. Wyatt removed the guard's weapon from its holster and tossed it across the floor, into a corner.

Tara ran up to the guard, her little shoes skidding as she stopped about seven feet away. Remembering Wyatt's instructions about acting crazy, she growled as ferociously as a nine-year-old could and pointed her gun squarely at the guard. She tried very hard to hold it steady.

Wyatt looked at her and pointed his fingers toward his

eyes again. He mouthed the words "stay focused" and ran toward the tellers.

Tara let out a small yelp, growled again, and shook her gun at the guard. It was working! He actually looked scared.

Wyatt waved his gun toward the blond female teller. "Hey sugar, why don't you give me some of that cash there? Nice and easy, all right?"

The flustered teller grabbed her purse and thrust it at Wyatt.

"Are you insane, lady, or just one of those perky, dumb blondes?" Wyatt threw the purse across the room and jumped up on the counter, waving the gun wildly. "Do you think I would come inside a bank to rob you of your own personal stash? I want the bank's money." He tossed her the duffel bag and she began filling it from her drawer.

He turned back to the customers. "Now class, do any of you know what happens to a bank when it gets robbed? Anyone?"

Unprepared for a pop quiz, the customers shuffled their feet and looked at the ground. He pointed the gun at a lady customer and cocked it. "Any idea?"

The lady, unhappy with the attention bestowed upon her, promptly fainted.

Wyatt looked over at Tara and winked. He turned back to the group. "Well, I'll tell you. Absolutely nothing. They fill out an insurance claim and get paid back every cent. It's a win-win situation. The only people to get screwed here are the God-damned insurance companies. And does anybody deserve it more? I don't think so."

He pointed his gun toward the tellers. "Well, of course, any idiots who get in my way deserve it too, so hurry up with my damn money!"

Wyatt jumped off the counter and pounded his fist onto its hard surface, startling everyone. "Just thinking about these fucking insurance companies makes my blood boil! You know what's wrong with those pieces of..."

Tara had been splitting her attention between the guard

and Wyatt's antics. But when he started ranting about the insurance companies she tuned him out, having heard it all many a time before.

She focused all her attention on the guard, like Wyatt had said, but noticed that something seemed different. The guard had moved about a foot closer. *Not good.*

Tara waggled the gun toward him. "You stay back now, you hear?"

The guard didn't look scared anymore. He gave a big smile—looking friendly—and she knew she was in trouble. She thought about calling out to her daddy but figured she should try to stop him herself. Then he'd be real proud of her.

She growled again.

But the guard kept inching forward. "Hey sonny, you be careful with that gun, all right?"

This was getting bad. She had to do something.

She remembered that lady fainting when Wyatt cocked his gun, so she decided to try the same thing. The guard stopped dead in his tracks. Wow, that sound was like magic.

She backed up a step so the man wouldn't be too close, but he kept with her, taking another step forward. She gave out a little scream, again, and yelled, "I'm warning you, now. Don't make me shoot you!"

Wyatt turned toward the commotion and pointed his gun at the guard. But he held off, waiting to see if his little pumpkin could handle it herself.

Tara started to panic. The guard was still moving toward her. She'd screamed, she'd cocked the gun, she'd growled. She didn't know what else to do—the guard was almost to her. So she closed her eyes and squeezed the trigger.

The gun roared, kicking so hard that she nearly dropped it. People screamed. The guard dropped to the floor, untouched and unhurt, but extremely frightened. He cowered on the ground, rolling around and covering his ears, saying he was sorry over and over again.

I did it. I stopped him.

Tara glanced over to Wyatt, hoping to see an amazed and

proud dad. Instead, he was clenching his teeth, grimacing. His right shoe had a blackened hole in it and blood was escaping onto the floor.

Her eyes started to fill with tears.

"Don't you do it, God damn it!" Wyatt shouted. He grabbed the duffel bag and limped over to her, trailing blood. "I've been shot and you don't see me crying, do you?"

Tara's chin quivered. "No."

"Good job." He grabbed her chin tenderly. "That wasn't your fault. You did great. We just need to get you some target practice."

Tara stifled her tears and gave him a little smile. That was the most praise he'd ever given her.

Wyatt turned back to the crowd. "All right, class. Good job. You all get an 'A' for your cooperation. And you know what that means?"

A few people shook their heads.

Wyatt gave them a wink. "It means no one has to die."

CHAPTER 2

Rule #1: Your gun is your friend! And one of the best friends you'll ever have, so take good care of him. Treat him proper and he'll protect you. But there's only one way...only one God-damned way to shoot a gun. With your eyes wide OPEN. And no tears, either. You do this right and everyone's happy. Do it wrong and I'll be getting stitches at the vet again. If that happens, no one's happy. I guarantee it.

Thirteen years later—Texas

Escaping the nasty scene at the Del Rio branch of First Nationwide Bank was Tara's first priority, but as she burst out the door she wondered—and not for the first time—if her daddy might actually be a homicidal maniac after all. She'd always given him the benefit of the doubt, but lately that was getting harder and harder.

Tara ran down the steps in her cowboy getup and fake mustache, cursing up a storm.

Top speed was essential, what with the alarms ringing at a deafening pitch. She reached the getaway vehicle first, a "borrowed" Chevy Malibu, and slid into the passenger side.

She watched with amusement as Wyatt, in his ridiculous ten-gallon hat, followed in her wake. His oversized frame wasn't built for running, and so he usually didn't when he was on the job. But this time things had gone to hell in a hand basket, so he was doing his damnedest. His fists pumped madly, and his snakeskin boots shuddered with each footfall as he rumbled toward the car.

Two ticks later they were on their way, keeping the Malibu just under the speed limit—attention being the last thing they wanted at this particular point.

Tara narrowed her gaze, thinking of Wyatt's exit line at the bank—"Say hi to the lord for me, would ya?" Then he'd shot those poor people and laughed. He'd actually laughed. When it hadn't been even the slightest bit funny. Just plain nasty.

He still cracked her up sometimes with his infamous orations during jobs, but definitely not on this occasion. *Rule #17* said you should say something memorable during the heist and give the witnesses something specific to remember. The funnier and/or crazier the better—anything to make it harder for them to remember something truly helpful for the police. It was one of the simpler rules, but she figured the devil must be in the details since they'd never been caught.

The sting of one of Wyatt's famous love taps snapped her back to the moment. Tara felt a flush in her body that rose to her cheeks. Rubbing her face, she aimed a fierce glare toward the used and abused face in the driver's seat. "Damn it, Wyatt, you can't just whack me upside the head anytime you feel like it. I'm not your little girl anymore. What was that for, anyway?"

Wyatt cackled. "For taking all the fun out of that Del Rio job. I was just hitting my groove when you got all righteous on me."

Was he serious? "Well…spraying bullets into the crowd took all the fun out of it for me. I mean, I understand the bank manager. It was *Rule #33* all the way. But the rest of those guys were innocent."

Wyatt smirked. "No one's innocent."

"You make it hard sometimes, Wyatt," Tara sighed. "You really do."

Wyatt kept silent as they pulled into the parking lot of a grocery store. With practiced ease, they both sprang out of the borrowed vehicle and hopped into their older, faded black Cougar. Wyatt threw his ten-gallon hat and the loaded duffel bag into the back seat and started the car. He revved the engine a couple of times, listening to its throaty roar, then took off down the Texas highway.

Tara removed her fake mustache and put it in its case, glad to have the hairy thing off of her face. Felt like a spider crawling on her lip. She didn't really care for dressing up as a scrawny male cowboy, but couldn't fault the logic behind Wyatt's system of rules. And the rules had saved their hides on more than one occasion.

She looked in the visor mirror and had a moment of déjà vu, remembering when she'd done the same thing thirteen years earlier, back when Wyatt was first teaching her the trade. Now, instead of seeing an oversized mask on an innocent face, she saw someone else's blood.

Tara groaned, feeling nostalgic for the old days when skipping school and robbing banks with her daddy had been fun and exciting. And as a bonus, Wyatt had practically never killed anyone.

At least, not in her presence.

But the intense adrenaline rush she got every time they pulled a job had faded to obscurity. Courtesy of Wyatt's shooting spree.

And the difference was night and day. She couldn't believe how powerfully she felt the loss. No amazing feeling when they got away with the money, and not a single loving feeling from her daddy. Hell, he never even let her call him Daddy.

She gazed cautiously at Wyatt, wondering why things were getting steadily worse. Bloodier. More dangerous.

But mostly she wondered why they weren't following his system anymore. "This is reckless, Wyatt. The Feds are primed—just waiting for us to make a mistake. We should be lying low, hiding out. Not crossing two state lines."

Wyatt's eyes twinkled with glee, reminding Tara of the Santa Claus poem about a right jolly old elf. Nobody, but nobody, enjoyed his work more than Wyatt. The nine-to-five grind of lawbreaking never seemed to get him down.

But Wyatt kept silent. His smugness made her want to punch him. "What's so important in Arizona?"

Wyatt grinned. "You'll see."

CHAPTER 3

Rule #16: Change your M.O. about as often as you change your underwear. No need to make things easy on the law.

"Say hi to the Lord for me, would ya?" The man with the ten-gallon hat shot the bank manager, spraying blood on his scrawny partner, then shot randomly into the customers lying on the floor. His partner clutched his arm, interrupting the bloodshed. With a last glance toward the security camera, the two ran out with a duffel bag full of cash.

FBI Agent Dawkins flinched and paused the videotape. He looked in disgust at the frozen image of the bank robbers in their cowboy disguises, then rewound the tape and watched, for a third time, the fuzzy surveillance video from the Del Rio branch of First Nationwide Bank.

For thirteen years, the cowboys had always hit small-town banks. Fewer cops to deal with, he guessed.

Of course, that was only if it was the same cowboys. They'd hit banks all over the south and their M.O. always changed, so it was hard to be sure. One year they'd even dressed as clowns, so his predecessors had subscribed to the theory that the earlier jobs had been the work of a circus midget, and not a kid at all. Which was asinine. They had to be the same guys.

Dawkins sighed. He'd always appreciated the fact that most criminals were dumb as posts. It made the job easier, more enjoyable. He'd even come to treasure the way they left an abundance of clues at the crime scenes—as if they wanted to be caught. It was that rare breed, the smart criminal, that always proved to be trouble.

And these cowboys were definitely smarter than the average bear. They'd stolen so many picnic baskets that Dawkins began to think of the big cowboy as Yogi and the scrawny guy as Boo-Boo. The case had recently been assigned to his team, and Dawkins was still searching for a handle—a way of looking at the case. Yogi and Boo-Boo.

Of course, that would make Dawkins the hapless ranger. Not a pleasant thought.

Dawkins sat in the dark video room of the bank, surrounded by walls of concrete and steel, and slammed back a fourth cup of coffee. His eyes flicked to the other monitor for a moment, watching the live picture feed of the agents dissecting the scene. A junior agent tripped over one of the bodies and cursed with unusual clarity.

Thankfully, there was good sound on this little bank's surveillance video—and because of it they had their first good lead. He'd throw a sound clip of the suspect's voice to the press and see if anything turned up. The odds were long, but maybe they'd hear from a disgruntled ex-wife, or an ex-partner who'd be happy to roll over on an old pal for a little reward money.

He checked his watch—11:04 A.M. As usual, the bastards had slipped through the roadblocks or gone to ground somewhere.

Dawkins downed another gulp of coffee and rubbed his temple. Six dead, seven hysterical survivors to deal with, and one of his worst migraines ever. Why Agent Blowhard had wanted to question the survivors here at the bank was anybody's guess. Probably wanted to enjoy the moment.

Special Agent Stratton, a.k.a. Agent Blowhard to anyone forced to spend five minutes with the man, burst into the room with a shit-eating grin plastered on his face. "That was unbelievable! Blood all over their clothes. And the stories they had to tell. Oh, man."

Dawkins removed his hand from his weapon. It was *not* a

wise career decision to shoot your superior officer—no matter how much he deserved it. Instead, he said, "I'm sure it was loads of fun. But did you get anything useful?"

"Well," Stratton screwed up his face in concentration. "You know I'm pretty sure this is connected to that job near Charlotte, about three months ago."

"You *think* so?"

"Now don't get snotty with me or I'll…" Stratton stopped abruptly as he noticed the monitor behind Dawkins with the suspect in mid-shooting spree. "Why the heck you watching this without me?"

Stratton elbowed his way past Dawkins and sat at the controls. He rubbed his hands together, the loathsome grin back in place. "Go somewhere and investigate something."

Dawkins left, disgusted.

Wyatt took one beefy hand off the steering wheel and smacked Tara. "Don't give me any more lip, girl."

Tara's cheek stung and she fought back tears. She would not cry. "I'm making sense, Wyatt. It's your system, so why the hell aren't you following it?"

He reached over to slap her again but Tara grabbed his arm. "If you hit me again, I'm out of here."

It was time to draw the line somewhere. No more hitting and definitely no more killing whenever he felt like it. And yet—that was easier said than done. Wyatt had never seen a line he wouldn't cross.

Wyatt put his hand down and rested it lightly on her thigh. "You know better than that. You're not out of here until I say so."

Tara flinched and pushed his hand away.

The hand clenched into a fist. "You're my girl. Just because you're all grown up now…well, that doesn't change a damn thing and you know it."

She knew better than to keep pressing. But he was wrong—

things had changed. At twenty-two, she knew she could take care of herself. She wondered if that was why he held on so tight.

The car stopped at the light. Tara looked around and saw a battered New Mexico town that was nothing more than a crossroads. Even so, she was delighted to see even a small sign of civilization. After miles of sand and tumbleweeds she could still taste the grit coming in through the air conditioning vents.

She caught her reflection in the storefront window and shivered at the bittersweet memories being stirred up once again—thinking back to the first time she'd ever shot anyone.

She took a deep breath and tried to shake off the memory, wondering why she was dwelling on the past so much. Memories could be painful.

Real painful.

Of course, Wyatt was the first person she'd shot. So sometimes, memories weren't all bad.

CHAPTER 4

Rule #7: It's impossible to overestimate how stupid people can be. The only thing that smartens 'em up is a large caliber gun barrel pointed right at their face. Even then you still got to be careful.

Pete Woods looked up at the blazing sun with intense loathing. He'd take the freak show of Los Angeles any time over this Arizona cactus farm.

The red rock of the Painted Desert was all right, he guessed. He hadn't noticed it too much as they raced down the highway in his red '78 Caddy convertible, what with his partner, Bull, bleeding all over his white leather upholstery. They'd barely made it to the Vietnam Vet's place in time.

Shit. Pete tried to wash the blood off, but no matter how hard he scrubbed, it left a stain behind.

Pete hopped out of the car, cringing when his friend squealed, and turned to the large ranch house where the shell-shocked veteran was putting his veterinarian skills to good use. It was pathetic, a three-hundred-pound tough guy screaming like a little girl. Shit, Bull was half Samoan and half Apache Indian, for crying out loud.

Pete leaned into the open window of the dank surgical room, into the overwhelming stench, and yelled, "Damn it, Crispin, can't you give him something to shut him up?"

Crispin's eyes blinked a few times behind his horn-rimmed glasses. A cigarette dangled from his lips. "Well, I've got horse tranquilizers and cow steroids," he wheezed. He hacked a couple of times, nearly dropping his ash into Bull's open wounds. "What's your pleasure, Bull?"

On a good day, Bull's eyes protruded from his face quite a bit more than a typical Indian, and now they bugged out even farther. "No way you're giving me any of those animal drugs. Last time my crotch swelled up like a balloon and my girlfriend left me."

"You kidding me?" Pete laughed. "That was a hooker. You never had a girlfriend."

"Well, she took my money and didn't give me shit in return. I think most people would call that a girlfriend," Bull said. He screamed again as the vet fished another shotgun pellet from his flesh.

"Hush, hush. Now, why don't you be a good boy like my friend over there?" Crispin asked. "He got run over by a car and he hasn't been any fuss."

Bull looked over at the steel table next to him and saw an armadillo with dull, lifeless eyes. The lower half of its body had been turned into road pizza by an eighteen-wheeler. "Hey, Crispy, quit fooling around. Tell me you know that thing is dead."

Crispin glanced over at the armadillo. "Nah. Just sleeping."

"Great Spirit protect me! I'm not gonna make it," Bull cried.

Pete slammed the window shut and walked back to his car. He turned the radio up loud in an attempt to drown out the high-pitched shrieking. He made another feeble attempt to wipe the blood off the leather seats—without success.

The gears started cranking in Pete's brain. Full of excitement, he pulled a micro-cassette recorder out of the glove compartment and hit the record button.

"What about feeding cows Scotchguard? Make the world's first stain-proof leather."

Pete smiled to himself. *Hell, yes!* That's why he was the idea man and Bull was the muscle. There was no way his buddy could have come up with a million-dollar gem like that.

At another squeal from Bull, Pete's smile melted away. The last idea before the Scotchguarded cows hadn't been all that great. In fact, breaking into the redneck's house had turned out to be idiotic—and not easy money at all. Something had brought the rancher home early. And of course, all rednecks had guns. In case they saw a lizard or fence post or something else they could shoot.

No more of these penny-ante jobs, Pete decided. If we're gonna get shot at, it's got to be for bigger stakes.

That's when he heard a news flash on the radio about a bank robbery gone wrong. Biggest massacre this year. But the interesting part was a sound clip from the bank robbery.

The voice was hauntingly familiar. "Say hi to the Lord for me, would ya?" It sounded like an ex-partner of his—that psycho Wyatt.

Pete grinned. A rich ex-partner, according to the reporter.

Because of the static in the broadcast, it was hard to be certain it was the Preacher. But the germ of an idea started to form.

Bigger stakes!

He leaned over to turn up the sound when a gigantic wolf-dog jumped onto the trunk of the Caddy. It growled with menace and...*Oh my God*...a hint of something else.

"Bull!" he whispered, remembering belatedly that Bull's brawn was on the operating table.

Pete's eyes opened wide and he fought hard to control his bladder. He stood frozen to the spot, none of the usual "brilliant" ideas coming to mind, his brain haunted by the memory of a disastrous dog-breeding scam. From painful experience, he knew all too well that the wolf-dog was after something else. And Pete figured the enormous beast was big enough to take what it wanted.

Ahh...keep it together. No sudden movements. As the lustful animal started toward him, he reached under the seat and pulled out his thirty-eight. The wolf-dog lunged and Pete fired prematurely, missing the animal by a yard. But the sound of the gunshot was enough, and the wolf-dog slunk off, limp and defeated, growling all the way.

Pete quaked in the car for a couple of minutes, trying to calm his nerves. Only in the sticks did you have to worry about shit like this. Must be why all these rednecks kept their guns handy—you never knew when you might be a victim.

With no sign of a return visit from the animal, he started to relax and got back to thinking about his new idea. This one should work. It was easy money.

AGENT DAWKINS HUNG UP THE PHONE AND GAZED OUT THE window of his office. Another crackpot—the fifth one that day. *Houston sun must be frying their brains.*

Each of them claimed to be the mastermind behind the Del Rio, Texas bank job. He shook his head. It was nauseating what people would do to get on TV.

The phone trilled and Dawkins glared at the thing with deep suspicion. It went against his better judgment, but he answered anyway. "What?"

He listened for a second and smiled. Not a crackpot. "Sanders. Tell me you've got some good news on that partial print." His mood soured as he listened to the response. "All right. Let me know if anything turns up."

Dawkins hung up the phone and thought, score one for Yogi and Boo-boo.

The job got to him at times, but there were plenty of feel-good moments to balance things out. Catching the bad guys and busting their scummy little heads was a pure and patriotic high. Since the fifth grade he'd known that flushing the toilet bowl of society was the right line of work for him. Nine times out of ten the criminals were so inept it wasn't even a challenge to catch them.

The problem was the numbers. There were way too many bad guys out there and not enough good guys chasing them. Even so, he knew he was fighting the good fight.

For Dawkins, being both black and smart had caused a little lag in his career development—courtesy of a fearful Klan-loving supervisor. But he hadn't let that stop him.

He had slowly but surely worked his way up the ranks until he'd hit his first real snag. A bigoted blood-lusting idiot, with impeccable political connections, had leapfrogged ahead of him, stymieing all forward progress in his career.

Agent Stratton walked into Dawkins' office. *Speak of the Devil.*

"Hey, guess what?" Stratton said.

"Mmmm, you forgot how to knock?"

"Cute. But no. I pulled some strings and got our boys bumped onto the Ten Most Wanted list." Stratton puffed out his chest a little, his voice dripping with a Texas accent. "You know what that means, right?"

"That Senator Stratton took our chief for a ride on his yacht and greased his palms?"

Stratton squeezed his beady eyes shut for a moment. "You are a bitter little man, aren't you? I can't help it that my father is an elected official of this great state of Texas. Just like you can't help being a smart, yet bitter Negro. But as I don't mind the colored folks, that's neither here nor there."

Stratton strutted in his thousand dollar gatorskin boots from one side of the room to the other. "With our boys on the list, this is now a *prime* case. And that'll mean way more visibility." Stratton nudged Dawkins in the shoulder and winked at him. "Probably even media. More guys to work under me and more resources."

The guy was brain-dead. Dawkins wondered if it was worth explaining the math, and then thought why not, it could be entertaining. "How much more budget do we get to work with?" he asked.

"We get a twenty percent increase. Not bad, huh?"

"And when your father and his fellow Senators funded us this year, how much did they decrease our department, in order to fund those tax breaks for themselves and their oil buddies?"

Stratton furrowed his brow. "How should I know? And those oil buddies are the backbone of this state!"

"It was a twenty-five percent cut. So getting a twenty percent increase doesn't help much."

"What's that got to do with anything? A twenty percent increase is pretty good, no matter how you look at it."

Agent Dawkins sighed. "Right..."

CHAPTER 5

Rule #6: Only rob banks in the sticks. In big cities like Los Angeles they'll have a tactical SWAT team on your ass in sixty seconds. In Hickville, there's just one old geezer with a badge and a potbelly. Yet, for some reason L.A. is the bank robbery capitol of the world. Go figure.

The next morning the Cougar skidded to a stop. Tara rolled her eyes. *A bit dramatic,* she thought. Then again, Wyatt always liked to make an entrance.

The engine revved a couple of times before puttering out. Tara gazed across the street and watched a couple of local characters, already half-tanked, stumble through the front door of a place called Joe's Tavern. It looked like a dive, but there probably wasn't much else to do in this little Arizona town.

She looked out her window and her heart skipped a beat. She *always* got excited when she first laid eyes on the prize. She couldn't help it. And 1st Farmer's Bank was surely the only bank in town.

But so what. If you let excitement trump common sense, you were as good as dead. That was something Wyatt had drilled into her for as long as she could remember. She forced herself to settle down, and all was quiet for a couple of seconds, like the calm before a storm.

They'd been arguing about it for a solid ten miles, something that wore on her nerves, but since she loved her old man she decided she just couldn't let it drop. "I know you don't want to hear it, Wyatt, but there's too much heat."

Wyatt clenched the wheel and shouted, "Just shut your trap for one minute before I lose my mind."

She fumed and thought, how could you lose something that you never had in the first place? With acute self-preservation instincts, she tactfully kept the thought to herself. Instead, she said, "Fine. Let's just concentrate on the business at hand."

She gave Wyatt a sidelong glance, checking to see if he was close to erupting. Of course he was. Lately, he was always close. Heck, last week a guy had tried to pick her up at a bar and Wyatt had nearly killed the poor fella.

She looked Wyatt over and saw that his temperature gauge was in the red, but decided to risk it anyway. "It doesn't feel right. We shouldn't be doing two big jobs back to back and you know it."

Instead of getting angry, Wyatt merely sighed. "Girl, you would try the patience of Job. This one's the big one for Christ's sake! The last one was pocket change, twenty thousand at most. This one's good for a quarter million at least."

Tara caught her breath. "You're full of it. We never got anywhere close to that amount before. And you think there's gonna be money in this little one-horse town? Not a chance."

Wyatt smirked. "That's where you're dead wrong, missy. Twice a year the hayseeds from four counties come here to cash their farm subsidy checks. And on those glorious days, this bank actually keeps cash in it. A lot of cash."

Wyatt lowered his head, as if in prayer. "Can you feel it? This here's a day of reckoning."

"Well…maybe you've got something here," Tara said.

For a moment, she looked at Wyatt in admiration, then frowned again. "But we still shouldn't have hit that bank in Del Rio. Two banks in two days? That's like stirring up a hornet's nest and then reaching inside."

Wyatt's mood darkened with the criticism. "Don't worry your pretty little head. I got it all planned out."

"All right," Tara agreed. "I just got one question. What the heck is a farm subsidy, anyway?"

Wyatt's eyes rolled. "You're not gonna believe this, 'cause it's even worse than the goddamned insurance companies."

Tara had heard him refer to insurance companies that way for so many years it had taken quite a while for her to realize that the phrase "goddamned" was not a part of their actual name.

Too late, she realized she'd prompted him for another one of his sermons and groaned inwardly. He wasn't nicknamed The Preacher for nothing.

"The goddamned government actually pays farmers not to farm, like they're on welfare or something. It makes me all twitchy just thinking about it," Wyatt huffed. "But I don't want to get all riled up about it right now so let's just drop it." He brightened up. "Leaves more money for us anyway. Enough talk. Better get yourself ready."

Since this was a scouting run, the idea was to look completely different than they did in their work clothes. She searched through her purse and pulled out her Scrumptious Raspberry lipstick.

Wyatt howled and punched the roof of the car a few times. Tara smiled to herself as she put on her lipstick. These were the times that he truly enjoyed life.

Wyatt gazed longingly at the bank. "Like taking candy from a baby."

He grinned and then cackled for a moment longer before calming down and putting on a dress shirt, tie and jacket. Like a chameleon adapting to its surroundings, his features became more mild-mannered as he got dressed. Tara watched him, impressed as always that he could change his character so completely.

Wyatt pulled his gun out and reluctantly placed it under the seat. Tara understood why. She often felt naked and uncomfortable without her weapon, and knew Wyatt was the same way. Like father, like daughter.

"Meet me at the bar afterwards," he said.

Wyatt headed for the bank, leaving Tara to put the final touches on her makeup. She had on a sexy, short black skirt and a skimpy top, which she promptly adjusted, positioning her cleavage for maximum effect. A killer outfit. She loved the fleeting moments that she got to dress up. It wasn't often, 'cause Wyatt went nuts when other men noticed her, unless it was on the job.

When she exited the car, she noticed a couple of guys her age laughing it up as they walked down the street. As always, she wondered about the life she was missing. One of the guys whistled at her as they turned into Joe's Tavern, country music blaring through the open doorway. She ignored them and got back to business. She went up the steps, entered the bank and walked over to the counter with the withdrawal and deposit slips, passing right by Wyatt. She ignored him completely, pretending not to know him.

CHAPTER 6

EXCERPT FROM MAX WILLIAMS AUDIOTAPE

Growing up, my pop always told me that women are either good…or bad. That there's no in between. Personally, I think that's bullshit.

Sometimes you just have to look deeper.

Max Williams flicked his lighter open, lit his cigarette and watched, with great interest, the sea of humanity that filled Joe's Tavern to the brim. The putrid stench of too many people using too little soap. In addition, they were sweating buckets of alcohol from their pores and were crammed into too tight a space. It could be overwhelming, but as it was about the only interesting thing to do in the little town, Max savored every entertaining moment.

The town of Stoneybrook was located at a crossroads of desert highways, which made it the logical stopping place for many of the bottom feeders of civilization. They were usually inclined to misuse the town and then toss it away like so much garbage. Max, stuck there his entire twenty-one years of life, found it an exhibition worth watching—and his best look at the outside world.

But nature called, so Max decided his favorite show would have to wait. At Joe's, he tried to hold his water as long as possible as the restrooms were famous for their olfactory assaults. The more the barflies drank, the worse their aim.

He strode over to the john and opened the door, holding

his breath. The extreme heat of a summer morning in the Arizona desert had joined forces with a busted ventilation system, and the smell of vomit and urine was already intense. Reeling, Max choked back tears.

Aw, shit. Over by the last graffiti-covered stall, some Neanderthal was beating the crap out of his buddy, C.J.

It was nothing new for C.J., as his small frame and bizarre manner of dress—white leather with fringes and pork-chop sideburns—made him a natural target. But Max still took it personally. Over the years, Max had stepped into the role of his protector more times than he could count. After all, what were friends for?

Max pounded on the door to get the Neanderthal's attention. "Hey!"

The guy wasn't huge, but next to a gaunt C.J., he seemed a giant. When the guy turned, Max could see that life had not been kind to him. One of his eyes had been clawed out and part of his nose appeared to have been bitten off. Max had once read about an angry wife that had cut off her husband's prized body part and figured this poor guy had similar problems. Under different circumstances he might have bought the guy a drink and heard his sad story. If he hadn't been thrashing his friend.

Max's gaze narrowed as he noticed C.J.'s wallet in his hand.

The guy said, "You got a problem?"

"Nah. It's all good." Max spread his hands out and spoke with a friendly, yet firm, tone of voice. At the same time he stood up straighter, making sure that his solid, six foot frame was visible, trying to show the guy that it wasn't worth it. "But you know, my pop taught me to never pick on the little things of life."

The guy worked at his chewing tobacco, dribbling a little juice onto his chin. "And why should I give a rat's ass what some snot-nosed punk's pappy spit out his pie-hole?"

"I'm getting to that," Max said. "You see...my pop claimed the little guys needed our protection. Now much as it galls me to say so, when the man's right, he's right. So you can just consider that guy you're stepping on under our protection."

The Neanderthal spat out some of his tobacco juice onto C.J. "Is that right?"

"Yeah. And I'll tell you what, you put that wallet back where you found it and we won't have any problems here."

C.J. looked at Max with gratitude.

The guy bristled, spat again, and then charged Max at full speed. With the natural instincts of someone who'd participated in a few fights, Max stepped quickly to the side and helped fling him past and into the tile wall.

The guy hit headfirst, then caromed off a puke-covered toilet and went down like he'd been shot. Max kicked him a couple of times for good measure and to make sure he wasn't faking. The only movement was the trickle of juice running down the man's face.

"You know something C.J.?" Max reached down, grabbed C.J.'s wallet and tossed it to him. "Pop always said that the best way to teach a bully to change its spots was to beat the tar out of them, preferably in front of a good crowd."

C.J. hacked a couple of times, searching for breath. "Does it work if you do it in the bathroom where no one can see it?"

"Hell, I don't know," Max said. "But at least we did our civic duty."

"This one doesn't seem too bright, maybe we should try a little harder," C.J. said.

He kicked the guy in the ribs one last time.

WYATT GLANCED AROUND THE BANK. HE SAT AT THE NEW Accounts desk, playing idly with the nameplate of the peon that worked there. He was tired of waiting. And he knew patience wasn't one of his virtues—that his personality was more along the lines of "Idle hands are the devil's playground."

When is that piece of shit manager gonna get here? He didn't suffer fools gladly. In fact, if that manager didn't get here in one more minute, he knew he'd have to adjust the plan for this afternoon and ice the idiot right quick. Maybe set an example for the rest—get everything off to a good start.

With his extensive criminal expertise, he knew that good starts were important to most jobs. He watched the bank personnel working away like busy bees and figured the pathetic pencil pushers probably didn't care much about good starts—or anything else for that matter.

He couldn't blame them. Their lives sucked.

He'd once had the misfortune of having a regular job. And the experience had been more than enough for his lifetime.

When he was younger, his cousin Vern had gotten him a job at the insurance company where he worked. Day after endless day filled with repetitive bullshit. And if that wasn't enough, as low man on the totem pole, they made him do the hatchet work.

His official job title was Quality Control, but what that meant was that he had to interview any poor sap who made a sizable insurance claim and find a way to trip them up—figure out how to void their claim. They paid a bonus for each one he rejected. And the regular pay was so low that he couldn't make a decent living without the bonuses.

He'd always had a few screws loose, at least that's what his dad had told him, and he'd never lived life on the up and up anyway so he didn't stay with the vocation for long. But he'd had a particularly hellish experience on his last day on the job.

A family that had suffered the misfortune of being burned out of their house, had then had their claim denied based on some fictional fine print manufactured by one of his co-workers. And seeing the human result of his company's handiwork left a foul taste in his mouth.

After he read through the file, with the family crying the whole time, he stamped their claim approved. The relief on their faces was a sight to behold.

He got the ass-chewing of a lifetime when his boss found out. He was reamed in front of the whole office. Although Wyatt had seethed with anger, when he was younger he had a lot more restraint. His killing was much less frequent and was even discriminating. He gave his public resignation in front of the office staff, then waited patiently for a month before sneaking into his ex-boss's house one night and giving him a private and more brutal response—Wyatt style.

His cousin Vern suspected and even confronted him, but nothing serious ever came of it. Vern and Wyatt both knew that family was family and you never ratted them out.

Of course, Vern never offered to help him find another job. But that was to be expected, considering the circumstances. Wyatt understood and decided he'd never play in the corporate world again. He preferred the ethics of a life of crime to the morally low, yet somehow legal, life of insurance "adjusting."

Wyatt was brought back to the present by the sound of oily laughter and a giggling young woman. The slick bank manager, Lou Stephens, appeared to be flirting with one of his employees. Obviously he was banging her. Pretty dangerous with today's sexual harassment lawsuits.

So he was a bit of a gambler and he liked the ladies—good to know.

Wyatt decided to change his approach and turned around in his seat, looking for Tara. She was at the counter. Wyatt watched her with a lecherous gleam as Lou approached and offered a sweaty palm.

"How do you do, sir?" Lou asked.

Wyatt nodded toward Tara. "If I wasn't married," he said, "that would be a rather tempting morsel. Wouldn't you agree?"

Lou turned to Tara and nodded appreciatively.

The female teller directly behind Tara noticed Lou and smiled. Lou blew her a nervous kiss and turned back to Wyatt, giving him a conspiratorial glance. "Well now, my wife there isn't too observant, thank God, but if she ever caught me looking at another woman...let's just say it would be a whole lot harder to work together. She can be a screamer, if you know what I mean."

"Oh yeah," Wyatt agreed. "Aren't they all?"

The two shared a small chuckle together, like old buddies. Wyatt figured he'd have to watch the guy carefully during the job. Anyone who had an extra female at the same place his wife worked was unpredictable. Maybe even had a death wish.

"Ain't that the truth," Lou said. "Now tell me, what can I do for you today sir?"

"Please, call me Jack," said Wyatt, handing him a business card he'd picked up off the street. "I've got a rather large commercial account that I'm thinking about relocating."

"Well you've come to the right place."

"Now, I'm sure you're right, but I'm talking about a long-term relationship," Wyatt said. "And I like to be *real* sure who I go to bed with, so to speak."

"Of course. Let me introduce you around, tell you a little bit about this place." Lou rose and dried his wet palms on his pants, a habit for the habitually moist man. He wandered off, beckoning for Wyatt to follow.

TARA NOTICED WYATT WALKING AWAY WITH THE BANK MANAGER and sighed, hoping against hope that the bank manager would still be alive at the end of the day. *He'd better be.*

She finished scoping the place. Wyatt hadn't been full of it after all. There was a temporary banner over one of the teller windows that read: *FEDERAL FARM SUBSIDIES, NOON TO FOUR, THIS LINE ONLY.* She drew on the back of one of the withdrawal slips the location of the security cameras in each of the corners, the two armed guards, and the eight teller windows—only half in use.

Now it was time to check out the guards. As she crossed to the exit, she passed by one of them and dropped her purse, scattering the contents all over the floor. The guard, who had been checking her out, bent over to help pick them up. He gave her a charming smile and kept his eyes on her cleavage the whole time.

Typical. She shook her head and noted the other guard watching enviously. Neither one was watching the door or anything else for that matter—their eyes glued to the sight of two breasts in a push-up bra. Like babies drooling over candy. She thought, and not for the first time, that the males of the species weren't properly suited for guard work.

CHAPTER 7

Rule #10: Partners suck. Well, not you, Tara. You're coming along just fine. Most criminals don't have the sense God gave 'em, or they wouldn't be criminals. But if you got to have one...a driver, safecracker or what have you...get a reference. And if no one will vouch for 'em, deep six 'em.

Using a miner's hat with a flashlight to shine the way, Crispin moved through the dirt tunnel that connected his house and veterinary practice to the barn and other places on his property.

The tunnels, though handy and comforting for many reasons, sometimes caused him to flash back to his time in the war. He had to keep telling himself that there weren't any Vietnamese around the next corner. He had his favorite M-16—the one he called Emmy—to keep him company and provide protection against the ramblings of his imagination.

He reached a junction and struggled to remember the way to the barn. His memory hadn't been that great since he'd taken one to the brain in his war days.

To his right he heard the tell-tale sound of clucking chickens. They sounded frightened.

Oh crap! That damn wolf-dog must be up there again. He scooted quickly down the tunnel toward his chickens, muttering all the way.

The beast was a loose cannon—a recent escapee from a stud farm that bred big, tough, guard dogs. He'd been the biggest of the monstrosities there, and had been repeatedly injected with massive amounts of hormones—both to make him less choosy with the bitches as well as keep him in a perpetually randy state. The perfect stud.

Wolfy, as he called the thing, had been loving up his chickens something awful. A couple of them had died from the severe affections of that insatiable giant brute. And the ones that hadn't died from the attempted sexual relations, got eaten. Crispin wasn't sure which was worse.

He stopped and listened again, but the sounds of the clucking fowl had faded dead away.

He poked his head through a trap door in the chicken coop, and was relieved to find only happy chickens. Not a maimed one in sight. "Hey Chicky, everything all right?"

He wasn't surprised when the chicken clucked in reply. They got along pretty well, since he didn't eat 'em or anything.

He looked around but there was no Wolfy. Must have been a false alarm. He decided to head back to the barn where Pete and Bull were hanging out. That was his primary mission, anyway. He would get Wolfy later.

After a night of recuperation, Bull was up and around now, healing nicely. But he and Pete were always whispering about something. And whispering made Crispin very nervous. He worried they were plotting against him.

A few of his human patients had tried to silence him before. His small graveyard out past the chicken coop was filled with the remains of criminals that had tried to kill him, worried he might leak something to the police about their evil deeds. And that was after he'd saved their lives on the operating table.

It was probably time to stop working on humans and just stick with his veterinary practice. People just didn't seem to deserve help anymore.

He certainly couldn't relate to criminals in today's world. They had no ethics whatsoever. If they'd followed any kind of code, they would have known he would never rat them out to the police. It was against the Hypocritical Oath, so it wasn't proper in Crispin's book.

So now they lay buried in his pasture. *Ah well, such is life.*

He slowed his pace and crept quietly down to the end of the tunnel. He wiped the dust from his glasses and peered up through the planks of the trapdoor. He listened carefully, Emmy at the ready. But they weren't planning to whack him after all.

"It's perfect. Easy money," Pete said.

"Perfect, huh. You said the same thing about the redneck job. And the dog job before that. And here we are. Broke and wounded. Maybe 'perfect' doesn't mean what you think it does," Bull said.

"Look. I'm just a bit rusty at these jobs out here in the sticks. If we could go back to L.A., we would. But this is a big time score I'm talking about."

"It makes me nervous, going after an ex-partner of yours. Makes me wonder how we might end up."

"It's not like that with us, Bull. You know that. We're tight. But this Wyatt guy, he was one crazy fucker, let me tell you. If he hadn't gone psycho and tossed me out of a speeding car, we wouldn't be having this conversation," Pete said. "I don't even remember how it came up. But somehow or other I said something about insurance companies being helpful to people and he just went nuts. Goodbye partner, hello asphalt. It took me about six months to heal from the road rash."

Crispin shoved his fist in his mouth, attempting to stifle his laughter. The picture he got in his head of Wyatt and Pete was worth framing. Wyatt had been one of his first human patients, and his anger could be dead funny when it was directed at someone else.

"Guy sounds kind of crazy. You sure this'll work?" Bull asked.

"Hey, I'm the idea guy, and you're the muscle guy. If we do it right, we'll have all the money of a bank job without any of the work. All we have to do is take out one big guy," Pete said. "How hard could it be? They won't even know we're coming."

Bull squinted. "What do you mean 'they'?"

"Oh yeah, he's got a little brat with him. Actually she's probably grown up by now. I even heard she's become quite a hottie."

Bull strained for a moment, concentrating. "You think she might like me?"

"Well...your career choices won't bother her."

Bull grinned. "I could use a girlfriend."

Crispin cringed. It was one thing to go after a homicidal scumbag like Wyatt, but Tara was a sweet angel. Even though his age—and Wyatt's temper—kept him from ever making a move on Tara, Crispin dreamed he could. He was, as most men were, smitten by her charm and good looks.

But since the guys weren't talking about killing or hurting her, he decided not to add them to his cemetery...yet.

CHAPTER 8

Rule #29: Males are easily swayed by the female of the species. It's sad, but true. So if a cop pulls us over for a busted taillight, or anything else for that matter, you use your God-given charm to talk him out of it. With a hundred watt smile, and a low cut top, you'll be able to talk your way out of just about anything.

Max took a sip of his beer and surveyed Joe's Tavern, noting how empty the place was. Word had just come across the c.b. radio that the INS was searching trucks for illegal aliens and most of the truckers had fled the town like rats from a sinking ship.

Max grinned. The majority of them weren't carrying illegals or they wouldn't be sitting here in a bar while the sun broiled their cargo to death. Apparently, smuggling contraband was still big business around these parts.

As Pop always says, 'To each their own.'

He leaned over the billiard table and took his shot. The eight ball bounced off two rails, then stopped just short of the pocket.

C.J. snorted and tapped in one of his three remaining balls. "How about Rachel? She's a looker."

Max shook his head. "No. Not enough smarts."

C.J. sank the four. "All right. Well what about Lauren? She's got the hots for you something fierce."

"You kidding? She's slept with half the guys in Stoney-brook."

"You're just way too picky, Max. Who else is left?"

"That's my point. No one."

C.J. lined up the cue ball using his good eye. The other was swollen shut, but otherwise didn't look too bad. He took his shot, but the fringe from his white leather coat got in the way and the ball missed the mark.

"Well, crap. At least I left the cue ball as far away as possible," C.J. said. "Oh, yeah. By the way, did I tell you I've finally figured out where the King is hiding?"

"I knew if anybody figured it out, it would be you," Max said.

He smiled to himself but kept his concentration on the pool table. He knew the table like he knew everything in the little town—in excruciating and mind-numbing detail. This table had a depression by the far corner pocket that caused the ball to curve to the right. He aimed accordingly, and sank the eight ball with ease.

He picked up a five spot from the table and decided he was way past due for a change of scenery. Maybe the beaches on the west coast. Or maybe Hollywood.

C.J. put another five on the edge of the table and started to rack them up for another game. He checked around to see if anybody was in earshot and started talking, keeping his voice low and serious. "You remember when Lisa Marie married Michael Jackson?"

"Yeah?"

"Everybody thought the wedding was a sham, right? And it was! Just not for the reason people suspected."

"Just shoot the ball, C.J."

C.J. shook his head and checked over his shoulder once more. He leaned in conspiratorially. "I'm talking about Never Never Land…where Michael Jackson lives. The guarded estate where *no one* has ever been inside…"

Max smiled. Any day of the week, he'd take quirky, loyal friends over cool and stuck-up ones. "You think The King is living in Never Land?"

"Shhhh. Keep your voice down. You want people to think I'm crazy?"

Max put down his pool cue and stared C.J. right in the eyes. "People already think you're crazy. Well…more like eccentric. Heck, that's one of your finest qualities."

C.J. nodded sheepishly.

"Your theory is a pretty good one, though, and I bet the *Enquirer* will be interested. But I don't think you should mention this to anyone else," Max said. "Some of these rednecks might not be so understanding. And they can be downright mean when it comes to things they don't understand. You get me?"

"Shit, I know that Max. Why do you think I was keeping my voice down?" C.J. downed his beer and signaled to the bartender for another. "So shut up and shoot. It's your turn."

Max grinned and lined up his shot, then stopped abruptly.

He turned, unsure what had grabbed his attention, and noticed an absence of movement by the front door. The barflies were looking out the window, frozen in place. Max frowned, wondering why they looked like they were holding their breath.

He understood why a moment later, when a young woman—whose beauty was completely foreign to those parts—walked through the door.

Max caught his breath and a hush fell over the rest of the men as Tara approached the bar. Young and old alike could share their appreciation of the fine specimen that had entered the lion's den. Entranced, and still holding his breath, Max watched Tara as the bar's resident stud approached her and tried to pick her up. Some harsh words were exchanged and Tara sat down alone at the end of the bar.

The cowboy stomped off, rejected and angry, cursing her for the lesbian she must be.

And just that quickly, the crowd dismissed her. After all, if the cowboy called her a lesbian, what chance would any of the others have? The noise level returned to its customary loud pitch as everyone got back to the real business at hand. Drinking the blues away.

For Max, nothing returned to normal. In fact, it might never be normal again. He couldn't take his eyes off her. The air was electric and every part of him felt alive—charged. The rest of the room went dim as he focused on her and only her.

Max realized he'd stopped breathing when he started to see stars. He took a deep breath and nurtured a deep suspicion that all physical symptoms of love, or lust, or whatever you call it, came from a lack of oxygen to the brain.

Slowly, her gaze moved across the crowd and onto Max. She stopped, sensing the electricity. Tara gazed for a moment and ran her fingers lightly up her arm and toward her shoulder, shivering at her own touch.

Max took another deep breath. *Damn, that's sexy.*

She crossed her legs, sliding one against the other, shifting her short skirt a little higher. Max caught a momentary glimpse of a small gun strapped to the inside of her thigh—partially hidden by her skirt. *Hell, yes!* Beauty *and* danger. Was there a more potent aphrodisiac? Max gave himself up for lost.

C.J. gave him a little shove. "You haven't heard a word I've said, have you? Wake up."

Max shook his head a little bit as he came out of it. The moment between them had passed, but they still stared at each other. He felt distracted and tried to think straight, but found he couldn't. He pulled out a pocket tape recorder and spoke into it, keeping his voice pitched low. "This is a crossroads, Max. Go right or go left?"

C.J. stared at him blankly.

"Pop would say she's trouble. As if that would somehow deter me."

C.J. snorted.

"She's out of my league so it could be brutal." Max paused, then said, "But hell…what isn't brutal in life?"

Max made his decision. He spoke quietly, under his breath, "This is it."

He pocketed the recorder, then turned to C.J. and handed

him his pool cue. He started toward Tara, then stopped and quickly turned back to his confused friend.

"Listen to me, C.J. Listen. This is very important. Do I look all right?"

C.J. was about to answer when Max cut him off. "Never mind. It doesn't matter." He strode over toward Tara.

C.J. watched him go. He sang to himself, "Only fools rush in," and started to comb his great big Elvis sideburns. "And people think I'm crazy."

AGENTS DAWKINS AND STRATTON HAD THE PLEASURE OF WORKing out of the Houston branch of the Federal Bureau of Investigation. And last year, to Dawkins' great amusement, one of the desk agents—or "mama's boys" as the field agents liked to call them—sued the government over second-hand smoke and successfully kicked all of the "degenerate smokers" out into a special courtyard to do their dirty work.

In Houston, the smoking and smog capital of the mighty US of A, this went over like a ton of bricks. Agents planned a mutiny over the violation of their constitutional rights. Surely, forcing them out into the smog to smoke must violate their freedom of speech, or right to bear arms, or some kind of Amendment.

Things might have turned ugly, if not for the major terrorist attack that week. While the rest of the nation mourned, solidarity slowly returned to the Texas branch of the FBI. Now, grumbling could only be heard on rainy days or when the temperature passed into the hundreds—which was most of the summer.

Dawkins didn't care one bit what people did to their bodies, but one of his greatest pleasures in life was the free time he got when Stratton took one of his many smoke breaks. In the twenty minutes it took Stratton to get down to the smoking pavilion, smoke his cancer stick, and return, Dawkins got his best work accomplished. The glorious silence of an absent buffoon.

He went over the tapes of the Del Rio job for what seemed like the hundredth time. In fast motion, while shuttling the tape, he noticed something he had never seen before. He rewound back to the right spot and watched it again. And there it was—a subtle swaying of the hips when the younger, scrawnier suspect was walking.

Unbelievable. Boo-boo was a she.

It made so much sense that Dawkins was immediately sure he'd figured it correctly. It filled in a lot of blanks. It also explained why the perps were constantly able to get past the roadblocks, among other things.

Stratton entered the room—huffing and puffing from the strain of climbing two flights of stairs after smoking outside in the extreme temperatures—his shirt pooled with sweat. Dawkins enjoyed the moment. A major break in the case and great discomfort for the idiot thorn-in-his-side.

"What the hell you grinning at?" Stratton said. "You like seeing sweaty men, is that right, Dawkins?"

He ignored the comment. Not even the buffoon could quash his enthusiasm. "What I've got is a good solid lead for this case. Check this out."

Stratton took a seat next to him while Dawkins quickly set up the tape. After they watched the video of the young suspect walking, Dawkins crowed, "Wasn't it amazing? Did you see it?"

Then Dawkins rolled his eyes, because Stratton obviously didn't get it. He sat there looking confused and maybe even a little suspicious.

Stratton said, "What the hell are you talking about?"

"His walk. *Her* walk. It's hypnotic. For those four steps, that sexy ass sways like a hula dancer's."

Stratton's face now showed signs of alarm. "A hula dancer?" He started to back away from Dawkins. "Did you just tell me that you thought that guy's ass was sexy?"

"I'm telling you, it's not a guy. It's a girl. And one that knows how to move, too."

Stratton's face turned beet red. "The hell he does. And if

you come near me, fruitcake, I'll call daddy, pronto, and get your butt shipped out of here."

Dawkins sighed. He should have known better, but now that he had dug the hole, he had to try to climb out. "Look, take it easy. I'm not into guys. Let's watch it again and I'll show you what I'm talking about."

"No way. I saw plenty already. And it's a guy."

Dawkins stared in disbelief. Stratton's overreaction was bizarre, to say the least.

Stratton said, "You want to watch it again, go right ahead. If you do, go pack your things because there will be no black homos working for me."

Black homos? What an asshole. Dawkins gave up, for now. "Okay, okay. It's not a girl. Sorry I brought it up. And I'm not homosexual, so relax."

Stratton did relax, visibly. "All right. We'll forget about this whole thing."

Dawkins thought for a moment and then couldn't resist a little dig. "Have you ever heard what they say about homophobes? About them having...um...well you know... deep-rooted latent homosexual tendencies?"

Stratton strained but couldn't quite grasp what Dawkins was talking about—too many big words. "No. But let's just drop it, okay? This isn't a subject that I care to even think about, much less discuss."

Dawkins chuckled quietly.

TARA WAS HAVING A NORMAL CONVERSATION WITH A NORMAL man. It was the first time in her life and she loved every minute of it. They didn't talk once about guns, ammo, or killing, or bank jobs, like she did with her old man.

Wyatt didn't take kindly to gentleman callers, so she hadn't had many opportunities with the opposite sex. The few times she had gotten away from Wyatt long enough to meet someone had been disappointing.

Mostly they were just interested in her body and had

nothing going on upstairs. So she tried them out—and wasn't really impressed with the whole sex thing. Maybe they weren't doing it right, but she wasn't sure that was really the problem.

She had a feeling that the real problem was that they were assholes. And impossibly weak.

She thought men should be strong.

The guys she'd met didn't make her blood race the way it did just talking to Max. She and Max were having an honest-to-God interesting conversation and a great time.

She discreetly checked out Max while he talked to her. His rugged looks not only got her heart pounding, but his broad shoulders suggested he had a well-chiseled body underneath his tight, black T-shirt. She imagined, for a brief moment, what it would be like to have his whole body pressed up against hers.

"Hey, you're not listening anymore," Max laughed. "And you've been staring. I'm pretty sure you were checking out my rear end."

He said it good-naturedly, but Tara blushed anyway. She took her mind out of the gutter. "Sorry. My brain wandered there for a minute." Tara leaned in closer to him, their bodies practically touching. "I thought for sure you'd say something stupid at some point in this conversation."

But he didn't. Which was something new for Tara. She stretched out luxuriously. *I could get used to this...*

She reached out and put her hand on top of his. There was a little spark of static electricity when they touched. She blushed again and looked away, laughing.

Max smiled along with her, mesmerized. "You're definitely not from Stoneybrook."

She started to reply, but stopped quickly when she noticed something behind him. *Shit.* Her mood went from relaxed to scared in a heartbeat.

Wyatt was approaching fast and he didn't look happy. More like suspicious and hostile. Possibly homicidal.

Tara quickly pulled her hand away. "Pretend you just asked me for a light or something," she said.

Max looked bewildered, then reached out and put a hand on her shoulder, concerned. "What? Are you all right?"

Before Tara could say another word, Wyatt grabbed Max's hand violently and started to bend it backward.

Tara groaned—the hand thing was one of Wyatt's favorite party games. He considered it a great way to command respect. And as a bonus he got to inflict instant, yet great, pain upon his enemies. He'd discovered the trick while fighting his little brother when he was eight. Wyatt's "Laws of Physics"—leverage was your friend. Part of *Rule #5*.

Tara knocked their hands apart and stood between them, her body touching Max's. Wyatt stared at her, enraged, and barely under control.

"Leave him alone, Daddy," Tara said. "He wasn't doing anything."

"What am I, blind? I'll deal with you back at the motel, missy."

Wyatt pushed her out of the way and turned to Max. He gave Max a little shove, pushing him back a few steps and knocking over a couple of barstools. This got the attention of the barflies—as far as entertainment went in the small town, a good fight was worth its weight in gold.

"Keep your filthy hands off her, maggot!" Wyatt sprayed him with spittle.

Max started toward Wyatt before Tara caught his eye. She shook her head emphatically. He got the picture and stopped.

"Look, pops," Max said. "I can respect that you're her father, but the little lady and I are..."

Max was cut off as Wyatt pushed him up against the bar, knocking over a whiskey and a couple of beers. One bulky guy looked forlorn, his spilled drink dripping from the bar. A skinny guy in chaps, his drink also somehow on the floor, howled in agony at the injustice of it all.

They both helped Max to his feet and stood behind him, ready to defend their lost alcohol, to the death if need be.

"We're with you Max," said the drunks.

Tara noticed the extra attention by the crowd. She whispered in Wyatt's ear. "Think about the bigger picture here."

She grabbed Wyatt by the arm and tried to drag him away, but he was stubborn, unwilling to be moved. "Come on," she said. "It's not worth it."

Wyatt looked around, finally noticing the attention. He made a reluctant decision and started to leave. Tara gave Max a quick, apologetic look.

"How will I find you?" Max asked.

Wyatt stopped in his tracks. He slowly pulled a small knife with a wicked point from his belt buckle, then whipped around and put the tip to Max's throat. His palm hid the knife from the view of the other patrons, but kept the edge pressed against Max's Adam's apple.

Wyatt leaned very close to Max's ear and whispered into it. "You don't. If I ever see you again, it'll be in tiny little pieces. You got me, maggot?"

Wyatt backed off and gave Max a wink, while Tara pulled him outside.

Max stood there for a moment, incensed. He was mulling his options when C.J. arrived at his side.

"I don't think you should mess with him, Max."

"You're absolutely right, C.J. But pop always said, 'No guts—no glory.' So let's go."

"You picked a bad day to start doing what your pop says," C.J. said.

CHAPTER 9

Exhibit 27—State of Arizona v. <u>XXXXXXX</u>
Excerpt from audiotape 1: Max Williams

My pop always told me that love was a crime...that they should lock up "people in love" and throw away the key. Especially the men. And hell, he may be right. But I think there's a bit more to it than that.

So this here's the story. The real story...not that bullshit you saw on the TV box. Now, don't get me wrong, I'm not saying we're innocent. But our hearts were in the right place.

Max paused and took a drag of his cigarette.

No...we're not innocent. But then hell...who is?

Wyatt slid into the Cougar, sweating profusely from the thirty second walk to the car. He noticed Tara wasn't sweating at all and snorted in disgust. Empirical evidence that she wasn't really his child. But he still loved her.

He turned the ignition and cranked up the air-conditioning. *Sweet nectar of life.* How people lived without the cool flow from this godly invention was beyond Wyatt's understanding. He felt pretty sure that a rise in temperature was directly proportionate to his loss of sanity and control. In fact, he held the heat wave of '66 solely responsible for the accidental killing of his little sister.

And now it was a hundred and ten and Tara was

pushing his buttons. Wyatt couldn't believe she'd picked up some drunk at a bar. Things had been getting out of hand with Tara lately. She was always sassing him. Riding him. She was in need of a little extra schooling, apparently.

He turned to face Tara and caught her staring over his shoulder. When she quickly looked away, he followed her glance and noticed Max and C.J. getting into an older Bronco convertible. Wyatt sighed and reached under his seat for his gun. He grabbed a silencer from the glove compartment and screwed it into place.

"Jesus, what an idiot," Wyatt said. "I'm gonna have to kill him."

"Now that'd make you twice the idiot, wouldn't it? We've got a job to do. You want the police breathing down our necks?" Tara asked. "With the biggest score of our life fifty feet from where we're sitting?"

Wyatt bristled. "This is your doing, missy, so shut your trap." He put the gun behind his back and into his waistband, then pulled his shirt out to cover it. "I'm just going to educate him a little bit."

Wyatt got out of the car and started his transformation back to the charming guy from the bank. He started to cross the street toward their car when the scrawny guy took notice of him. That wispy freak with the Elvis complex looked ready to crap his drawers. Then the maggot took notice and reached under his seat. He emerged from the car brandishing a tire iron.

"Well, well," said Wyatt. "The little pig's got some guts after all."

"Just back off and you won't get hurt," Max replied in a calm, even tone.

Wyatt looked around and saw that no one else was nearby. *Hick towns. Gotta love 'em.* He chuckled for a moment before pulling out the gun with the silencer, aiming it first at the freak and then the maggot. He could hear the freak whimpering in the car.

"Would you mind a little fatherly advice?"

"Yeah, I would," Max said. "I get enough of that already."

"That was what you call a rhetorical question," Wyatt said. "So listen up. Guts don't mean shit when you run up against someone smarter than you."

Wyatt tapped the gun against his temple, indicating his large noggin. He pointed it back at Max and cocked the gun.

C.J. whined in the car, "Don't shoot us, man."

Wyatt pointed the gun at C.J. "Never attract the attention of a predator, son."

Max tensed as if to jump, causing Wyatt to chuckle. But since the purpose of the exercise was to teach, and not to maim, he calmly lowered his aim and shot out both of Max's tires on the driver's side.

"Next time," Wyatt said, "show a little more respect for your elders."

Wyatt walked back to his car and got in. He grinned as he peeled away, tires screeching and smoking.

MAX AND TARA WATCHED EACH OTHER AS SHE PULLED AWAY. He stood there, dazed, before hurrying over to the car parked next to his. The new Porsche belonged to the only oil-man in town, an unhappy seventy year old hoping to regain his youth through fancy foreign cars and silicon blondes.

Max opened the door and whipped out his buck-knife. With one swipe he cut the ignition wire.

"What are you doing?"

Max stripped the wires and started twisting two of them together. "What's it look like? I'm putting an old skill to work."

"Are you crazy?" C.J. asked. "You can't seriously be thinking of following him."

"Not him. *Her.* You coming?"

Max started the car and gave it some gas. The engine roared.

C.J. jumped in, full of nervous energy. "Old man Hurley ain't gonna be happy you took his car."

"He'll be drinking for a couple more hours at least. We'll get it back before he even notices."

PETE AND BULL FLEW DOWN THE NEW MEXICO HIGHWAY AT ninety miles an hour. The registration on the Caddy was legit, so all they worried about were speeding tickets. And useless pink papers didn't cause them to lose much sleep—since they knew they wouldn't be around long enough to pay them.

But the mood had turned ugly. A two-hour wait to get through a roadblock on the highway had Pete and Bull boiling with rage—and the Caddy's A/C had broken down the day before.

Pete had tried his hardest to annoy the cops at the roadblock and dish back some of the hell they'd just been put through, but none of them took the bait. The border cops had pissed off travelers before and knew they sometimes had to let people blow off a little steam.

One of the cops had even searched their trunk for aliens. Bull had worried for miles about the implications of the search. He'd heard plenty of talk about Roswell and Area 51 and had been on edge since they hit New Mexico. He'd even tried to talk Pete into going the long way to Del Rio, Texas, but Pete wasn't having any of it.

But if cops were inspecting people's cars, Bull figured that aliens must be as common around here as flies on a dung heap. He'd have to keep a sharp lookout.

After twenty minutes of nervously checking over his shoulder and scanning the underbrush, Bull's fidgeting began to get on Pete's already ragged nerves. "Quit jumping around. What the hell's the matter with you?"

"Something's been bothering me, Pete," Bull said. He jumped, startled, as a rabbit ran across the highway. "Why would they think we had any E.T.'s in our trunk? I mean, it's not like we live in this infested place. We're just passing through."

"What are you talking about? What's an eatie, anyway?"

"You know, one of those extra testicle creatures."

Pete looked at him blankly, unsure where the conversation was going.

Bull tried again. "You know what I'm talking about…from outer space."

The light dawned for Pete. "Shit, they weren't looking for space aliens. They were looking for Mexican aliens. Like the ten thousand sons of bitches that sneak across the borders every damn day."

Bull stopped scanning the bushes, relieved about the aliens, but annoyed with Pete's crack about the Mexicans. He thought about pointing out to Pete that the Indians and Mexicans had lived on this land first, but he kept his mouth shut. He'd known this particular white man for many years and knew the past meant nothing to him. Such contempt for the land he lived in.

Most white men were so arrogant that he gave serious thought to beating their heads together—making their spirits one with the land. It could only improve things.

And while Pete was definitely arrogant—and whiter than nearly everyone, with his jet black hair making it seem like he'd just crawled out from under a rock—he wasn't as bad as most, 'cause he'd made Bull lots of money over the years.

Pete had all kinds of crazy ideas for making money. Sometimes they even worked.

So instead Bull changed the subject. "You know, that probably explains these signs I've been seeing on the road. They're like those signs of wild animals crossing. Only they've got people crossing."

"Yeah, those are the aliens all right. Making a mad dash for life, liberty, and the pursuit of minimum wage jobs. I should get two points if we pop one with the car."

Bull grimaced, and figured he'd better talk about

something else, quick, before he was overwhelmed by the urge to bust Pete's skull like an overripe melon. It wouldn't be good for their friendship. Bull knew Pete always liked talking about his ideas, so it was a natural for a diversion.

"Tell me again how you figure to catch this Wyatt guy," Bull said. "I still don't get it."

"For crying out loud, I told you already." Pete sighed dramatically, then proudly launched into a shortened version of his latest scheme. "When Wyatt, Tara and I worked together, they had particular habits. A system for doing jobs. And after a job, we all laid low at an associate's house until the heat was off. It's a small world...and I know most of the same guys they know. We just look for them near where they pulled their last job. We look till we find 'em. Piece of cake."

Bull nodded. It was about time they had an easy job.

He squinted, spotting some movement in the bushes up ahead. *WHAT IS THAT?* As soon as he thought the question, his mind jumped to the answer and his eyes opened wide.

There, at the edge of the highway, an extraterrestrial was rising from the brush. Bull felt a rush of relief when he determined that it wasn't the space kind of alien at all—merely the illegal type.

But then the Hispanic man skittered across the road in front of them.

"Look out!" Bull shouted.

Pete stomped on the brakes, but too late. The man bounced onto the hood and over the car. Pete brought the car to a stop, then turned around to look at the guy lying behind them. He wasn't moving.

"Shit. That was freaky," Pete said. "I guess I get two points though."

Bull looked over at the contemptible pale face beside him and started punching.

Max slowed down the Porsche and watched the Cougar pull into the parking lot of the Hideaway Motel. He frowned as her ultra-violent pop waved his hands wildly, arguing with Max's dream girl.

It was contemptible, treating her like that. But he had a feeling she could hold her own against him—or anyone else for that matter. There was just something about her. She was like a gorgeous cactus flower. Pretty on top—prickly and dangerous underneath.

Max drove past to the corner, then turned the stolen car around and doubled back.

It would've been easier if he'd gotten her name. Then it would have been simplicity itself to call her room at the motel there. Leave the psycho out of it.

But even with all that talking, it had never come up. Of course, they had been interrupted. Hard as it was to believe, it appeared her father was a heck of a lot worse than his.

As they neared the motel, Max slowed down the car for another peek, hoping his buddy wouldn't get too twitchy. No such luck.

"Hey, let's give it a rest now," C.J. said. "We can come back later. We don't want to run into the crazy guy, right?"

"Well, it wouldn't be wise to go up against a guy with a gun," Max said. "Not without a plan."

They heard the sound of the siren just as the flashing lights hit them. Max looked in the rearview mirror and noticed a Sheriff's car behind them. *Shit.* His pop was gonna kill him. Max turned back to the Cougar, but his girl was gone.

C.J. slumped down in his seat. "This day blows. I want to go back to bed," he whimpered. "Hurley must've noticed his car is gone."

Max glanced back at the Sheriff's car. "Do you think he saw me?"

C.J. sniffled, then gaped at Max with suspicion.

"What's it matter if he saw you or not?"

Max grinned. "If we can ditch him, we can drop the car and no one will be the wiser."

"Are you crazy? Just pull the car over and let me out."

But Max didn't pull over. He stepped on the gas and

thought, *Let he who's without sin cast the first stone.*

He made a quick right and avoided a pedestrian by a wide margin, but only narrowly missed a parked car. The patrol car kept up with them easily. He needed a plan.

"Jesus H..." C.J. cried, "this is not the way I want to get to Graceland."

"The 11:45 train should be here."

C.J.'s mouth dropped open. "And? Your point is?"

Max turned into an alley and headed away from town. C.J. grabbed onto the door handle, ready to jump if Max slowed enough.

"Look, you know what'll happen," Max said. "This'll be the straw that broke the camel's back. He'll beat the crap out of us."

Max headed down the two-lane highway at top speed. He checked his mirror—the patrol car, with its American-made big-block engine, easily kept pace with his snazzy foreign sports car.

Crap. In town the Porsche was great, but out here on the open road the police cruiser would have the advantage. Then he grinned—life was all about timing. Way up ahead, the crossing gates for the train tracks came down and partially blocked the highway. The 11:45 freight was on its way.

C.J. looked at the train, then back to Max. Then back to the train, then to Max. "What are you gonna do?"

"We can make it," Max said.

"No way! We can't make it!"

"We can do it."

Max lost a second and a half braking for a rabbit that bolted in front of them. But you had to watch out for the little guys in life.

The train was getting closer to the intersection. Max sped up, the accelerator pressed to the floor. The train was too close.

C.J. looked ready to pass out. He put his hand on the door handle and wondered if jumping would be less painful.

"We can make it..."

Max said it, but he couldn't convince himself. The point of no return was approaching and Max didn't care for the odds. It was too close to call.

"ELVIS, HERE I COME!"

"Shit!"

Max slammed on the brakes and went into a skid. C.J. threw his hands in front of his face, bracing for impact. Max regained control of the car and used the skid to turn the car parallel to the train. The car came to a halt, mere inches from the train cars going past.

Max stared at the Sheriff's car as it skidded to a stop. "That didn't work as well as I'd hoped."

The Sheriff jumped out of his car and stomped toward the Porsche. His face was beet red and the spit was flying as he approached the car. A large bloodhound jumped out of the police car and followed along.

Max dreaded the upcoming conversation. In fact, he figured it would probably make his personal top-ten list of shittiest moments.

At his pop's bidding, he'd actually made the list when he was twelve. The exercise was purportedly for his better mental health or some such nonsense, though truth be told, it hadn't really helped him deal with his mom's death. Even time had barely helped with that.

Max looked over to check on C.J. He looked ill. "I'm sorry, C.J. I guess I didn't really plan this well. But don't throw up in the car, all right?" Max said. "We should return it like we found it. It just wouldn't be polite to old man Hurley."

Max started to say more, but Sheriff Williams ripped open the door and yanked him out by his shirt collar. Max didn't protest as he was dragged to the rear of the car. The dog howled alongside, licking Max's face.

"Be quiet, Duke," said Williams. "What the hell is the matter with you, Max?"

C.J. stumbled out of the car and started retching.

"C.J. Get over here. Now!" Williams said.

"He had nothing to do with it, Pop," Max said. "I made C.J. come with me."

Williams backhanded Max across the face.

Max kept silent, but Duke howled again. Williams continued to hold Max by the scruff of the neck with his other hand.

"Don't you backtalk me boy. I'm so furious with you I can't even stand it."

"Look, Pop, I'm sorry..."

Williams backhanded him again, provoking another sympathy howl from Duke. "Just keep quiet, Max. You stole Hurley's new car. You almost killed yourself. And you endangered the lives of innocent civilians while running from me. *Me!*"

Max figured he probably shouldn't aggravate his pop. But then again, that was what they did. It practically defined their relationship. "Come on, give me some credit. I didn't get anywhere near those other people. It was some pretty decent driving, don't you think?"

Williams raised his hand again, then shook his head. C.J. slunk over next to Max and cowered. Williams noticed the fear in C.J. and then looked back at his own upraised hand.

"All right. All right," Williams said. "Timeout. We need a timeout."

Williams took a couple of steps back and began to pace. Max heard him count slowly to ten and gave C.J. a wry smile.

His pop had a self-acknowledged tendency toward anger, and had latched onto the concept of the "timeout" like it was a life preserver for a drowning man. The prized concept had spewed forth from his collection of highly revered self-help books. Max hated to admit it, but it did have a calming effect on him.

But it didn't on C.J. Maybe 'cause he was from outside the family. Whatever the reason, poor C.J. found the behavior way too disturbing and more than a little bit confusing.

Williams relaxed a bit when he finished counting. He

turned back to the two of them, still looking mean, but no longer out of control.

"All right. What the hell is going on here? Why did you steal the car?"

There wasn't an answer that would please him. Max maintained his silence and lowered his gaze. Duke rubbed up against him, playfully.

"Don't push me, Max. I'm having a hard time as it is."

C.J. piped in, "It was a woman."

"Jesus, Max. If I've told you once, I've told you a hundred times. Use your brains. Isn't that how I've raised you?"

Max looked into his pop's eyes. Williams gestured toward Max's privates. "Don't ever let the little guy be in charge. You know what I'm saying?"

Williams took a deep breath and then began again. "I'm sorry I hit you, son. I was angry, but that's no excuse. Can you forgive me?"

What the hell. You only get one dad. Max said, "Sure, Pop. No problem."

EVEN THOUGH MAX KNEW BETTER, HE HELD OUT HOPE THAT HIS dad wouldn't lock them up. That hope lasted from the time it took to walk from the front door of the tiny police station until they reached the lone holding cell in the corner—about thirteen seconds.

The drunk that was sleeping it off smelled of something awful. Or maybe it was Duke. The smell was strangely reminiscent of the time Duke had eaten a dozen hot dogs.

The drunk had a book entitled *Help You—Help Yourself* lying next to him, but was in no shape to read it. There was a stack of them on one of the desks. One per customer. His pop's way of offering a bit more than the usual legal remedies.

The cell door slammed shut, and its clang echoed around the station. Max wondered if there was a more dismal sound.

"You're locking up your own son?" C.J. asked.

"Shut up, C.J. You broke the law. I just enforce it."

C.J. sat on one of the beds and put his head in his hands.

Max started to follow when Williams reached in and grabbed his arm. He pulled him closer to the bars for a little privacy.

"You haven't pulled a stunt like that for a while, now. I thought we had an agreement."

"You're right, Pop, and I'm sorry. But it's not about that. That's not what's going on here," Max said. "It's just…it's time for me to get out of here. See what else is out there."

Williams sighed. "We've been over this and over this. I know I'm a little hard on you. And I know things haven't been the same since your mother died…"

"It's not about you. Or Mom. It's just time, that's all." Max looked out the barred window. He could see clouds stretching for miles and miles. "It's a big world, Pop."

The red-headed dispatcher, Lorna, dropped the phone from her ear and piped in, "Sheriff, you better get a move on. It's going down right now."

Williams looked sadly at Max for a few seconds and then took off. Duke thumped his tail a couple of times and raced after him.

CHAPTER 10

EXHIBIT 28—EXCERPT FROM AUDIOTAPE 2

I never believed in love at first sight…I don't think any-
one ever does until it happens to them. Hell, I thought
I'd been in love before. Turned out it was merely a mild
form of the disease…more like puppy love.

Max sighed.

But this was the real deal. When she walked through
the door…everything changed.

Till death do us part.

Sheriff Williams and his dog, Duke—both of them
wheezing from the two-block run from the station to Daisy's
back yard—stood watch over a litter of the cutest little bloodhound puppies, proud as could be. "Aerobic exercise" was an
evil phrase that was in neither his nor the dog's vocabulary.
   "Damn fine work, Duke. You, too, Miss Daisy."
   Williams' grin turned sour. The buggers were darned
cute, but then again, so was Max when he was a pup. All
babies were cute. But that hadn't stopped him from turning
into a punk teenager when he grew up. Williams couldn't figure a better way to describe being a single parent raising a
teen than "hell on earth." He was darn glad the teen years
were behind him, though the twenties weren't priming to look
much better.
   Given the recent events with Max, it was hard for Williams

to enjoy the moment. The whole situation had him rattled.

He'd racked his brains for a solution on the run over, but had come up empty. The lack of oxygen to his brain hadn't greased the wheels any. But he had an inkling which book to turn to—*Rough Love, A Parent's Guide to the Proper Use of Force.* There was a lot of good stuff in there.

One of the little puppies yelped, stepped on by its brothers in the quest for food. A lesson learned early in life for that one.

The little things were squirming around everywhere, crawling on top of each other. Williams shuddered and turned away from the seething mass of bodies. They reminded him of an unfortunate incident from his childhood—when his older brother had forced him into the crawl space under the house and he'd fallen into a nest of tarantulas.

Williams felt those kinds of memories should be kept locked away in the dark parts of the mind. He counted slowly to ten and relaxed. He hadn't thought of that in years. Must be the stress. He resolved then and there to pick up an extra self-help book this month, maybe even one of those books that were on CD so he could listen to it on patrol.

Williams heard a loud bang from across the alley, as some drunken fool stumbled out the rear door of Joe's Tavern. The drunk shuffled around the dirt parking lot, searching for his car, but the extreme amount of alcohol that he'd imbibed kept it mysteriously hidden. As the man wandered aimlessly, he began to sing. Duke looked on and joined in with a howl of his own.

Sheriff Williams sighed and rolled his eyes. "Now don't you start up, Duke. Jeez, you'd think Withers would get tired of spending the night in the cage." He started on over toward the drunk.

"Every time the temperature hits a hunnert and ten, the flies crawl out of the woodwork," Williams said. He got a mental picture of the crawling flies and shuddered. "Come on, Duke."

In the dim motel room, Tara slid on some baggy jeans and slipped the room key into her front pocket. There were only about forty rooms in the motel, but the number for their room was 999—a weak attempt by the owner to make the crappy motel seem ritzier than it was.

She stared at a lump of black mush on the wall and thought, *Oh, yeah. Real ritzy.*

A previous tenant had probably smashed a cockroach, and no one from the Hideaway Motel had ever bothered to clean it off the wall. Typical of your average fleabag dive. Stains everywhere and a hot-plate to serve as a pathetic excuse for a kitchen. She'd spent too many years of her life in places like this. At least this one had a cool name.

Tara felt a flush of heat course through her body, remembering her conversation with the guy in the bar. *Now that would be someone to hide away with.* Her heart raced just thinking about him.

Reluctantly, she shook it off and started thinking about the job ahead—and her heart started pounding again. It was magic hour. The biggest heist of her life just twenty minutes away. And counting.

She had already wrapped her breasts tight and removed all traces of makeup. Grabbing a lighter, she set her drawings of the bank aflame and tossed them into the garbage can. Best not to leave any incriminating evidence behind—part of Wyatt's system. In case they didn't make it back.

She put on a loose leather biker jacket and smeared mud lightly over her face—each step erasing another bit of her femininity.

Wyatt entered the room, humming a little ditty to himself. He wore his cowboy outfit—from chaps and spurs to his black, ten-gallon cowboy hat.

He pumped his fist in the air. "Is this a great country, or what?" Wyatt said. "All the farm subsidies from four counties in one little podunk bank!"

Tara matched his mood. "Along with a couple of the

stupidest guards I have *ever* had the privilege to meet!"

"Oh yeah," said Wyatt, "and have I mentioned the money?"

Tara smiled. "Only about a hundred times."

"Well it's ripe for the picking," Wyatt said. "And we're just the ones to do it."

He turned the dial on the radio and found a snazzy little country song. Wyatt grabbed hold of Tara and started dancing a jig.

She laughed it up, enjoying one of his rare happy moments, and they danced around for a couple of minutes, whooping and hollering. As they danced, Wyatt's hand casually descended a few inches until it rested on Tara's rear. She winced and elbowed his hand to the side.

"Stop it, Daddy. How many times do I have to tell you?"

Wyatt stopped dancing immediately, the party spoiled. "Don't you call me that. You remember what Aunt May said."

She certainly did. The second worst day of her life. The only one worse was the day her mom was killed. "Just keep your mind on the job," she said.

A change came over Wyatt. Lately, he'd been taking this jealousy thing to unhealthy extremes. Tara watched the storm clouds gather in Wyatt's head and tried to think of a way to distract him before the storm broke, but the lightning in his eyes flashed and the thunder boomed.

"Now that's rich, pumpkin. Since we left that little shit hole bar the job is the one thing you haven't been thinking of! It's written all over your face."

Little bits of spittle flecked against her cheek as he spoke. Wyatt took a step closer to her.

"You think that punk could take me on?"

"If you would ease up on the leash a little bit, *Wyatt*, I just might find someone," Tara said. "But maybe that's the whole point, isn't it?"

Wyatt leaned in real close to her and grabbed her chin. She could see his stubble and feel his breath.

"I raised you. And I know what's best for you," Wyatt said. "And that punk ain't it. Don't try to make this into something disgusting."

He pressed up against her, nostrils flaring. Tara looked him in the eye, keeping hold of her anger. But she felt nervous. For him to show this much emotion before the job didn't bode well for things to come.

After a moment, he let go of her chin. "That's a good girl. You've got ten minutes to finish getting ready while I go grab us a work vehicle."

Wyatt slammed the door on his way out.

She yelled out after him, "Damn it, Wyatt. You better not kill anybody this time."

She didn't know if he heard.

MAX FIDDLED WITH HIS TAPE RECORDER AND GLANCED AROUND the cell. With the addition of the latest drunk, it was beginning to get a little crowded. One guy had passed out and was leaning up against C.J., who was doing his best to ignore him. He sat there on his corner of the bed, engrossed in his free literature.

"You know," said C.J., "I think I would like to 'help me—help myself.' This stuff ain't half bad."

"Yeah, that stuff's hit and miss," Max said. "But if you read enough of that bullshit, you just might find somethin' that works for you."

"Yeah, but this shit is really deep. Listen, it says here that if I learn to 'help me' by letting out my true feelings, it'll unlock my inner happiness, and therefore 'help myself.' That's…like… genius or something."

Max yawned—having heard it all before. His pop never met a self-help book he didn't like, and Max had been subjected to every manner of book-taught guidance known to man.

Even one book meant for dogs. His pop was nothing if not thorough. "Knock yourself out, C.J."

The one notion from the freakish collection of books that had stuck with Max was the habit of putting everything down on tape, a technique learned from the book *How to Love the Inner You*. The book said to write everything down on paper, but that had proved a little tedious.

Max had thought the whole idea was corny, but it turned out the process of laying everything out helped keep the things inside in decent order. And he considered it time well spent.

A daily portrait of his thoughts and views.

In the holding cell he had nothing but excess time on his hands, so he pressed the record button on his micro-cassette recorder and began to lay it out there. "When you're born the whole world is open to you. But as time goes by, opportunities seem to dwindle. One day you wake up and life isn't up for grabs anymore. Your life has become a prison. Made of dreary jobs and dismal relationships…"

C.J. broke in. "You're right about the dreary jobs thing. But you sound kind of crazy, Max, talking to a machine like that. And what does that mean—life is a prison?"

Max hesitated, momentarily embarrassed. "It's a metaphor, C.J. Now let me finish."

"Sorry." C.J. shrugged and got back to his book.

Max took a drag off his cigarette and started again. "There are some great movies with people breaking out of prison. Of course, not all of them make it. But it's better to die trying than to give in."

WYATT APPROACHED THE BEAT-UP VAN LIKE HE OWNED THE THING. It was one of those models from the seventies with stripes down the side and black bubble windows in the back, a hippie love mobile.

He jimmied the door open and stepped inside. With a

smirk, he noticed the bed in the back of the van—definitely a love machine.

Then came the easiest part of the job. He pulled out a hammer and whacked a big screwdriver into the ignition. Much quicker than wiring it. He twisted the screwdriver and started the van.

The tires squealed like a pig as the van peeled away.

Rule #3: Never use your own wheels. This was a subsection of *Rule #2: Keep your personal life and your professional life separate. Use some low-life's car, and better still, put it back where you found it before anyone's the wiser. The poor sap will be the one who gets picked up and strip-searched and probed. Your orifices will remain sacrosanct and unviolated. Thank you, Lord, for your protection.*

Max decided the first thing he'd do when he got released was search for the girl. He stood at the front of the cell, arms hanging through the bars, while C.J. stood next to him, grinning like a fool. Things were taking a turn for the better.

"Damn it, Mr. Hurley. Come on, now," Williams said. "Why on earth wouldn't you want to press charges?"

Williams paced from side to side as if he was the one who was caged. "What do you mean, 'No harm, no foul?'"

C.J. whispered to Max, "Can't he still keep us for evading him or something?"

"Not really. Judge Roy's told him, on many previous occasions, that it isn't proper for my pop to be the one pressing charges against me. Makes the law look unprofessional or something."

"Hot dog," C.J. said. "The King must really be watching out for me."

Rule #9: *Wear something that covers your face, like a bandana or pantyhose. Better still, use a disguise. But if your mask slips and they catch sight of your real identity, take 'em out. If they look at you funny, they're paying too much attention to you. Take 'em out. If they're in your way, they annoy you, or they just breathe funny, feel free to take 'em out. It's important to remember that most people are assholes. If you take 'em out, you might be doing the world a favor. You've met these people—societal cleansing can be a good thing.*

Later, the criteria for "Take 'em out" became extremely lengthy as Wyatt discovered there were more, and more, and even more reasons to kill people. A seemingly infinite number of reasons. So, it became a rule of its own—the final rule—#47: *When in doubt, take 'em out.*

Tara checked her false beard and moustache. They'd paid good money for one of those Hollywood hairpieces from the movies, so the facial hair looked pretty real. She hid her long hair under a baseball hat and smiled, remembering the first time she'd done that very thing. She rubbed a little more dirt onto her face and neck, then put on a pair of leather motorcycle gloves to cover her hands.

It's a miracle, C.J. thought. We're going to be freed.

He watched Max's dad fidget with the phone cord while he talked.

Williams said, "Look Mr. Hurley, won't you reconsider?"

While Williams listened to the response, he shot Max a baleful glare. Though the force of the gaze wasn't aimed at C.J. he cringed anyway, then gave a sideways glance toward Max and chuckled. Max didn't even seem fazed by the glare, looking his pop straight in the eyes. Heck, he'd probably stared down the barrel of a Williams stare so many times that the look had lost its power.

"I *know* he's my son," Williams said. "That's the point. I think he needs to be taught a lesson."

Max looked disappointed, and C.J. felt for him. He couldn't

believe what he was hearing. If that's what it was like to have a dad, C.J. thought, he wasn't missing much.

RULE #12: *NEVER DO A JOB UNDERMANNED OR WITHOUT ENOUGH firepower to do the job proper—Wyatt style. If you need extra guys, get 'em. "Professional" criminals are kind of like a family. Well…a dysfunctional family, not like you and me, Tara. Just call around to the people you trust until someone can recommend a driver or some extra muscle or whatever else you might need. Have plenty of ammo. And know your weapons inside and out. That way nobody gets accidentally shot in the foot. Again. That really hurt, damn it. And it was mighty unprofessional.*

Tara checked her little semi-automatic and put it in her thigh holster. Since she was now wearing pants, she wore it in plain view on the outside of her thigh. She loaded a forty-five semi and a sawed off shotgun and packed her jacket pockets with extra clips and shotgun shells.

Wyatt loaded a snub-nosed revolver and slid it into the ankle holster in his boot. He loaded a revolver and a sawed off and grabbed a bunch of extra ammo for each. He loved the soothing effect of holding a precision steel machine in his bare hands. Powerful.

Tara said, "Yee haw, cowboy!"

MAX WATCHED HIS POP SLAM HIS FIST ONTO THE COUNTER, scaring the petite dispatcher, Lorna. From the hungry way she looked at Williams, Max figured they had something going on the sly. Or maybe not yet consummated.

"Look, all I'm asking is for you to delay your decision until tomorrow morning," Williams said. "That way, they spend the night in the cell. It would do 'em some good."

C.J. sighed. "He's like a bulldog. He really has it in for you."

Max shook his head, disagreeing. "Naw, he's just misguided. He thinks he's doing the right thing."

Williams slammed down the phone. He slumped at his desk, ignoring Max and C.J. He picked up the *Rough Love* book and thumbed through it, looking for answers.

RULE #8: ALWAYS HAVE FUN! A GUN IN YOUR HAND. A SPRING in your step. The cool wind blowing against your face. That's what life is all about.

And remember, for every lucky person that gets a gun pushed in their face, that'll be the most exciting thing to ever happen in their insignificant lives. Even the ones that wet their pants will get a kick out of it. So you have a blast, too!

The beat-up van stopped quietly in front of 1st Farmer's Bank. Wyatt pulled a bandana over his nose and mouth. Tara used a Lone Ranger-style mask to cover her eyes—and her disguise was complete.

They both looked at each other for a moment, shotguns raised. Wyatt's eyes were a little manic with excitement. On the job, there was never a dull moment for Wyatt.

Tara kept cool and professional, but a touch of excitement peeked through her veneer.

"Let's do it!" she said.

CHAPTER 11

EXHIBIT 27—EXCERPT FROM AUDIOTAPE 1

*One of my favorites is Rule #36: To make your point—
cock your weapon. The sound of the hammer being
pulled back will inspire an automatic attitude adjustment.*

Max flicked his lighter open, lit a cigarette, and
then continued.

That's just beautiful.

Wyatt and Tara walked slowly into the bank, keeping
it casual until the last possible moment. Or until someone
screamed. They split up, each heading for their respective
security guard—with Wyatt idly wondering if anyone would
provoke him today. He hoped so.

Wyatt glanced over and watched Tara approach her guard.
She moved with such grace and beauty—finely tuned precision from years of practice. Damn, he was proud of her. They
made a great team.

He also knew that it helped to have a good strategy and
gave himself a mental pat on the back for coming up with a
foolproof system. *If you want success, you have to have a good
system!*

He'd picked up that little gem of an idea at one of the
insurance seminars from hell he'd had to endure. One of the

perks of the day job he'd had way back when. Only fantasies of killing everyone present at those abominations had kept him awake during the interminable lectures.

Wyatt reached his rent-a-cop. It had only been a few seconds, but the waiting seemed to stretch into forever.

The security guy never even noticed a big man with a mask and gun approaching—the fun part about robbing banks in the sticks—and Wyatt appreciated the guard's "blah-zay fair" attitude while he whacked him on the back of the head with the butt of his shotgun. And yet, he was also agitated at the lack of employee standards rampant in today's corporate world.

Tara was almost to her guard when the guy noticed Wyatt knocking his partner out cold. The guard caught sight of Tara bearing down on him and reached for his weapon.

Tara remained in character—and her talent rivaled that of any method actor—as she called out in a gruff, manly voice, "HOLD IT!"

The guard proved to be hard of hearing, or just plain stubborn, because he didn't stop. He pulled out his weapon right as Tara arrived.

She always found it annoying when they didn't listen, because out of necessity she'd have to introduce the guy to a little pain. She took the stock of her shotgun and smashed the side of his face. He dropped to the floor in a heap, out for the count. His gun went skipping away to hide in the corner.

At this point, patrons of the bank started to notice the show going on around them. Wyatt always felt it wasn't really a proper robbery until somebody screamed or fainted. Luckily, a woman soon kicked it off right and started a high-pitched, deafening shriek. Now the fun would really begin.

Wyatt kicked his guard's gun a couple of feet away, out of easy reach, as the customers began to panic. Crowd control was crucial. He wanted them scared, but didn't want them running around like chickens with their heads cut off. That way led to chaos.

Wyatt fired a shot into the air to secure everyone's

undivided attention. For emphasis, Tara cocked her gun and leveled it at the crowd.

Wyatt did his best to come across as a menacing psycho. It wasn't as much of a stretch as he imagined.

Rule #26: Let 'em know you're crazy. Feel the crazy. BE the crazy. It's not just fun and games. This shit works. And the job will be that much easier if you can pull it off. After all, who wants to take on a two hundred and fifty pound psycho?

"LISTEN UP! The first person to cause me any problems, or make me even a tad bit upset, GETS TO MEET GOD FACE TO FACE."

The crowd backed away from him in unison. That was better.

Tara leapt up onto the bank counter. The crowd backed away from her, too.

From Tara's vantage, they looked like a school of fish darting, in concert, away from a predator. She turned away from them and corralled the bank tellers and the bank manager, Lou Stephens. That was the slimy guy Wyatt had told her to watch out for. She herded them toward the rest of the crowd.

Wyatt took a deep breath and reveled in the moment. This was the perfect way of life for him. His form of religion—his church. And it was wondrous and holy. He approached an imaginary pulpit and spoke to his captivated flock. Or was it a captive flock? Either way worked for him.

Wyatt grinned under his bandana as he spoke, "Now you all are God-fearing citizens, am I right?"

He put the barrel of his gun right into a customer's face, then laughed when his chosen target half fainted from being the center of attention. The man tried to speak but couldn't get the words out, like his mouth had suddenly turned dry as the Mojave Desert. He feebly nodded his assent.

"Then get *down* on the floor and pray for your deliverance!" Wyatt proclaimed. "And you might just live through this."

"Amen," Tara chimed in, like a chorus in a gospel church. "You just might live through this."

Wyatt and Tara gestured with their guns and the customers moved to the floor.

"And pray do it quietly," Wyatt said.

"Quietly," Tara chorused.

"You don't want to attract my attention..."

"Hell, no," Tara added.

"...if you catch my meaning," Wyatt said.

He aimed one of his fingers at the flock and mimed pulling the trigger. "Let me get an Amen."

The crowd was quick to respond, and in stunned amazement, murmured "Amen."

Tara followed with her own "Amen." She glanced over to the bank manager. A woman who was not his wife was crowding up against him, but he didn't seem like he was up to anything.

Lou Stephens' little squeeze was hanging on a little too tight for his comfort. He worried the good times might be dead and gone, that his wife was sure to figure out he had a thing going with the nubile blonde from New Accounts. He decided he'd better take things in hand and calm everyone down. For the sake of the employees and the customers, not to mention his own hide.

"Just do as he says everyone," Lou said to the crowd and specifically his honey. "Stay quiet and this will be over before you know it."

Wyatt came up behind Lou and smacked him across the back of his head, then laughed as Lou fell to his knees. "I just said you don't want to earn my attention. Don't tell me you fell asleep during the sermon?"

"I hope he's not a sinner," Tara said. "We don't like sinners."

Wyatt whacked him again, cackling.

Rule #23: Weed out the troublemakers. Isolate them or immobilize them. Or take 'em out. Dealer's choice.

Wyatt figured *Rule #23* could be applied properly in this particular situation. He gestured for Lou to hop up onto the deposit slip counter.

"Now you sit on top of this counter here. And as punishment for your deplorable behavior," Wyatt looked straight into Lou's eyes, "you will be the first to die if there are any problems."

Lou staggered up and sat on the counter, stranded on an island in the sea of customers. Wyatt raised his gun as if to whack him again and Lou flinched, looking miserable. Wyatt nodded, satisfied, and figured Lou would now try his best to be a good boy.

With years of practice and study, Wyatt found he had a knack for looking at people and figuring out if they were gonna be trouble or not. This was a trait he apparently shared with the President of the United States. Leader of shit-kickers and rednecks everywhere.

He'd heard the President spewing on TV a few years back. The guy had been alleging his mastery of the Russian leader and how he'd looked into his eyes and seen the goodness in his soul or some such crap. But, in this particular instance, the President hadn't been lying after all. A unique circumstance, to be sure.

After that, Wyatt started paying close attention to people. He noticed that it was indeed possible to use his considerable experience and figure people out just by watching 'em.

Lou sat on his island. Feeling queasy, he pondered his ill fortune and wished fervently that he'd listened to his departed mama and treated his wife with more respect.

Or, even better, that the women of his life hadn't been positioned on the floor so close to each other. His honey kept looking to him for support and his wife, Marge, was getting suspicious. He tried to ignore the girl and instead grinned sheepishly at Marge.

Wyatt noticed the exchange and pointed to the wife. "You. Heifer. Get your big ass behind the counter there and start filling this duffel bag with large denominations."

He tossed her the bag. It landed on her head and appeared to quiver as the body below it trembled.

"Are you deaf? I said MOVE IT!"

He grabbed her roughly and yanked her up, then frog-marched her over to the *Federal Farm Subsidies* window.

"You've got sixty seconds to fill that bag. At sixty-one seconds, I start breaking fingers."

Marge looked forlornly at her chubby fingers and started filling the duffel bag.

Tara spotted movement out of the corner of her eye. She jumped down from her perch on the teller counter and landed next to one of the customers. She jammed the barrel of her sawed-off into his face.

"Don't you move, slimeball. Don't even breathe funny. And keep your hands where I can see them."

The guy, who had been mining a stubborn nugget in his nose, froze and left his hands right where they were. Tara looked back to Wyatt, who gave her a wink of approval.

Lou used the distraction to give Marge a couple of very subtle hand signals. The two had developed a special code for cheating in their bridge club. After all, it hadn't been easy to remain the Stoneybrook Bridge Champions for three straight years—they'd had to use every possible advantage.

Marge understood the crafty gestures and seized the moment. She pushed the button for the silent alarm that was under the counter. It started flashing out of sight. She continued to load the bag with stacks and stacks of greenbacks.

SHERIFF WILLIAMS SHOOK HIMSELF OUT OF THE FUNK HE WAS IN and stared at Max and C.J. He rose from his desk and pulled his keys out. Max knew the moment was hard for his pop.

"It burns me up, but I've got to let you out."

A red light started flashing on the side of the wall, along with an obnoxious buzzer.

Williams glanced at it quickly, then to Officer Lorna. "The bank. Get all units down there, now! Then notify the Feds."

He tossed the keys to Max, then hurried over to the shotgun case.

"Pop, it'll be quicker if you run through Daryl's place."

Williams ran out the door, shotgun in hand.

Max opened up the cell door and started after him, then glanced back at C.J. sitting on the bed. "Aren't you coming?"

C.J. winced before giving him a pathetic grin. "Naw. I've had enough excitement for one day."

Max wondered if it was even possible to have too much excitement. He doubted it strongly as he bolted through the door.

MARGE TRIED TO KEEP HER COOL AND COMPLETE HER TASK in the time allotted. She hesitated and looked at her fingers, terrified. She clucked nervously, worried she was running out of time and wondering if the police would make it there quickly enough.

That horrifying cowboy criminal clapped his hands twice. "Chop, Chop! Come on sweetheart! Your sixty seconds are almost up," Wyatt said.

Marge trembled even more and accidentally dropped a bundle of hundreds onto the floor. She quickly reached for it, but the cowboy stopped her. Then the beast put his hand on her shoulder and leered at her. Oh goodness, the desire in the man was plainly evident.

"I got it honey. Don't stop what you're doing. I guess I make you a little nervous, huh?"

The man moved his hand slowly down her oversized body as he talked to her. She knew she should have been repulsed by the psychopath in front of her, but it had been too many years since Lou had looked at her or touched her like that. The bastard said she'd gained too much weight. The real reason, she suspected, was that he was sleeping with that blonde slut from Credit. She'd been dangling all over him since this wretched ordeal began.

She jumped nervously as the cowboy in his ten-gallon hat moved down to the ground. She'd heard that men who wore large hats were compensating for a lack of size in other, more private areas. She sighed—only the tiny ones ever seemed to find her attractive. She stepped forward and covered the alarm switch with her ample body.

SHERIFF WILLIAMS RUMBLED DOWN THE STREET AS QUICKLY AS he could—winded, but still moving fast.

Max hurried after, about two blocks behind his pop, but almost tripped when a toy poodle darted in front of him. He leaped over the yipping mutt, noticing that he didn't have the urge to protect all little things in an equal manner. Those little dog-like creatures, with their French haircuts, painted toenails and ear-shattering barking, violated all that was good and decent. Even so, he made sure not to run over the diminutive critter.

Williams reached the front of the bank and dove to the ground. He landed with a thud, then scooted up to the large-paned window next to the front door and peeked inside.

WYATT KNELT ON THE FLOOR AND PICKED UP THE BUNDLE THAT had dropped there. When he looked up at Marge, he noticed she had a funny expression on her face and that she'd changed her body position. Wyatt used his presidential deductive powers and found the evil in her soul.

He pushed her out of the way and saw the flashing yellow alarm light. Why were people so stupid? He rose, wondering if Marge could see her death in his eyes.

Rule #13: Stupid people must be punished. If it doesn't interfere with the job, rid the world of these foul creatures that use up our precious resources. Deep down, society just might thank you for it. Not out loud, of course.

Wyatt looked over to Tara, apologetic. She'd been pretty fussy lately with his killing people. Not at all appreciative of the lengths he went to protect her.

But you did what you had to. Tara would just have to understand.

Wyatt looked at the nameplate: Marge Stephens. "Well, well, well. Would you believe Marge, here, set off the alarm?" Wyatt asked the crowd. "It would seem that both Marge and her husband don't listen too well. Either that or they just aren't too bright."

Wyatt turned back to a petrified Marge. "You must have mad cow disease or something. This could have been so easy. I'm afraid it's gonna cost you."

Wyatt turned casually to her husband, Lou, and fired into him, the impact blowing him off the counter and onto the floor. Marge and some of the customers started screaming in terror.

THE BLOW TO THE GUARD'S HEAD HAD BEEN PAINFUL BUT HE was still conscious, though dazed and confused. He'd inched toward his gun. But once he reached it, unnoticed, he hesitated. He'd always figured his job was just for show. And since he'd never actually shot anyone before, he was slow to work up the courage to stand against the gun-wielding thieves. When Lou's body landed on top of him he decided it was time. He closed his eyes and said a quick prayer.

GOD HELP US! WILLIAMS BACKED AWAY FROM THE LARGE WINdow, shocked. He put his back to the building and pumped his shotgun, loading a shell into the breach. He took half a second to mentally prepare, then started for the door. He stopped when he heard fast footsteps coming up behind him and whirled his gun toward the sound, looking for an accomplice.

Max came to an abrupt stop, breathing hard.

No! Williams pushed him back out of the way, and toward a cinder-block wall. "Get down, Max!"

Damn it. He did it again. Tara couldn't believe it. Wyatt just couldn't keep his gun in his pants. She felt tears start to form and quickly clamped down on her emotions. She swept her gun across the floor, but no one else was moving.

Wyatt turned away from Lou's corpse and back to Marge. She was sobbing. He grabbed her wrist and held her hand down against the counter.

"It's been sixty seconds. And just like I promised..."

Marge started to struggle, but Wyatt smashed his gun onto her hand, breaking her fingers.

Visions of the last bloody job swirled in Tara's head, and she figured she had to get him out of here before he started shooting into the crowd again. She grabbed the duffel bag and started to zip it up. "Come on!" she said. "We've wasted too much time here! Let's get going."

Wyatt hopped over the counter and froze, startled, as Lou's dead body started to move. *Shit!*

Wyatt pumped another shell into his shotgun, ready to fire as many rounds as necessary to keep Lou's body in its naturally deceased state. But a security guard popped up from underneath the body and raised his gun to fire.

Relieved, Wyatt shot the guard's arm, blasting his weapon and a couple of his fingers into the corner. Wyatt cackled, watching the guard back toward the door and brace himself for impact.

Wyatt was about to put the guy out of his misery when he spotted the sheriff sneaking in right behind the security guard. He held off for half a second, then fired his shotgun into the guard's chest. The powerful impact lifted the guard up and into the air, crashing into the sheriff and smashing them both through the plate glass window.

All right! A two-fer.

As he headed for the door, Wyatt turned to Tara and said, "Give me a five count, then follow."

Tara backed slowly toward the door. She fired, unloading her weapon into the surrounding furniture and counters, keeping the gunfire well above everyone's heads. Her shots did some serious damage to the bank's corporate image.

OUTSIDE, SHERIFF WILLIAMS GOT UP FROM THE GROUND SLOW-ly, a bit dazed as he shook off the glass. Max rose from behind the retaining wall where he'd taken refuge, and saw a tall, heavy-set cowboy with a shotgun burst through the broken window. He ducked back down and yelled out, "Watch out, Pop!"

Too late, Williams raised his gun, but the blast hit him in the middle of the chest.

Wyatt jumped into the beat-up van and turned the key, listening to the delightful musical sound of gunfire from inside the bank.

Max hopped over the wall and into the open. He ran to his pop and leaned down to check if he was still breathing.

Tara ran out of the bank and over to the van, the whole time cursing Wyatt's name under her breath.

She noticed Max and raised her weapon to shoot—and then hesitated. *It's him!* She knew she should take him out, or Wyatt would go berserk, but she held back and didn't shoot.

He was oblivious to her presence, his attention focused solely on the dead man in front of him.

She lowered her gun, intrigued by this tender side of him she hadn't seen in the bar. She got into the van, taking off her mask and hat as the van peeled out. Her long hair, hidden by the hat, flowed out the window.

She watched Max in the mirror as they pulled farther and farther away. Until there was nothing left to see.

MAX RIPPED OPEN HIS POP'S SHIRT TO EXAMINE THE WOUND and apply some pressure, hoping to staunch the blood flow, and was immensely relieved to find himself staring at a bulletproof vest.

Williams coughed as Max helped him into a sitting position. He coughed again and then smiled, noticing a tear in Max's eyes.

"See, I knew you still cared," Williams said.

Max rolled his eyes before answering. "That's never been our problem, Pop."

CHAPTER 12

Excerpt from audiotape 2

Another thing my pop always told me was that when you have a woman on your mind, there's not much room for anything else. I think he nailed that one, 'cause all I could think about was her. With all the excitement of the bank heist, I should have had other things on my mind. But I waited outside her motel, like a love starved puppy, and never caught sight of her.

I knew I might never see her again, but I made myself a promise that if I did, she wouldn't slip away.

"Oh, this one's good," Pete said.

Bull watched him fumble around looking for his tape recorder. Pete had a tote bag full of tapes of his amazing ideas. *Pete's Greatest Hits, Volumes 1–27.* But the magic had begun to fade and Bull had lately begun to wonder if all those hours of tape were as amazing as Pete thought they were. His latest one, about grabbing his ex-partner's cash, was getting them nowhere, fast.

They'd gotten nearly all the way to Texas before finding out on the radio that Pete's old crew had just hit another bank. Back in Arizona. And they'd just driven four hundred miles in the opposite direction.

They could've dropped the whole thing, but ignoring a quarter-million dollar take went against their principles.

Now they were driving back through the land of sand, cactus, and freaky aliens from outer space: the damned rectal-probed state of New Mexico. Bull didn't know why aliens were fascinated with people's assholes, but he knew *he* didn't want to be violated, and that New Mexico was one place he never wanted to see again. He dreaded this fearful stretch of highway with every part of his being.

Feeling powerless and impotent, he prayed to the spirits for protection from the aliens. Unfortunately, Bull wasn't sure if his ancestors would respond to his prayers again so soon. He knew the spirits, in their mysterious ways, had already watched over and guided him earlier today. They'd stepped in and kept him from bludgeoning his partner to death.

Somehow, they'd caused Bull's stitches to rip open and bleed, which in turn had made him stop and think about what he'd been doing to his partner. He knew it was no small feat for the spirits to accomplish that, but looking back, he felt it was something that was probably best for everyone involved.

If anything, the beating made Pete and Bull's bond stronger. The brawny partner keeping the smart one in check and vice-versa, striking a balance in nature.

So, they'd smoked a little of that soothing and illegal leaf, in the Indian tradition of peace pipes, and decided to make up—giving each other some man-style hugs, which Bull likened to little pats on the back.

Pete dug out his little tape machine and spoke into it. "What if you took milk and cookies and combined them into a thick, tasty drink? Maybe one of those breakfast drinks with vitamins and minerals added to it, so people would be suckered into thinking it's nutritious. Market it to the whole family as a combo everyone loves with all of today's modern convenience."

Bull's jaw dropped. Every time he started to doubt Pete, he came up with some extraordinary idea, just like that one.

At times like this Bull knew, deep in his soul, that if he stayed around Pete long enough, one day they'd strike a path to glory and riches. Even in his marijuana-induced fog, he realized everyone loved milk and cookies.

AGENT STRATTON STRUTTED THROUGH THE BOILING HEAT AS he approached 1ˢᵗ Farmer's Bank. He wasn't strutting because he'd bypassed the slow FBI system and gotten his team to the bank bandits' latest crime scene in less than an hour. He was *definitely* proud he'd wheedled use of his daddy's private jet for his own personal gain, but it wasn't why he strutted.

He *always* strutted. In his head he played the Bee Gees' tune from *Saturday Night Fever* whenever he walked. If there was a cooler flick to ever grace the silver screen, he hadn't seen it.

In the seventies, he'd even bought one of those white suits with the wide lapels, hoping to impress the chicks. And for about six weeks the suit had been a regular babe magnet. Then the earth stood still—and disco died. A tragedy of epic proportions in Stratton's book, and soothed only by repeated viewings of his favorite film.

Stratton and Dawkins entered the air-conditioned bank and looked at the carnage. A half dozen other agents spread out to check the area. Stratton had a gleam in his eye, enjoying the view, but he noticed that Dawkins looked a little green around the edges.

What a homo, Stratton thought. If Dawkins didn't enjoy something like this, he was in the wrong line of work.

To his way of thinking, the crime scene was amazing, even better than sex. He worked hard to suppress a grin. He'd noticed that people tended to look at him in a peculiar way when he smiled or laughed at the crime scenes.

Oh well, fuck 'em. The blood, the destruction and the bodies were too awesome a sight to hold back. He chuckled and spoke out of the corner of his mouth to his partner.

"Dawkins, go set up the video. And this time, make sure you let me know when it's cued up."

"Yes, sir. You got it. I'll come get you the second I've got the bloodshed ready to view."

Stratton noticed, but emphatically ignored, Dawkins' disgusted expression as he wandered off, carefully stepping around the body of the bank manager. The body count wasn't high, but the damage was impressive and the blood had flowed like a river. He made a mental note to get a copy of the surveillance video for his private collection.

Stratton looked around for the local yahoo in charge. Where was that bozo?

He'd been in contact with the ground forces while he was in the air and had ordered the city sheriff to corral the witnesses and set up the usual roadblocks—looking for two men, of course. He hadn't bought Dawkins' crackpot theory that one of the evil duo was a woman. Heck, the previous theory about circus freaks made more sense than that. And if Dawkins was so smart, why was he still a powerless peon at the agency?

After a couple of minutes of fruitless searching, Stratton figured out who the native chief of police was. He strutted over and puffed out his chest, trying to present an image of a man in control, but instead doing a spot-on impersonation of a bloated puffer fish. In his most condescending tone, the one reserved for maids and waiters and the like, he said, "Are you Sheriff Williams?"

Williams gave him a once-over, then wrinkled his face, obviously disapproving of him.

My god, these peasants have nerve.

"Yeah, I'm Williams. And you're General Patton?"

Stratton's eyes narrowed. Dawkins had once told him he had a Napoleon complex, whatever the hell that meant. While he wasn't sure of its meaning, he knew it was disrespectful. He wondered if the Patton reference was similar. "Special Agent Stratton," he huffed.

He thought up a few choice words for the sheriff, but held them back. He felt torn—on the one hand, he wanted desperately to tell this low-life to shove it up his ass. On the other hand, he knew that Williams had been shot and Stratton was dying to see the wound up close and personal. Morbid curiosity won.

"Hey Williams, let me ask you something before we get into any of the usual procedural stuff. Man to man, you tell me what it was like."

"I'm not sure I follow you."

Stratton glanced around, conspiratorially, and said, "Come on. It's just you and me. Tell me how it felt. I'm just itching to hear all about it."

"I have no idea what you're talking about," Williams said.

Stratton leaned in close and whispered, "I've never been shot before."

Williams frowned. "Are you kidding me?"

"Did it bleed? Can I see it?"

Williams took a step back from Stratton as Agent Dawkins approached the two and interrupted their scintillating conversation. "The tape is cued up to the carnage, as requested, *sir*."

Williams shook his head in disbelief and turned from Stratton to Dawkins, who shrugged an apology.

"Stratton, I'm not going to show you a damn thing," Williams said. "I think you're one sick puppy."

Stratton bristled. "Well this sick puppy is in charge. You know...I don't care for your attitude. And since this case falls under federal jurisdiction, get the hell out of my crime scene."

Stratton gestured to a couple of his agents to remove the spluttering sheriff. As they ejected him from the bank, Stratton called after him. "You know, since we've got it covered here, why don't you make yourself useful and man one of those roadblocks with your men. You can consider that an order."

Stratton turned his back on the impotent sheriff. He had some juicy things to do. Important "Special Agent" stuff. He had to interrogate the frenzied and emotionally devastated wife of the dead bank manager—always a treat. He had to check out the video of the bloody heist—which he was pretty sure he'd give a rating of two-thumbs-up. And he had to assert his superiority on some of his lesser agents—one of his favorite pastimes.

All in a day's work.

Tara looked out the tiny motel window at the beautiful desert sunset and cried as softly as she could. She'd locked herself in the seedy bathroom of their luxury suite because she didn't want Wyatt to hear her from the other room. That would only make matters worse. And they were bad enough already.

She couldn't decide what she should do. It had been just the two of them for the last thirteen years. Ever since mom had been killed. But now she wasn't sure.

Since the bank heist she'd been on auto-pilot, following the system religiously. She'd taken off her male disguise and clothing and replaced it with a short skirt and a pastel tank top. She'd placed her guns on a towel after cleaning them thoroughly per *Rule #21*.

She knew Wyatt had returned the van to the spot where he'd borrowed it, with the owner none the wiser. The Cougar had been parked about a block away, ready for a quick getaway, and she'd wiped down the place for prints in case anyone ever linked the two of them to this room.

Earlier, they'd arranged to bunk down at Chester's place for a week or so, until the heat died down. Chester was part of Wyatt's network of buddies. The guys in his network would let them hide out as long as they got a minor cut of whatever job they'd just finished. For a bunch of lazy, no account lawbreakers, it beat working for a living.

Everything was going according to plan except the constant killing. Or maybe, Tara figured, that had been Wyatt's plan all along. It was like an addiction or something.

Fatalities were an unfortunate side-effect of her line of work, like when someone got cute and interfered during the heist, but this was getting way too disturbing and uncomfortable. The bastard was killing people on every job! It had become routine for Wyatt.

But it wasn't routine for *her*. She didn't want to be like him. She didn't *have* to be like him. It's not like it was genetic or anything.

The man probably wasn't even her father. At least, that's what Aunt May had said, and she should know—she had been privy to all Mama's secrets. At the time, Tara had hated Aunt May for saying that, but lately she'd grown to appreciate the woman's point of view.

Now, she felt a little crazy—like Wyatt—and needed to find a release so that she didn't end up like him, too. She punched the mirror, cracking it.

A little better. Tara looked down at her bloodied knuckles and then back up to the mirror. She could see her fractured image in the splintered slivers of the glass. Twenty segmented images of Tara stared back at her. *Which one should she be?* Or did she even have a choice? She wasn't sure if the apple could fall far enough from the tree or not.

She started as Wyatt pounded on the bathroom door. "Tara, get in here. We've got to have us a little talk."

Unbelievable. His voice was already slurring. He always tapped a bottle of whiskey after a job, but today it sounded like he was going strong. Celebrating like someone just released from a ten-year stretch in prison. Wyatt could crave his whiskey like a man lost in the desert craved a drink of water. And as he'd always been a mean drunk, she wasn't looking forward to joining him in the other room.

She made up her mind. It was time she got out and forged her own way. Made her own system. Her own set of rules.

She'd known it for a while now, but hadn't been ready to admit it. Maybe 'cause she knew damn sure Wyatt wouldn't let her go without a fight.

Wyatt pounded on the door again. "Tara, get your ass out of there!"

Tara wiped the tears from her face. Crying never helped

anyway. *You make your own help.* She looked down at the weapons cache and at the little .22 that was sometimes strapped to her thigh. She put it on and lowered her skirt to cover it, hoping violence wouldn't be necessary. But as she knew Wyatt better than anyone, she realized it was a distinct possibility.

She remembered the time, at one of those fancy burger places, when Wyatt had gone off on one of the food servers. He'd been in a bad mood, as usual. And the poor bastard had served him a well-charred burger, with pickles, after he'd distinctly asked for a pickle-less hunk of meat. Wyatt had waited two hours, in the rain, for a bit of societal cleansing—that's what he'd called it anyway. And that was for a misplaced deli-sliced dill.

She took a couple of deep breaths, opened the door and walked into the bedroom. The drapes were drawn, keeping out prying eyes. In the dim light, she could make out Wyatt in his boxers and T-shirt, sitting on the bed, counting the money and cackling to himself.

He took another pull from the whiskey bottle and yelled out, "Tara! Oh. There you are."

He took another drink and frowned. "You and me got to have us a little talk. I'm getting worried about us." He hiccupped. "About *you* anyway. This last job was messy."

"Messy?" Tara said. *Is he serious?* Apparently, in his drunken stupor, she was going be blamed for the bloody mess from an hour ago.

"Things weren't up to snuff," Wyatt said.

"Are you talking about the guard that you supposedly knocked out, but ended up shooting at us, or the fact that you wasted three people, including a cop?"

Wyatt quickly stepped up and slapped her across the face. He gestured to the money spread across the bed.

"We've got two hundred and fifty thousand reasons why I did okay." He stumbled about, enraged. "I'm talking about the fact that you didn't waste that punk."

"And why would I? I'm not like you, Wyatt. I don't kill without good reason."

Wyatt arched his eyebrows and chuckled a little. "You don't believe that," he said. "You and I are cut from the same cloth. I raised you."

Wyatt took his finger and traced a heart on her breast. "The same blood runs through your heart as mine. We're family."

Tara looked him straight in the eye.

"It's not the same blood," she said. "We aren't the same."

Tara glanced down at the finger still lingering on her breast. She looked at the offending digit with the same disgust she'd have showed if she found a rat dropping in her food. *It was definitely time to leave.* She could smell the hundred-proof fumes coming from his mouth as she said, "That's your twisted fantasy."

Wyatt looked down and pulled his finger away. He threw the whiskey bottle past her head, smashing it against the wall.

"Have I ever asked anything of you?" Wyatt said. "Except that you do your part so we can make a living?"

He began pacing like a caged animal. "And on the day of our biggest score, you screw it up."

Tara narrowed her gaze. He was working himself into quite a lather—a typical Wyatt warning sign.

"That Romeo punk from the bar is the only person in this shit hole town who might've recognized us...and you let him live. Now why would that be?" Wyatt began to pace with even more energy and anger.

Shit. The fast pacing was another sign of a Wyatt Armageddon.

Wyatt slurred, "I've been blind. This wasn't sloppiness. I've gotta face facts. I taught you *better* than that."

Wyatt threw a chair out of the way and rushed back to her side. He grabbed her by the chin and looked into her eyes.

She stared back, but couldn't find anything familiar. He was gone—crazed and inhuman.

Worse than that, he was giving her the look he gave his victims—right before he killed them. She'd seen the look many times in the past, of course, and it was always bad news. But never before had Wyatt directed the look toward her. *This is bad.*

Growing up, Tara had always worried that Wyatt would hit her or, even worse, abandon her someplace like Aunt May's. But she always knew she could deal with those kinds of problems, even as a ten-year old. Working the cover position in bank robberies had always made her feel capable of handling life's little tribulations.

But, for the first time, Tara feared for her life—and from the person who raised her. As a little girl, she'd faced down people with guns without hesitation or fear. And now she was worried about a drunk and unarmed man.

Once he snapped...well...it was best not to think about it. And there was no way he wouldn't snap—he was too tightly wound, was too jealous, and had drunk way too much alcohol. A ticking time bomb.

Wyatt punched a hole in the wall right next to her face. *This is worse than bad.* She had to start thinking pre-emptive strike since Armageddon seemed just around the corner.

Wyatt left his fist in the plastered wall as he said, "You must really be aching for this guy."

First thing was to stall him. "I would never do that to you, Daddy. I love you too much for that." She gave him a big fake smile. "It was just a mistake. I should have killed him. It was *Rule #47*, plain as day. Take 'em out. I know I should have and I'm sorry."

Wyatt calmed down a bit. Or maybe not.

To Tara, it seemed more like the eye of a hurricane—and that there'd be just as much danger on the other side.

"I wish I could believe you," Wyatt said. "But how can I. You've obviously shown me your true colors." Wyatt removed his hand from her chin and placed it on his belt buckle knife. A tear rolled down his cheek.

He trembled and clenched his hands a few times, then Tara saw Hurricane Wyatt start to build again.

"Maybe we should make a new rule. *Number 48,*" Wyatt

slurred. "About giving me the respect...and loyalty...and love that I deserve. Can you do that?"

He's going to kill me and he wants love? Tara felt the rain start to whip around her face. She glanced down at the knife and said, "I can do that."

Wyatt shook his head and slowly pulled the knife from his belt. "Your mother couldn't."

He jerked his other hand free of the plaster and took hold of her hair in a tight grasp. "And you can't either."

Shit! She looked at the knife and figured it was time for a pre-emptive strike, but found it easier said than done. She'd never drawn a gun on Wyatt before and it was much harder than she thought it would be.

Tara closed her eyes and tried to gain a little more control of herself. She decided to think of it like a bank job. Like when she had to act crazy to maintain control of the situation. Because, of course, then it would be all right to attack her father.

Well...here goes nothing.

Per *Rule #14* about applying pressure to sensitive areas—fingers, private parts, etc.—she aimed accordingly and kneed him, hard, in the groin.

Wyatt immediately dropped his handful of hair, distracted in spades.

She backed away from a writhing Wyatt to gain a little elbow room. He was still too close, but she hoped the alcohol would slow his reflexes enough.

Just a job. Just a nice, happy, bank job.

Taking a deep breath, she reached under her skirt and grabbed the gun strapped to her thigh. She drew the gun quickly, but Wyatt saw it and lunged for her, raging. He tackled her onto the bed and started ripping at her clothes, screaming at her.

"You conniving little slut! You'd betray me for a punk you've just met..."

She struggled to get away, but he was too strong and too heavy.

Wyatt used his forearm to hold her down and the other

to twist away the gun. He screamed at her non-stop, incoherent.

"I'm your father. I would have loved you forever," Wyatt blubbered. "And you betrayed me."

He grabbed the gun and started to raise it. Tara clawed for the telephone beside the bed, but couldn't quite reach it.

"Now you better pray for forgiveness…'cause it's gonna cost you," Wyatt cried. "It's gonna cost you everything!"

Desperate, Tara kneed him again. From underneath Wyatt, she didn't have the leverage for a solid strike, but the soft hit on an already tender area was apparently painful enough to give her a little space.

She reached over and grabbed the phone—which was heavier than most since the motel didn't want people stealing their prized possessions—and slammed it into Wyatt's head.

He dropped to the ground, stunned, then struggled feebly to get up. Tara hit him again. And again. And again. Just to be sure.

Tara fell to her knees, crying the tiniest bit. She shoved his limp body, making sure Wyatt was definitely out.

He was, thank God. Then she had a panic attack and checked for his pulse. Luckily, he had one—so she thanked God one more time.

She reached over and caressed his head, feeling tender for a moment. Her hand came away bloody. She wiped it off on his shirt and then wiped away her tears.

She was glad he couldn't see her crying. That wouldn't have made him very proud. He probably *would* have been proud of her doing whatever was necessary to protect herself…if it hadn't been *his* head that had gotten bashed in.

She packed her things and changed her ripped top. Per *Rule #15* she wiped her prints off the phone. She doubted she'd ever give up the rules. Probably just change them a little. Make 'em a little better. A little less violent.

She grabbed a couple of guns, then reached for the duffel bag and started filling it cash. But then she hesitated. She didn't want the money.

Amazing.

She packed away a few thousand only—a little money for the run ahead—then scattered the rest of the two hundred and fifty thousand around the room, with most of it landing on top of Wyatt's still form.

She grabbed the remaining weapons and put them in the duffel bag as well. Best not to leave Wyatt with an easy means for her destruction just lying around. He'd find replacements, but at least it might delay him a little bit.

She had a brainstorm and decided to take all his clothes, including the boxers and shirt he was wearing. Just to make things a little more difficult.

At the door she turned back to look at Wyatt one last time. Naked, he seemed out of his element, kind of like a giant beached whale. She shed a final and solitary tear.

"I do love you, Wyatt," Tara said. "Just not in the same twisted way you love me."

She blew him a kiss and walked out, saying over her shoulder, "You're damn lucky I do love you and that I don't go *Rule #47* on your ass." She slammed the door.

But she didn't have the heart to take him out per *Rule #47*–though she knew she should have.

'Cause she had no doubt Wyatt would follow.

CHAPTER 13

EXCERPT FROM TAPE 3

Pop told me that there were moments—and for some people maybe even just one—that would change your whole life. If you had the courage to take the chance. Most people let that chance go by and regret it for the rest of their lives.

Seize the day. Carpe diem.

"I'm telling you it's not a coincidence," C.J. said. "There have been more Elvis sightings this year than ever before."

Max only half-listened. C.J. was always spouting off about Elvis. And his favorite time to eschew his latest theory was while they were playing pool at Joe's Tavern. Most of the time, his friend's entertaining conversational skills made for a good way to pass the time. But tonight, Max kept looking at the door, hoping she would walk through it.

Max missed an easy shot at the nine-ball. Since his mind just wasn't in the game, C.J. enjoyed the longest winning streak of his life. He sank the nine, winning his third straight.

"All right!" C.J. said. "Now most of the sightings...well *some* of the sightings are within a ten mile radius of Michael's estate. I know Jackson and Lisa Marie aren't together anymore, but you tell me I'm not right."

Max racked the balls and checked the smoke-filled room again. Instead of finding Tara, he found a large guy with the build of a football player staring at him from across the bar.

When Max caught his eye, the guy raised his beer in greeting. Max raised his beer in return, puzzled, because he didn't seem familiar.

Max would have gone over to check him out, but then Tara walked through the back entrance. She was wearing that sexy, short skirt again. *Yeah. There's something about her, all right.*

She stepped inside the bar and looked around. When her gaze found his, they stared at each other for a brief moment, then she beckoned for him to follow and walked right out the back door.

He liked how sure she was of herself—as if she knew he'd follow. And, of course, that's exactly what he wanted to do.

He wouldn't waste one more second here in this bar. He turned and nodded to his friend, who'd been watching.

"Good luck," C.J. said.

"Thanks."

As Max headed for the door, C.J. put a hand on his shoulder.

"Watch yourself. She makes me a little nervous."

Max grinned. "Everyone makes you nervous, C.J."

C.J. laughed sheepishly and let go of Max's shoulder. He grabbed a pool cue and held it like a microphone. He raised it up to his mouth and spoke in his very best Elvis impersonation.

"Thank you. Thank you very much," he said. "And now, for my next little number…"

Max left the building and headed for the dirt parking lot behind Joe's Tavern. He took a deep breath of the cool night air. It was the only time the desert temperatures were comfortable.

He hesitated, looking past beat up cars and pickups for a sign of her. And there she was, sitting on his Bronco like she owned it. Good thing he'd had the shot-out tires replaced that afternoon.

Max felt a tap on his shoulder and figured C.J. must have come out for something. He had just enough time to notice that it wasn't C.J., before the large football guy from the bar sucker-punched him. He noticed the guy had a tattoo of a snake on the back of his fist and got to see it up close when it punched his face.

Max hit the gravel face first and tasted a little dirt. The football guy pushed his knee into Max's back, pinning him to the ground.

"Listen up," Football Guy said. "This here is a message of LOVE from your father." The guy whacked him across the head to punctuate the word love.

Max groaned loudly. "Let me guess. Rough Love. From that book, right?"

"That's right. Your father LOVES you." Another whack. "I'm just here to make sure you get some consequences for your actions with the stolen car this afternoon. A little lesson in authority."

Max groaned again, his face pressed into the dirt. A little trickle of blood dripped onto the earth.

"It'll be nothin' major, just my fists. Because he LOVES you."

Football Guy whacked him again on the word love.

"No permanent damage, I promise," the guy said. "And don't resist, 'cause it'll just take longer and then I might lose my temper."

Football Guy pushed his face harder into the ground and Max decided he'd had enough—it was time to act. He briefly lamented that this would be the second person he'd have to beat up today and pondered the general crappiness of the world. His pop would say, "If life gives you lemons, make lemonade."

But then again, his pop apparently believed that being rough with your kid was the equivalent of love.

Max tensed, ready to heave the guy off and defend himself, when he noticed a pair of sexy legs with a thigh holster approaching.

"Uhmm. Excuse me," Tara said.

The guy turned his head to Tara and then back to his intended victim, ignoring her.

"Back off sweetie," Football Guy said. "This has nothing to do with you. Just my little friend here."

Max relaxed, wondering if she was as dangerous as she seemed, and figured he'd probably find out any second now. If she *was* dangerous, she'd take advantage of the guy's dismissal of her and make a move.

He was right. From his vantage point, he noticed her calf muscles tense, and then one leg shot into the air.

Tara kicked the guy in the face, knocking him to the ground. Max wiped the dirt off his chin and rolled onto his side to watch the show.

Tara quickly stepped over to the guy's hand and stomped on it, breaking a couple of fingers.

Football Guy roared in pain and lunged to his feet. But Tara pulled her gun from its hiding place and pointed it at the guy's face.

"This is my fiancé," she said, winking at Max. "So this has everything to do with me, okay?"

Max cautiously raised himself to one arm. *Yep. She's a keeper.*

The guy stood there, glaring at her. When he didn't respond the way Tara wanted, she cocked her gun.

"That was not one of those rhetorical questions."

"Okay. Okay."

Tara said, "If I see your face one more time, I'll do more than break fingers. Understand?"

"No problem."

Football Guy backed slowly away to a safer distance, and then sprinted away, running for dear life. Max and Tara burst out laughing. She gave him a hand up and replaced the gun in her holster. Tara appraised him with a glance.

"I was hoping I'd see you again," Max said.

"So was I."

They stared at each other. And though it seemed unlikely, Max thought that underneath, she was a little bashful and coy. That didn't seem to fit with her dangerous side, but he figured she was probably better with guns than with people.

"That was pretty impressive," Max said. "I'd like to make it up to you."

She smiled and said, "I'd like that."

As they walked back to his Bronco, he noticed her attitude changing. Her demeanor became less shy and went back to being cool and sensuous. Back to being sure of herself.

"But there's something else. If you're up for it," she said. "I think I'd like something more than that. Like maybe a ride to California."

Max stopped in his tracks and looked at Tara. She was serious.

"You sure?" Max said.

"I've never been more sure."

Max barely hesitated before responding with a grin.

"Then let's go. Hell, I knew the moment I saw you that we'd be going places."

As they reached the car, he noticed that her bags were already in it—as if she knew he'd agree. *Damn, she's sure of herself.* He found that completely sexy. He knew it was soon, but wondered if she'd mind if he kissed her.

As they got into his car, she leaned her whole body into him and gave him a deep, long and meaningful kiss. As they continued, their body heat quickly began to fog the windows. Max realized he'd forgotten to breathe again when he saw stars. As they broke away from each other, he marveled. Underneath her cool, hard exterior, she felt so soft and alive.

Max started his car and turned on the defroster.

She smiled seductively at him. "Should I call you sugar bear? Stud? Or what?

Max grinned and replied, "I'm Max."

"Tara."

She put her feet on the dash and made herself at home as the Bronco pulled away.

"THAT WAS A HOOT AND A HOLLER!" AGENT STRATTON SAID.

Dawkins kept his groan to himself, knowing it was

usually best to agree with the blowhard. "I can see why you enjoyed it."

Stratton had just finished up with Marge Stephens, the widow with the broken hand. Dawkins didn't share his obvious glee in watching human suffering. Instead, he kept quiet and took copious notes of everything, even events that were already being recorded. He knew the little extra details he wrote down paid off once in a while.

And he had a hunch things were finally starting to break their way.

After ten brutal years during which the agency hadn't much hope of catching the duo—during which they'd embarrassed the agency time and again—they were actually getting some decent leads. It was just a matter of time now. If he spun it right, he might even be able to get assigned away from Agent Blowhard.

Dawkins decided that he'd have to hone his people skills and find a way to manipulate Stratton into following the right leads. He hadn't got him to buy into his discovery that one of the duo was a woman, so that would be the first step.

An eager young FBI agent, edgy from too much adrenaline, burst through the door, bumping into Dawkins and spilling his coffee.

"Damn, son. Where's the fire?" Dawkins said.

"Sorry, sir. But I had to tell you right away..."

"There's a fire?" Stratton asked, looking ready to bolt at a moments notice.

"No, sir. I had to tell you, sir, that we got a line on the getaway vehicle, sir. The van—it's parked on a side street, right here in town, sir. At this very moment."

Dawkins was about to tell the kid to lay off with all the sirs and to not get too excited, that it couldn't be the right one, when Stratton shot out of his chair like a firecracker and spilled the rest of Dawkins' coffee.

"Hot damn! We got 'em!" Stratton said. "Get all the boys rounded up. No locals, though, just the Feds."

"Wait a second, Stratton," Dawkins said. "No disrespect

intended, but you might not be familiar with the case history. In ten years, there has never been a viable vehicle lead. They always switch cars, or something of a similar nature."

"Oh, no. This is it!" He turned to the junior agent. "Did you find out who it's registered to?"

"Yes, sir. It's registered to a Billie Gates, sir. He has eight priors, sir, including wife beating, drunken driving, and...," the youngster paused for dramatic effect, "...one count of second degree robbery of a liquor store, sir!"

Stratton threw Dawkins a look that said "see, told you so," before turning back to the junior agent.

"See if you can find a local media guy. If they don't have one in this town, then grab anyone with a video camera. We'll surround the place, but wait to go in till you find one." Stratton grinned, picturing the arrest. "With the right publicity, this'll take our careers up a couple of notches."

Dawkins grinned as well. With a little luck, and some extremely embarrassing publicity, Stratton could be removed from the case by next week.

TARA SLID ACROSS THE SEAT, COMFORTABLE AND CLOSE TO MAX. They blew past a sign that said, "Now Leaving Stoneybrook— Come Back Again."

Not likely, Tara thought. It had only been about twenty minutes since she left Wyatt. But now that they were on the road, she felt a little less nervous about him catching up to them.

She put her hand on Max's thigh and enjoyed the feeling of driving through the desert night—free to do whatever she wanted. To be with a man her own age—one that lit her fire, turned her inside out. To pull jobs without randomly killing people. To enjoy her chosen profession like she used to. The possibilities were endless.

She got all hot and bothered, sitting there thinking about it. She settled into her seat and ran her fingers slowly over her bare shoulders, giving herself goose bumps. She savored the sensation and smiled at Max. This was going to work out just fine.

Or would it? She frowned, picturing the big dude in the parking lot taking Max down to the ground with just one hit. The guy had sucker-punched Max, to be sure, but Tara still began to feel uneasy. If Wyatt caught up to them, would Max even have a chance? From past experience, it was hard to bet against Wyatt.

She was completely drawn to Max, of that she was sure, and he was obviously enamored of her. But could her new beau handle himself in tough situations? It was a good question. And the answer was critical to their survival. She decided to test the waters and see how his brain worked. Check for compatibility.

"You know, Max. It won't be an easy trip…dangerous might be a better word to describe it."

She watched him closely for his reaction, but didn't see any fear or nervousness. *A good sign.*

Max didn't even hesitate before responding with enthusiasm. "Hell…that sounds perfect." He stroked her bare thigh. "If we're lucky, danger will just…spice things up…make things more interesting."

He turned from watching the road to look her in the eye. His deep blues were piercing. "Count me in."

She liked it. It was a good answer. Tara was sure he had the right attitude. But, of course, attitude wouldn't be enough. He'd have to pass a much stricter test.

One with guns.

BILLIE GATES SAT HIS REDNECK ASS INTO THE FAMILIAR GROOVES of his favorite chair. *Damn!* What was that smell?

He looked around the trashed living room. But there weren't no piles of dog shit lying around, smelling up the joint. Where the hell was that smell coming from?

He glanced with sudden suspicion toward the kitchen. That woman was trying to kill him! Lately, he couldn't remember why he'd gotten one of those imported brides from the damned Internet. *It sure as hell weren't because none of the local white women never gave him the time of day.*

"DOREEN!" Billie said. "You better not be making me any of that Chinese crap! I want some pork chops, damn it!"

There, that should put the old witch in her place. Once in a while, ya had to show 'em who was boss. He might have to give the little lady a lesson tonight. Get the leather belt out.

Then Billie heard two things that chilled him to the bone. The first was the sound of Doreen screeching obscenities at him in her native Chinese while standing in the doorway, holding a carving knife. He figured she was about to launch herself at him and try to kill her way to freedom in the U.S.

The second was even more chilling. He turned to the front door as he heard someone on his porch yell "THIS IS THE FBI...OPEN UP," followed by the sound of one of those battering ram things, trying to bust the door down.

He went down in a heap, tackled from behind by his wife just as the FBI burst through the door. A bright light shone in his face as the agents wrestled his knife-wielding bride to the ground. The light came from the top of one of those video cameras, like on that TV show *Cops*.

Shit! His buddies would never let him live this down.

He turned away from the camera to the front door and saw his worst nightmare come to life. There, bold as can be, was a Negro with a gun and badge. In his house, damn it. Billie didn't think things could possibly get any worse.

Then the light hit him again and an agent came to his side. The camera panned to the agent and moved in, getting a nice close-up shot of Agent Stratton.

Agent Stratton turned dramatically to the camera and said, "All right men, search the house thoroughly. Leave no stone unturned."

The agent turned to Billie and said, "Billie Gates, you are under arrest."

And if that wasn't bad enough, Agent Stratton turned to another agent and said, "Agent Banks, I want a full cavity search of this man. We'll get to the bottom of this, no pun intended."

The videographer captured it all then panned back to Billie Gates, who began weeping uncontrollably.

CHAPTER 14

My pop was a good man...though his advice got to be a little cliché at times. But he was not a good father. I don't fault him for it. My mom had done most of the parental-type work. When she died, he was so unprepared for the job he took to reading self-help books like they were the gospel. Timeouts, Rough Love...you name it, he bought it. Hook, line, and sinker.

"Why are we stopping?" Tara said.

Max steered the Bronco into the station and stopped at a gas pump. He gestured toward the fuel gauge, which was on empty.

"There's nothing but a hundred miles of empty desert till the next station," Max said. "Not a place to get stranded."

Tara glanced at her watch. She figured it had probably been about thirty minutes since she clocked Wyatt. She'd hit him pretty hard, so she thought she had another half-hour, or maybe longer, before he woke up. Their odds of a successful escape would dramatically improve if they left town quick.

Max got out to fill the tank. She heard him talking to himself but couldn't quite hear what he was saying. When he noticed her watching, he abruptly stopped talking and hid something in his jacket pocket. Maybe one of those little tape recorder things.

He looked a little embarrassed and she wasn't quite sure

what to make of it. But if that was the worst quirk he had, it was better than just about all of hers.

She hoped Max wasn't one of those idea guys like her ex-partner, Pete. The guy had been a damn fine driver, but a regular nut job when it came to the ideas he put down on tape. She laughed, thinking back to an idea of his about genetic engineering. Combining dogs, hamsters, and cats together into the perfect pet. To get an animal as happy as a puppy, as clean as a cat, and small enough to fit in your pocket or keep in a cage in your kid's bedroom. But after reading about the sheep-cloning disaster in England, Pete's hopes had been dashed and he'd moped for a week.

She checked out the shabby Convenience Mart. It had seen better days. In fact, it was extremely run down. Tara smiled—it might not even have security cameras.

She checked around, noting there were no other customers—and not a single car on the highway. This could be the right time to test Max, to see if they were really a match.

She hopped out and leaned against the car. "This one's on me."

"All right," he said. "Pick me up a soda, would ya?"

"You got it."

She hesitated—nervous Max wouldn't be able to handle her way of life. That the ride would be over before it even began.

She muttered to herself as she began walking toward the entrance. "Should I do it? Or shouldn't I?"

She knew it was better to have her questions answered now, but dreaded it all the same. She stopped at the doors as a tumbleweed rolled by.

This place didn't have one of those automatic doors like most have now-a-days. She checked the corners of the building—no security cameras on the outside. She made a deal with herself.

"If there are cameras inside, I'll let it alone. If there's not..."

Tara heard door chimes as she entered the store. *Rule #11* said to check out your sites thoroughly. She did so, pretending to be browsing. The cashier wore a muscle shirt and curled a large barbell in one hand. He leered at Tara appreciatively.

She headed for the soda fountain and checked out every corner of the place. Not a single camera.

She sighed, thinking that they really did make these places convenient. Twenty-four hours a day, seven days a week—cash ready for the taking. Convenience Mart.

For a brief moment she thought about giving up the criminal lifestyle, since Wyatt was now in her rearview mirror instead of riding beside her. But what else was there? Settling down with Max to raise a few pups? Work an office job? She shook her head. Heck, even if she wanted to quit, it wasn't like she knew how to do anything else.

So let's see if Max can adapt. I bet he can. She pulled out her gun and walked purposefully to the front of the store and the cashier. The man was about her age, muscular, blond, and looked dumb as a post. He set down his barbell and checked out her figure. Tara noticed that his eyes were glued to her chest and hadn't even noticed the gun in her hand. He let out a little wolf's whistle.

"Hey sweetheart, am I glad you walked into my life," the guy said.

Tara whipped the gun around and up to his temple. "You glad now?"

The man's eyes opened wide as she read his name tag. "Hey, Rick, you've got thirty seconds to show me if you've got any brains in that well-chiseled body of yours. Fill that grocery bag with everything you've got."

Rick looked nervously at the gun and then back at her breasts, a bit of drool dripping from his mouth. "Chicks and guns, huh?"

When he smiled, Tara figured that chicks and guns were probably an incredible combination of his two favorite pastimes. She'd seen plenty of his kind before. Add a Mustang convertible and a keg of beer, and Rick would think he'd died and gone to heaven.

He inched closer. "Aw, come on baby. You think I'm gonna let a little thing like a gun get between us?"

Tara looked at him for a moment, her gaze traveling slowly across his muscular physique. She sighed, wondering why brawn always seemed to equal stupidity.

"No. You probably wouldn't," Tara said.

She slowly lowered the gun to the counter, keeping her hand on it, and leaned toward him. Exposing a little cleavage.

"You're much too manly for that," Tara said.

Rick smiled and leaned toward Tara. She moved in, as if to kiss him...and WHAM. She whacked him in the head with the gun.

Men are way too easy to fool, Tara thought. She grinned. If breasts could distract them from a loaded gun pointed right in their face, they deserved what they got. A Darwinian test for the male of the species.

She grabbed his head with both hands and slammed it into the barbell on the counter. He raised his head back up—nose bloodied and a look of terror on his face.

"I think you're beginning to understand," Tara said. "So, like I said before...you've got thirty seconds to fill this bag. Then I get violent."

She pointed the gun at his private parts. Rick cringed and started whimpering.

When she cocked the gun, the melodious sound of the hammer being pulled back inspired the cooperation she was looking for. As it usually did. Tara always found that the response to that horrifying sound was an automatic attitude adjustment. Like she'd waved a magic wand and then presto—when she said jump, people said how high. The reality was that it was more of a trained response. Like Pavlov's dog. Rick heard the magic bell and hurriedly filled the bag with money.

Tara basked, enjoying herself. It had been a while since

she'd really enjoyed her chosen field. Her adrenaline was pumping. She was in the zone. Everything was crystal clear. She focused on the bead of sweat that ran slowly down Rick's nose and dropped to the floor.

Chimes went off again as someone entered the mini-mart. Tara swiveled and pointed the gun toward the door. Max stopped dead in his tracks, halfway through the door. She'd forgotten all about him. The whole point of the exercise.

She realized that her gun was aimed at Max and quickly pointed it back at Rick. "Sorry about that," she said.

Max calmly took in the situation. Tara hoped he wasn't spooked. That he wouldn't take off. But he just glanced at her hands and started toward the cooler.

"Did you forget something?" Max asked.

He pulled out a soda and headed back toward the door, looking Tara in the eye the whole time. He didn't seem spooked at all. Just a little disappointed that she'd forgotten about him.

And she *had* forgotten his soda. She'd forgotten he was even there. Here she was, testing him, when maybe she was the one that needed a little work.

She caught her breath, remembering something she'd read in one of those beauty magazines. The number one reason men fooled around was that their women didn't pay enough attention to their needs. It had been followed by an article: "Ten Sure-Fire Ways to *Really* Turn Your Man On." In her limited experience, it hadn't taken much effort to turn men on. But she'd memorized the strange sexual ideas, hoping to try them on someone special at some point in the future. Max was the first real candidate. But they'd only known each other one day and here she was blowing it already.

Max opened the door, making the chimes go off again. That sound was getting annoying.

Rick, seeing his last chance about to walk out the door, cried out, "Hey, Max. Where you going? You remember me, right? We went to high school together."

Max paused in the doorway. "Oh, yeah. How's it going, Rick?"

Rick half-frowned and half-smiled. "Hey, don't leave me with her, man!"

Max turned to Tara and looked right at her while talking to Rick. "Don't worry, Rick. She won't hurt you."

Max turned back to Rick. "You remember that liquor store that got robbed a couple of years ago?"

Tara noticed that Rick was starting to lose it. His hysteria was mounting. "What are you talking about?" Rick asked.

"The guy working the store that night…hell…guys bought him beer for a month, listening to his stories. He was famous."

Rick laughed painfully—with the familiar grimace of someone in a dental chair waiting for the drilling to begin.

"Now that's you," Max said as he walked out the door.

"Max!" Rick called out. "Max!"

But Max was gone. Rick turned back to Tara, whimpering again.

"Too bad you can identify Max, huh?" Tara said. "The cost of fame is pretty high, I guess."

Rick started crying in earnest. "No! We're buddies. You wouldn't kill one of Max's friends, would you? Please…"

The big guy was really crumbling. It was kind of pathetic.

Rick continued, "I'll say that it was two skinny Mexican guys…and that their faces were covered up…"

If Wyatt was here Rick would be dead already. From outside, Max honked the car horn. The loud sound made Rick jump about a foot in the air, his eyes bugging out. Near his groin, a wet spot grew larger and larger. Tara glanced down at his pants and grinned.

"Relax, Rick. I was just playing with you. Any friend of Max is a friend of mine."

He glanced up, hopeful, as Tara said, "But we do need a little lead time. So adios, tough guy."

Tara took the gun and smashed him across the face, knocking him out cold. Now that was the proper way to knock someone out. Way better than the job Wyatt had done at the bank.

Rule #32, The Proper Way to Bash Someone's Head: Grasp the gun firmly, yet gently. Swing in a downward arc, using the force of gravity to help add force to your swing. Always follow through. In this case, gravity is your friend. At Tara's insistence, Wyatt later added to the rule: *And only swing once, if you want to avoid a murder charge.*

MAX AND TARA DROVE DOWN THE HIGHWAY IN AN UNCOMFORTable silence—Max focusing on the road and Tara focusing on him. She felt hesitant. This was new ground, dealing with regular people, and she wasn't really sure what to do.

"Max, I'm really sorry."

He cocked his head. "Are you sorry you forgot my drink, or that you pointed a gun at me?"

"Well, the gun thing, that's just what you do in the middle of a robbery. You've got to cover everything. The whole point is to make sure nothing goes wrong."

Max shrugged. "Makes sense."

"And don't worry, even though the gun was pointed your way, I haven't shot anyone accidentally since I was nine."

Max turned toward her. "Did you say nine?"

Tara nodded, slightly embarrassed. "Yeah…it was like a…training accident. I shot my dad during my first job."

Max quickly turned away from her and back to the highway.

Tara watched him putting the pieces together and figuring out that she and her dad were probably the bank robbers. He seemed like he was dealing with it pretty well, but she figured this was probably the moment of truth.

"Rick's okay, right?"

"Of course he is. I'm not like Wyatt."

Max nodded.

"Look, I really am sorry I forgot your drink back there. I've had…an unusual childhood. And thinking of others doesn't come natural to me.

She grabbed hold of his hand and held it close. "Now that's no excuse, so I swear to you, on my mother's grave, that I'll never forget you again."

Max thought for a minute before giving her hand a squeeze. He smiled before glancing back to the highway. "Okay."

Tara could have jumped in excitement. That one word held so much promise. She cuddled up next to him and put her head on his shoulder, content as a cat lying in the sun.

"For a second, I thought you were a little upset," Tara said.

"You kidding?" Max put his arm around her. "I'm hooked."

Tara watched his eyes, wondering if he was fooling with her, but she could tell he wasn't.

Max continued, "And I know this might sound strange, but every little thing I find out about you—including the disturbing bits—just gets me *further* on the hook." Max shook his head. "You've got my mind going crazy, wanting to know everything about you."

Tara shivered, warmth filling her body. He knew just what to say. Her engine primed, she snuggled closer and began kissing his neck.

"Trust me," she said. "You don't really want to know everything. You just think you do."

She knew *exactly* what she wanted. She kissed him on the lips, running her hands up and down his body. She began to reach between his legs when she felt the car swerve. Poor Max was distracted.

She glanced ahead, checking for oncoming traffic, and saw the red and blue lights of a police car flashing in the distance. The car was blocking the road and a cop was waving at them to stop.

Her emotions went from hot to cold in an instant.

Max pulled the car to the side of the road and shut off the

engine. He shifted uncomfortably in his seat, rearranging himself.

"Wonderful," Max said.

Tara reached into her purse and pulled out a couple of handguns. She threw one into Max's lap and checked her weapon.

Max put up his hand. "Whoa, relax. I'll handle this. It's just my father."

Tara groaned as Max reached behind his back and put the gun in his waistband. He winked at her and exited the car.

Tara now put two and two together, remembering Max with a cop at the bank. *Shit.* She cocked her gun and opened her window to hear their conversation.

Williams stood in front of his patrol car. "Where do you think you're going, son?"

Max leaned on the trunk of the Bronco, keeping his distance from his father. It was a good choice and Tara liked his instincts. Part of *Rule #25* was about keeping good space between you and your adversaries.

"Well, Pop, since you're here...I might as well tell you in person," Max said. "I'm gone...out of here."

She and Max were both flying the coop. She smiled, appreciating the similarity to her own situation.

"Cut the crap, Max. I know you're upset about the guy I sent over to the bar," Williams said, "but you're not going anywhere."

"Watch me."

She shook her head. If his father had sent that thug, then Max's daddy must be a little crazy, too. But it also meant that she and Max had even more in common than she'd thought. And according to the beauty magazines, that was a good thing.

Max edged back toward the car door.

"Whoa, whoa," Williams said. "Hey, hang on a second. Time out."

Tara held back a laugh. Like you could call a time out in real life.

Max stopped and shook his head.

Williams said, "Look, I know that Rough Love stunt was out of line. But I've run out of ideas."

"You don't need any more ideas, Pop. I'm not your problem anymore," Max said. "You always told me that every man has to choose his own path...it's time to choose mine."

Tara watched the sheriff sigh and come to grips with Max's news. If only Wyatt had been so agreeable.

A bloodhound barked and poked its head out the window. Williams reached into his car and pulled out a book with a red bow on it. "I've been dreading this day, son. But you're right."

He handed Max the book. *On Your Own: A Moral Compass to Guide Your Path, by Jack Handy.*

Max gave his father a hug and Williams walked back to his car. *An actual hug.* She tried to remember the last time Wyatt had given her a hug that wasn't repulsive.

As Williams got to his car, his radio crackled and Lorna the dispatcher broke in. "Sheriff Williams?"

Max cursed and looked around wildly.

Tara knew what was coming and glanced down at her gun, hoping she wouldn't have to use it. She watched Max intently, wondering what he would do.

Williams gestured for Max to stay put and reached for his radio. "This is Williams. Go ahead."

"There's a code thirty at the Gas/Mart on Highway 40," Lorna said.

Williams shook his head slowly. "And what's the bad news, Lorna?"

"I'm sorry to be the one to break it to you, but your son has been positively identified as a suspect."

Williams tossed the radio back in the car and walked toward Max, pulling out his handcuffs. "Boy, you must have a couple of screws loose."

Max pulled the gun from behind his back and aimed it at his father. Williams slowed to a crawl, but kept moving.

The radio crackled, "Sheriff Williams...Sheriff Williams? Are you okay?"

"Pop, don't even try it. I'm not going to let you arrest me again."

Williams kept inching forward. "Give me a break, Max. You're rebellious as hell. And I'm ashamed to say it, but you've obviously got a little criminal streak that I haven't been able to break. But in all the stunts you've pulled over the years, you've never hurt anyone. Son, you wouldn't hurt a fly."

Max cocked the gun. Tara smiled, pleased to see a little backbone.

"Come on, Pop. After years of hell...after hitting me, throwing me in jail...after hiring a thug to beat the crap out of me... you think I couldn't shoot?"

Williams was now a couple of feet from Max.

"I may be a bastard and a rotten father," Williams said, "but I'm the only father you've got. And you know I love you."

Williams stopped, just in arm's reach of his son. Max hesitated before reluctantly uncocking the weapon and pointing it away from his pop.

"Shit," Max said.

Tara looked away, disappointed, before slowly aiming her gun out the window toward Williams. On the one hand, it was nice to know someone who didn't kill first and ask questions later—like Wyatt. On the other hand, was Max strong enough?

Williams breathed a small sigh of relief and reached for Max's gun. As his hand stretched slowly out, she shot him, nicking the flesh of his palm. It was a relatively minor wound, for a gun shot, but it bled freely.

The dispatcher's voice could be heard on the radio, now in a state of panic.

Williams clenched his teeth as his face reddened. He squeezed the bleeding hand in an attempt to staunch the blood flow, while under his breath, he counted to ten.

"And just what is your problem, missy?"

Tara narrowed her eyes and then ignored him. She turned to Max, who appeared sheepish but still met her gaze straight on.

"Get in the car, Max. I'll take care of this."

With a hangdog expression on his face, Max got in the car. Tara turned her attention back to Williams. There weren't any rules she could apply here. He was her beau's father and the only rule pertaining to family was not to rat them out.

She said, "I'm not one to apologize for necessary actions. But I do wish I hadn't hurt you…you being my boyfriend's daddy and all."

Williams raised an eyebrow.

Tara thought over her options and came up with a messy, but workable, solution. It would mean breaking the family rule, but it would also be the best way to keep Wyatt off their tail. And of course, he'd broken the rules first when he'd tried to kill her back at the motel, so she wouldn't feel too guilty about it.

"I tell you what," Tara said. "Just so there're no hard feelings, I'll tell you where you can find one of the men who robbed 1st Farmer's Bank."

Williams' jaw dropped open. "Is that right?"

"Sure. Being as how we're practically family, I'd like to help you out."

"How on earth would you know where those men are?"

Tara, with years of criminal practice, thought up a story on the fly. "I had a run-in with one of them. He held me hostage today. And it wasn't pretty. Through sheer luck I managed to untie my ropes and bang him upside the head with the telephone. I don't know how long he'll be out, so you don't have much time."

Tara could see that Williams wasn't buying her story. But as *Rule #37* told her, *Don't ever change your story. A changed story is like a shoe with shit stuck to the bottom of it. Sooner or later, the cops will remove the shoe, and all you're left with is the shit.* So she stuck with it.

"Look, I'm not messing with you. He's at the Hideaway Motel, room nine ninety-nine. All the loot is there with him. And he's not gonna want to give it up, so it'll take every man you've got to take him in. He's dangerous as hell."

Tara climbed back into the car. Max started her up and shifted into gear. Williams ran up to the window, causing Tara to point her gun at him again.

Williams gestured for her to relax. "Take it easy, missy. I've already been shot twice today. And that's twice more than any other day of my life."

He turned to Max and said, "Like I've always told you... you've got a choice, son. You can choose the path that leads to heaven, or you can choose the path that leads to shit."

Williams looked pointedly at Tara, who rolled her eyes at the innuendo. It was something her daddy would say. She wondered if maybe Williams and Wyatt were long lost brothers or something. Separated at birth by some freaky hospital mix-up.

Max put his foot on the gas and the Bronco sped off into the night.

Tara said, "I hate being called missy."

THE CAR RIDE WAS QUIET AS MAX AND TARA WERE BOTH LOST in their own worlds. Max had the feeling that he was on the hot seat, that he'd really blown it, and that Tara was mad about how he'd dealt with his pop.

Man, she was something else. There wasn't anything ordinary about her. That gas station thing had been intense, and a step above any of his other crimes, but it had also been pretty cool. He'd actually enjoyed it. And gotten pretty turned on watching her handle herself with his pop and with Rick at the convenience store.

He shook his head, clearing his thoughts. It wouldn't do to ignore the negative side. After her revelation about Wyatt's whereabouts and the money, he was now positive Tara had robbed the bank with her crazed father. And that was a little scary. People had died there.

Her father definitely had some deeply disturbing tendencies. Homicidal tendencies. And apples never fell far from the tree.

But on the positive side, she hadn't killed Rick—or anyone at the bank for that matter. And she'd only nicked his father's hand, leaving him with no permanent damage. That was sweet of her.

He had a brief fantasy of Tara and him robbing a bank together.

"I don't get it," Tara said. "You couldn't just wing him?"

He was right. She was ticked off.

Tara continued, "How hard can it be? I mean, I know his hand looked bad, but it wasn't. All we're talking 'bout is flesh wounds, here. Nothing serious."

Max chuckled. "I know, I know. Take it easy. I'll remember that next time." Max paused, and then said, "I promise."

He likened it to her promise at the convenience store—not to forget him—and hoped she knew that it was his turn. That he was making his own promise.

Tara slid over and rested her head on his shoulder. Max put his arm around her and leaned over to kiss her, but she grinned and playfully pushed him away.

"Oh yeah...weakness in a man gets me all hot and bothered," Tara said.

Max heard the playful tone in her voice but also heard the hint of truth behind it. She gave him a peck on the cheek and put her head back on his shoulder, closing her eyes and drifting off.

Max drove on in silence. He barely heard Tara say under her breath, "A girl needs to feel protected."

CHAPTER 15

EXCERPT FROM TAPE 3

My pop always told me that it was much harder to be with women, than to be without them. But that it's balanced out by the other rewards.

I guess there's some things you just have to take on faith.

Pete gave a nod to Bull, then watched him pound on the door of the tattered ranch-style house.

A rat ran over Bull's foot, causing the big guy to lash out with his boot, startled. Pete wheezed with laughter as Bull kicked a field goal over the front porch railing. The rat sailed end-over-end, bounced off a shed wall and into the dirt, then skittered away, healthy as can be.

Pete shuddered. He'd heard those things could survive a "nukular" winter.

"Three points," Pete said.

"Yeah, if you say so."

Pete frowned. His partner had been sketchy since New Mexico. He hoped it was just that alien shit Bull was worried about and not the run of bad luck they'd had lately.

At least they'd made it back to Arizona in one piece. And there was a good chance they'd meet up with Wyatt right here at Chester's place—find the pot of gold at the end of the rainbow.

Except nobody was home.

Pete tried to recall if any of Wyatt's other buddies lived nearby, but came up empty. Must've had too much Jack Daniels. Or maybe it was the joint he'd smoked. Either way, he couldn't come up with another good possibility. Wyatt *had* to have come straight here from that bank in Stoneybrook.

Bull pounded on the door again. "It's hard to believe there's a quarter million in this place."

Pete shushed him as the door squeaked open and a gun barrel poked through. Chester was fiftyish, wore a dirty bathrobe that had seen better days, and had a twelve-gauge pointed right at them. A patch covered one eye and the other was one of those lazy eyes that seemed to always point north. Pete put his hands up in what he hoped was a non-threatening way.

"Take it easy, Chester. It's me, Pete."

Chester raised the eye patch to reveal a healthy eye underneath. It darted back and forth, suspicious, but the eye apparently approved, for the patch went down and the gun was set inside the door. The lazy eye still pointed north.

Chester spoke with a squeaky and raspy voice. "Pete. Been a while."

"Yeah. It's good to see you again, Chester."

"Chet."

Pete blinked. Chester had never been one to waste words and it tended to make conversations a little difficult. "I'm sorry. What's that, Chester?"

Chester pointed at himself and said, "Chet."

Pete nodded in understanding. "Oh, I got you. Okay, Chet, this here is Bull."

Bull grunted and shouldered his way past Chet and into the house, knocking the slender man backwards. Pete followed him in, taking care not to bump into Chet as Bull had.

What a dump. It was dark inside, with just a single bare bulb burning. Brown, stained sheets were stapled over the windows, preventing them from being opened and leaving the place dank and musty smelling. In the corner, across from a ratty couch, an old television played one of those horrendous reality shows.

Reality shows were Bull's favorite, so he took a seat on the couch, making himself at home.

Chet spluttered and reached for his shotgun. Pete jumped in and put a hand on his shoulder.

"Take it easy, Chet. That's just Bull's way. He's in a bad mood or something—don't take it personally," Pete said. "I'll vouch for him."

Chet hesitated, thinking it over, his lazy eye floating toward the right.

Pete cringed—he'd always felt a little creeped out by the whole eye thing. Even worse, in his peripheral vision he spotted a rat scurrying along the wall. *Disgusting*—the place reminded him of a haunted house.

Chet nodded to himself and then backed away from the shotgun. He scurried over to the couch, like one of his rat friends, and sat beside Bull.

"What you want?" Chet said.

"Didn't Preacher tell you we were coming?"

Chet grunted a negative.

The grunt was an affirmation of Pete's guess. This was the right house. He put on his best poker face and tried to keep the glee from his voice. "Well, shit. I don't know what the hell's the matter with Wyatt these days. He should have told you we were on this job."

A grunt for a response.

Pete sat on the arm of the couch next to Chet, and leaned in to whisper, "This one required some extra help. It was kind of a big one."

Chet grunted and gestured toward Bull.

Pete replied, "Yeah. That's why Bull was along. We needed some extra muscle."

Chet grunted again and settled in to watch the show.

"They arrested Billie Gates?" Williams asked. "What on earth are they thinking?"

Officer Lorna's laughter came through the radio, "I thought you'd appreciate the humor, pumpkin."

Damn it, she called him pumpkin on the air. He checked around to see if any of his officers had heard, but they kept themselves busy, pretending not to have noticed.

Officer Lorna continued, "And what's more, someone captured the humorous moment on video. It's gonna be on prime time in half an hour."

"At least that'll keep 'em out of my hair for a little while." Williams chuckled. Agent Stratton was a pompous windbag. Served him right.

A police car drove by and parked in front of the sign for the Hideaway Motel. Williams ignored the car and turned to the police station's pride and joy—a nondescript, late-model cargo van filled with the best cop toys the town could afford.

Departmental funds were always tight in the small town, but about six months ago they'd been lucky enough to find a whole batch of surveillance equipment on eBay. Spy stuff from a retired CIA agent. Why old CIA equipment was for sale to the highest bidder, Williams could never quite figure out. Anyone could buy the stuff. And when he'd seen that Mohammed Abdul Aziz from Saudi Arabia was the highest bidder, Williams had felt some civic pride at outbidding the man. A potential terrorist in Williams' view. And in the process, Stoneybrook got some necessary equipment for their police force.

He opened the side door of the police van and checked out the monitors inside. One video feed showed the door of Room 999 and Officer Perkins, in a flak jacket, crouched in front. The picture came from a nifty little remote-operated camera on the roof of the van. The other monitor showed only static. Williams, forgetting his hand was injured, banged on the set. He winced and looked at the bandaged hand—and still couldn't believe Max's girlfriend had shot him.

He looked up as Officer Johnson approached the van and handed him a picture. The entire Stoneybrook Police Force was here at the motel and Williams fervently hoped that the rest of the town could keep from running amok till they were finished.

"Here's a digital picture of the person who rented the room," Officer Johnson said. "We searched through the whole tape, but she never turned her face toward the camera. Like maybe she knew she was being taped or something."

Williams checked out the picture. It was obviously taken from a high-angle security camera and showed only the back of a woman's head. Just the barest glimpse of her face. But Williams was sure it was Max's girlfriend. He sighed as he looked at the picture.

"I hope you aren't messin' with me, missy."

BULL AND CHET WATCHED TV IN RAPT ATTENTION, GLUED TO the set like flies to flypaper. It was one of those slutty dating shows—the kind that made Pete want to vomit. He wondered how people could stomach that crap. He paced back and forth, anxious for Wyatt to show up.

Pete had read somewhere that these reality shows made tons of money, and though he couldn't see why, a flash of brilliance caused him to break out the tape recorder. He spoke quietly into the machine, keeping his new idea away from prying ears.

"Instead of reality shows, reality *advertising*. Maybe have Bull crash a car into somebody who's holding a can of Coke. Capture it all on a home video camera with a shaky quality. Reality advertising."

Pete clicked off the recorder. There was a car commercial on the TV and Chet tilted his head toward Pete and laughed. His laugh sounded like a barking seal.

Pete waited for him to stop, wondering how the man could even watch TV with his good eye covered by a patch. Chet kept on cackling until Pete interrupted him. "What the hell is so funny?"

Chet wheezed and pointed at Pete. "Wyatt." He pantomimed a heave-ho gesture and pointed again at Pete, barking with laughter yet again. "Pete." Another bark. "On the highway."

Pete turned red. "Now that was a long time ago. Wyatt and I have gotten over our little dispute."

Bull reached over and clamped a hand over Chet's mouth, stifling the laughter. He pointed toward the TV—the show was back on. "Shhh. They're gonna show us if Mandy picked Kevin or Jay."

Chet quieted down and said, "Wyatt's late."

Stunned, Pete turned from the show and back to Chet. The lazy eye was pointed right at him. "You should have said that in the first place," Pete said.

Pete thought for a moment. Wyatt was never late. He followed his system to the letter.

While Pete couldn't remember most of Wyatt's rules, he was pretty sure there was a rule about punctuality and professionalism. That meant that something had happened. And Wyatt wasn't coming. Pete groaned—he no longer had visions of sugarplums dancing in his head.

Bull was gonna be pissed. There'd been too many losers lately. If this idea didn't pan out, Bull would thrash him within an inch of his life. Or worse.

He tried to think, but couldn't come up with anything. Pete bemoaned his sorry state. Here he was—the idea man—out of ideas.

Chet saw an Indian on TV and looked over to Bull and started barking again. He pointed at Bull and said, "Sitting Bull."

Bull grabbed Chet by the throat and choked off the laughter mid-bark. He leaned in close to Chet's face and flipped up the eye patch. The eye darted around as if trying to escape.

Bull said, "Indians aren't like what you see on TV."

Pete figured it would be better if Bull took his anger out on Chet, so he chimed in, "It's rude to stereotype, Chet."

Chet nodded, his good eye roving back and forth between the two men.

"That's right," Bull said. "I don't care for your...," he searched his brain for the word Pete had used so readily, "stereo-pipes...or whatever."

Bull eased up enough to let Chet breathe. "For instance, you probably think I'm named after the great and mighty bull, right? But that would be typical white man shit—that would be wrong."

Bull left one paw on Chet's throat and used the other to take a pull of his beer. "When my mother looked at me, right after I was born—after I'd been squeezed out, she thought I looked like a dog. Like a *pit* bull. Not a cow. You see how stereo-pipes can be full of lies, right?"

Chet's eyes were shut tight, but he nodded his agreement.

Bull squeezed again, cutting off Chet's air, and then was interrupted by a news bulletin: "We interrupt this program to bring you breaking news from our Crime Watch reporters. In a few minutes, we'll show you exclusive footage of the capture of a criminal mastermind—the man behind the 1st Farmer's Bank robbery. Our Crime Watch report will show you the daring raid and capture. Stay tuned, immediately following *I Want To Sleep With A Billionaire.*"

Bull relaxed his grip on Chet's windpipe and looked murderously at Pete, who immediately felt the pressure. Pressure can turn coal into diamonds, and for Pete it had the same effect. At that moment, the light bulb turned on and he came up with an idea. A fantastic and wonderful idea. He assumed a worried expression for Chet's benefit.

"This is bad. Real bad. They caught Wyatt." Pete turned to Chet. "He told me what to do in this situation. In case of emergency. He told me to get the package you've got stashed for him. You know the one I'm talking about?"

Chet grunted an affirmative. His face was turning purple from a lack of oxygen.

"Bull, let him go. He needs to go get the package. Right, Chet?"

Chet nodded and Bull released Chet's throat. The man scurried away after the package.

Bull moved closer to Pete and whispered, "What package?"

"Rule #42: Never put all your eggs in one basket."

"What shit are you talking about?"

Pete wheezed in excitement. "It's some crazy thing Wyatt came up with. He's never really liked banks—never been impressed with their security. And he's not a believer in any kind of insurance, like FDIC, that bank insurance. So he keeps stashes of money all over the country. His own personal savings accounts. Maybe twenty thousand in each."

"The man left twenty large here?" Bull looked around, skeptical.

"Not just here. Texas, Georgia...all over the southern states."

"That's crazy."

"Well, this is Wyatt we're talking about."

Chet scampered back into the room like a rat on speed. The package was the size of a lunch box and wrapped in brown paper.

He ran up to Pete and held it out, then stopped. He grunted with a questioning tone.

Pete spread his hands. "Come on. Who'd be stupid enough to fuck with Wyatt?"

"Hard to tell. You're pretty stupid." Six words, including a contraction. It was the longest statement Chet had ever made. He hesitated, then passed over the package. His eye bobbed before settling in position, facing north.

A POLICE CAR SAILED INTO THE MOTEL PARKING LOT AND screeched to a halt next to the police van. Sheriff Williams yanked his half-bandaged hand away from Officer Johnson and put his finger to his lips.

"Let's try not to wake the suspect, all right?"

Officer Dilbert cringed as he got out of the car. "Oh, man. Sorry, chief." Then Dilbert slammed the door, eliciting a growl from Williams. "Oh, man. My bad."

In a town the size of Stoneybrook, good help was hard to find. Williams shook his head. "Jesus, Dilbert. Did you get the warrant?"

Dilbert handed it over and said, "Yeah. But the judge weren't too happy about it. I had to reach him at his mistress' house. He said, and I quote, this better be the guy or you're up that creek with no paddles, ya know what I mean?"

"Yeah, I know what you mean."

"I can explain it if you want. The judge explained it to me."

"No, I got it, Dilbert."

Williams turned back to the monitor with the static and pounded on it again. He rolled his eyes heavenward and muttered under his breath. "High-tech equipment doesn't mean a hell of a lot if nobody has brains enough to run it."

Stoneybrook's Police Department had the same stringent hiring practices as other cities. Felons couldn't be considered— which eliminated half of Stoneybrook. And anyone who'd used drugs even one time, was disqualified—which eliminated the other half. Combine that with a job where people were likely to shoot at you, and a low turnout was not only possible, but a statistical certainty.

Out of necessity, intelligence was not ranked as highly as Williams would have liked. The standards were sincere and lofty, with an unintended consequence: it was actually likely that there would be at least one gun-toting moron on his force. Probably more.

Williams keyed his radio to ask a seemingly obvious question. One that would offend a smart officer—which, unfortunately, was a group that had excluded Perkins from membership. "Hey Perkins, are you sure you've got that spy camera switched on?"

Williams grabbed the remote for the camera on top of the van. He zoomed in toward Perkins in front of Room 999.

Perkins shook the long, thin snake-like camera and jiggled the power connection before noticing the on button. He glanced around nervously, not realizing he was on camera himself, then grinned sheepishly and turned the camera on.

On the other monitor, the static disappeared and a fish-eye view of Perkins' face appeared—close enough to count his nose hairs. His face was distorted and he looked perplexed.

Williams keyed his radio mike again, "Got it."

On the monitor, Perkins smiled and turned the wiry camera away from him. The picture swung away from his face and slid underneath the door. Williams and Dilbert watched the image as the periscope camera snaked its way across the floor.

"Come on," Williams said, "be there."

The camera rose off the floor, higher and higher, until it crested over the edge of the bed. There was Wyatt, out cold, blood running from his forehead. Naked and covered with money.

"Yes!" Williams pumped his bandaged fist in the air.

Dilbert whistled his appreciation. "That's a hell of lot of money for a naked man."

"Hell, yes!" Williams said. "And it's time to relieve him of his burden."

Williams spoke into the radio, "Perkins, pull that camera out of there and fall back into position with Sammy and get your gas masks on. Dilbert, you and Johnson take the back window. Come on, let's look lively, now!"

WYATT LIFTED HIS HAND TO HIS EYES AND WIPED THE BLOOD OUT, then groaned as his eyes fluttered open. He shifted uncomfortably to a sitting position and looked around the room.

His gaze settled on the bloody phone.

Wyatt's eyes narrowed, dreaming up ways of catching her and making her pay. A particularly pleasant and malicious thought entailed a beat-up Tara begging for forgiveness and begging to come back to him. That made him grin.

He absentmindedly scratched himself and realized he wasn't wearing any clothes. A quick glance told him all his clothes were missing. *Clever girl.* She was following *Rule #18: Make it as difficult as possible for people to follow you.*

Then Wyatt felt something unnatural in the pit of his stomach—maybe indigestion, maybe worse.

He wasn't sure what the feeling was until tears started streaming down his face. The only other time he'd cried was when he'd found his wife dead and Tara shot. And this felt almost as bad. He couldn't believe his little Tara had actually left him.

"My baby..."

Wyatt picked up the phone that she'd hit him with and caressed it, lovingly. *That's my girl.*

She'd followed the rules perfectly when she hit him.

He gave his face a little smack, an attempt to knock some sense into his brain. His gaze turned to the money lying all around him and he shouted out, "What the hell you crying for?"

Wyatt picked up a hundred-dollar bill and raised it to his face. He rubbed it softly on his cheek and brought it to his nose, sniffing deeply. He smiled—money always had a pleasant smell. "It's not like this is the worst day of your life."

Wyatt spun around as something crashed through the window and thudded on the floor. Two canisters hit the ground and smoke started pouring from them.

His pity party melted away as anger took hold of him. He took a deep breath before the gas got to him and rolled to the floor.

He quickly looked around for his gun, but it was not in sight. *Damn.* She must've taken it. For a second, he felt pride—his little girl was a smart cookie.

Rule #39: Fail to plan—plan to fail. But you know, even the most thought-out plans can go wrong. So if things go to hell, make sure to take the road less traveled. The unexpected route. Improvise.

Wyatt grabbed the mattress off the bed and put it in front of him, using it as a makeshift shield.

The door slammed against the wall as Perkins and Sammy burst into the room. Wyatt had a split-second to notice their eyes, bulging with fear, as he charged them with the mattress in front.

The officers fired again and again into the mattress, their shots missing their intended target entirely and exploding harmlessly into the walls behind him.

Wyatt smashed the bulky mattress into the officers, banging their heads into the wall. The officers slid to the floor in a heap.

Shots from outside dug into the wall, spraying Wyatt with bits of drywall and wood. He stuffed the mattress into the doorway, blocking the shots.

Wyatt rubbed his eyes, which were watering from the tear-gas. He looked around and spotted the large covered window on the back side of the room, near the bathroom. He looked solemnly at the money. It was so hard to leave it behind.

He turned abruptly and headed for the window, grabbing a handful of bills off the floor on his way out.

OFFICER DILBERT COULDN'T BELIEVE WHAT HE WAS HEARING. His partner actually wanted to climb through the suspect's window. *Impossible!*

Dilbert spluttered, "The sheriff said we're supposed to stay right here and cover the back window to the alley."

More shots rang out. One wild shot went through the glass and past their heads.

Johnson replied, "They might be in trouble in there."

Dilbert knew that was just an excuse. Johnson had once told him, in secret, that he wanted to shoot a perp more than anything in the world. He probably figured this would be his best chance and wanted to make the most of it by sneaking in the back window.

Dilbert was about to reply when the conversation was rendered moot. A giant naked man hurtled through the window.

Dilbert noted how similar he was to a majestic whale bursting from the ocean, heaving its massive body out of the water. He noticed this in the four-tenths of a second it took before the naked man crashed into them, knocking them to the ground amidst a shower of glass.

Unfortunately for Johnson, his fantasy of killing a criminal came to an abrupt end as one of the pieces of glass skewered his throat, perforating the carotid artery.

The wild man grabbed Johnson's gun and pushed it into Dilbert's face. "Use your radio, and tell them you're chasing me north down the alley. Now."

After a last gurgle from Johnson, Dilbert did as requested. "Sheriff, he got away from me. He's headed north down the alley."

The man nodded and then bashed him on the head, leaving Dilbert stunned and harmless. He fell to the ground, his brain more useless than it was normally, and watched the man grab him by the ankle and drag him down the alley. Dilbert lost consciousness as the man picked him up and threw him into a dumpster.

CHAPTER 16

EXCERPT FROM TAPE 1

*When I first heard Rule # 47, I just about called it off
right then and there. I mean, what kind of person can
make a rule like that? When in doubt, take 'em out?*

Would you want that person chasing after you?

Dilbert woke up with something hard and metallic
wedged in his mouth and a sharp pain on the side of his
face.

He felt another sharp pain as Wyatt slapped him
again. Dilbert whinnied in alarm when he realized that
the hard, metallic thing in his mouth was a gun.

"Wake up, scumbag. I need some information," Wyatt said.
"But if I hear that horse noise from you again, or any sound that
rises above a whisper, I'm gonna pull this trigger and make
some nice, pretty artwork all over the inside of this garbage
can. You don't want to look like a Picasso, right?"

Dilbert nodded his head in agreement. He watched Wyatt,
fascinated. He'd never come across a hardened criminal
like Wyatt before. Just drunks and whatnot—where
he'd mostly been at risk of being barfed on. He'd had to clean
the vomit from his squad car more times than he cared to
remember.

But this man was different. You could see it in the black-
ness of his eyes. Dilbert had the uncomfortable impression

that his life held less value than a cockroach to the criminal crouching beside him.

Dilbert looked ruefully around the dumpster, which reminded him of a roach motel, and thought, *Roaches check in but they don't check out.*

Dilbert heard the sound of feet running past the dumpster. Wyatt put his finger to his lips and shushed him.

"Now, you've got three seconds to tell me what I want to know before I start with the pain."

Dilbert believed him. His worst fears realized, Dilbert's eyes widened and he began to stammer. It was hard to talk with a gun in his mouth. He flashed back to elementary school, when the teacher had called on him and all he could ever do was stutter. The other kids had laughed at him, of course, and the humiliation had only made him stutter all the more. A vicious circle.

When Wyatt cocked the gun and covered Dilbert's mouth with his meaty hand, Dilbert abruptly came back to the present. The sound of the gun had completely the opposite effect of the kids' laughter—breaking any potential repeat of his childhood trauma.

With a mental clarity he'd never before experienced, he decided that he'd best stammer more quietly. And cooperate fully with the predator before him, in the hope that it would lose interest in him before it killed him.

Wyatt mouthed the word "three" and took the gun out of Dilbert's mouth. A rag was stuffed in. Wyatt grabbed Dilbert's pinkie finger.

"This little piggy went to market," Wyatt said, snapping the finger backwards.

Dilbert's face bulged as he stifled a scream. He whimpered pitifully, but kept the sound as quiet as possible. Wyatt pulled the rag out of his mouth.

"You didn't even ask me anything," Dilbert said.

Wyatt shook his head in disgust as he said, "Do I tell you how to do your business?"

Wyatt pushed the rag back into Dilbert's mouth.

Dilbert's eyes bulged again and he mouthed, "No, please, no."

Wyatt grabbed the ring finger this time. "This little piggy should've stayed home."

Wyatt bent the finger back until it snapped. Dilbert wept, ready to pass out from the pain. Wyatt smirked and put the gun to Dilbert's cheek, tracing the path of a fallen tear. With his other hand, Wyatt ripped Dilbert's badge off and gestured at his own nakedness.

"You don't mind if I borrow your uniform?"

Dilbert nodded pathetically.

Wyatt continued, "Now, I want to know *who* told you where I was and especially, how to find said individual. And you'd better get on your knees and pray to God, 'cause I sure hope you know the answers."

Dilbert hoped so, too.

"Let us pray," Wyatt murmured.

DILBERT AWOKE FOR THE SECOND TIME WHEN THE LID OF THE dumpster opened up.

Williams and Perkins looked down on him, their faces full of horror and sadness. They were staring at the fingers on his left hand, each of which pointed in an unnatural direction, like a spiked Mohawk on a punk rocker. Dilbert was alone in the dumpster and dressed only in his underwear and a tattered police hat.

"You alive, Dilbert?" Williams asked.

Dilbert felt around his body with his good hand and found only superficial wounds. He *was* alive. And checking out of the roach motel, after all. He felt luckier than an illegal immigrant winning the lotto!

Then Dilbert cringed, remembering his conversation. At one point during the ordeal he'd confessed his sins in prayer, and now he felt the need to confess one more to Williams.

"I'm so sorry, Sheriff. I told him about Max and the girl. He's going after them."

AGENT DAWKINS WINCED AS STRATTON ROASTED THE SHER- iff. It wasn't pretty—Stratton's speech was stuffed with slanderous slurs about redneck sheriffs and small-town cops. His shouting was spiced with profanities. If Sheriff Williams had been black, Stratton probably would have sprinkled the conversation with some choice racial epithets, as well.

Williams simmered in anger.

Dawkins didn't envy the sheriff. Of course, if Williams had actually caught the cowboys, Yogi and Boo-Boo, then the guy would be the hero—instead of the sacrificial goat.

"And why the hell didn't you call this in?" Stratton said. "You've been instructed to cooperate with our department in this matter."

"We weren't sure we even had the right guy. What do us redneck cops know anyway?" Williams said. "We'd heard, and on TV no less, that you'd already got your man. Billie Gates, right?"

Dawkins hid his smile behind his hand as Stratton splut- tered in apoplexy.

Dawkins had come to appreciate the way Williams han- dled himself. A fellow professional. Someone smart enough to keep his anger in check and able to smoothly shift the heat right back to Stratton.

And the man had actually cornered Yogi in a motel. That in itself was no small feat.

Junior Agent Speedo ran over, toting a cell phone. "Agent Stratton, I've got *Senator* Stratton on the line for you."

Stratton glared at Williams for a moment, then grabbed the phone and stalked away.

Dawkins picked up two cups of coffee from Speedo, handed one to Williams, and then shooed the junior agent away. "I like the way you turned that back to Stratton," Dawkins said. "With any luck, the Billie Gates incident will get him in trouble with his old man, the illustrious Senator Stratton." He poured some cream in his coffee. With a chuckle, he added, "Is it illustrious? Or preposterous? I get those confused."

"With that blowhard I can see why." Williams took a drink. "Let me guess. The story goes like this: Politician gets his idiotic son bumped up a few levels, past decent agents, probably thinking the moron would be perfect in a leadership role. But the guy trips up his subordinates, annoying the hell out of every poor soul stuck in the same division as the dipshit. I'd even bet the guy couldn't find his own asshole if he didn't have a smarter and more seasoned agent working under him who could point him in the right direction. Am I close?"

"Sheriff, you're a damn gifted storyteller," Dawkins said. "Not that I want to hear a sad tale like that without a few beers to wash it down."

Dawkins liked the amiable, by-the-book sheriff and his perceptiveness. But he wasn't buying the story Williams had just told Stratton about receiving an anonymous tip. That a girl who'd been imprisoned by Yogi, and subsequently escaped, had called in with Yogi's location. Something didn't quite add up.

And since Yogi was the only one in the room when the bust went down, and an unknown girl had rented the room, Dawkins put two and two together and figured the girl had to be Boo-Boo.

There were a couple of things he couldn't figure—whether Yogi and Boo-Boo had really split up, and what the sheriff was covering up.

But he knew Williams was hiding something.

Dawkins tried a little fishing. "I've got one for you. About a young woman who robs banks disguised as a scrawny young man. With a psychotic partner."

Williams hesitated. "Hell...I don't know. That might be a true story. Too hard to tell."

Dawkins sighed. It was worth a try. He pulled out a business card and handed it to Williams. "Look, we're close to these guys for the first time in a decade. We've got DNA from the blood, cops who can describe his features, and possibly fingerprints left in the room. So, if we could put idiotic special agents aside, I'd appreciate a call to my private number if you find out any other information."

"Professional courtesy, huh?"

"Something like that," Dawkins said. He wasn't sure he was getting through to the sheriff. "Look, these cowboys have robbed at least twenty banks. That's just the ones we've tied them to. They change their M.O. every couple of years so it's hard to get a clear count, but it's probably closer to forty. And while their tendencies have always been a little violent, lately things have been different. The big cowboy has been killing people right and left. He's a freaking psycho."

Now he was getting through. Williams looked decidedly uncomfortable.

Dawkins drove the point home. "And what's worse, he's not just ruthless. This bastard is smart. He figures shit out. That's why we've never gotten close before. And why he's still going to be hard to catch."

Williams didn't budge. The sheriff tried to hide it, but was obviously worried about something.

Dawkins left the man alone to think it over. He had a hunch the sheriff would come around sooner or later.

CHAPTER 17

EXCERPT FROM TAPE 2

Our first night together, Tara and I talked till morning. We tiptoed around the issue of bank robbing—never quite bringing it up. I guess it's not really a topic of conversation for a first date. We were amazed at how similar our fathers were—considering my father was a cop and hers was a psycho criminal.

But still, she must have had an interesting child-hood.

Tara ran as fast as her gangly twelve-year-old legs allowed. She'd almost reached the van when she heard the pop-pop sound of gunfire behind her and ducked behind a retaining wall. It didn't sound loud and booming like in the movies—more of a Jiffypop popcorn sound. She screamed as the cinder-block wall seemed to spit pieces of rock at her.

Someone was shooting at her!

The van was only fifty feet away, with Pete sitting behind the wheel, the engine running.

They'd started using a driver after the disastrous job in Alabama, when they'd come outside of the bank, money in hand, to find their getaway vehicle being towed away. Sure, they'd broken the law by parking in a no-stopping zone, but some Nazi tow-truck driver had actually hooked up their car in the short amount of time it took to rob the bank. Less than three minutes. The bastard must've been waiting in ambush.

Tara thought those kinds of tactics should be illegal.

Pete yelled, "Get over here. I'll cover you."

She'd always figured Pete was a coward since he never actually went inside the bank, but decided to revise her opinion. There he was, waiting calmly, while bullets ricocheted around him. It was admirable really. She mentally changed her opinion of him to Reliable Pete.

Tara cocked her gun and pointed it toward the bank doors, ready to run for the car. Wyatt stumbled past her, blood dripping down his arm from a bullet wound to the biceps. As a security guard chased after him, Wyatt squeezed the trigger of his shotgun, dropping the man to the ground.

Tara's eyes opened wide, watching the guard bleed onto the pavement. She knew it had happened before, but this was the first time she'd actually seen Wyatt kill someone.

As she stared at the body, Wyatt grabbed her by the shoulder and threw her into the van. Pete stomped on the accelerator like it was a spider about to crawl up his leg.

"OF COURSE, THAT WAS THE FIRST TIME I'D SEEN MY DADDY kill anyone, but it wasn't the first dead body I'd ever seen," Tara said. "Unfortunately, the first was my mama. And if she hadn't been killed…"

She reddened, then looked away from Max and out the window of the diner—at Max's Bronco, at the big sign on the edge of the parking lot. At anything that wasn't Max. The sign read: *EZ EDIE'S MOTEL & DINER, a place to sleep and eat. What more could you want?* That was a dumb question. What kind of slogan was that? There were lots of things she wanted. Like her mama back, a father that wasn't a sociopath, a couple of million dollars, Max's lips all over her body. She could make a list in a snap.

They'd talked until dawn before deciding to come down for breakfast. Then they'd talked for a couple more hours. And she'd enjoyed every minute of it. She was feeling great—lively, energetic. She was beginning to think they were two peas in a pod.

Max spoke up, breaking her train of thought. "I still can't believe you've been robbing banks since you were nine—and that you've never been caught."

"Why?"

"Because that's not the way the world works. You rob banks, you go to jail."

"Maybe that's the way your world works," Tara laughed. "In my world, it's the *47 Rules*. And they say: If thou followest the rules, thou *shalt* get away with it."

She thought Max's expression was priceless. Part skeptical, part hopeful. A bit of conflict showing. He was at a crossroads and hadn't quite decided which way to turn. She put it another way.

"Look, *Rule #4* is simple: *Use your brains*. But that's easier said than done. Prisons are chock full of losers who don't use the tools God gave them—either that or they never had smarts in the first place. Prisons are ninety-nine percent filled with stupid people. And the last one percent are just smart people that got greedy and then *turned* stupid. Your father's a cop, so you know I'm right. And that's why Wyatt and I haven't been to jail before. We use our brains."

Tara took a drink of coffee and continued, "Wyatt...well...he may be crazy, but he's crazy *and* brilliant. And I'm no slouch. And neither are you, come to think of it."

Max shook salt and pepper onto his plate of food before asking the million dollar question. "And the rules are?"

Tara tilted her head. "I'm not sure you're ready for the rules."

She grabbed the ketchup bottle and smothered her plate of eggs and potatoes. She offered it to Max, but he shook his head and grabbed the Tabasco, covering his eggs with it. She liked sweet, he liked hot.

Her eye was drawn to movement outside—a newlywed couple running toward their car, which had a sign on the back that read "Just Married." They were as happy as newlyweds typically were. Before real life struck them with the force of a sledgehammer.

A hellish place for a honeymoon. She wondered what could possibly be enchanting about this sandy Arizona locale. They must be on their way to the Grand Canyon or something.

She turned back to Max, who was also watching the couple. Max glanced back, meeting her gaze, then quickly looked away.

Tara's eyes lit up in amusement. *What was that?*

"Don't even think about making an honest woman out of me, Max," said Tara. "Down that path lies danger...fire... destruction."

Max laughed. "Wouldn't dream of it."

But Tara was good at reading people, and again, she could see the smallest hint of something else. She smiled and said, "You little shit. Don't lie to me."

"I won't."

Tara reached over and grabbed his hand. She pulled back one of the fingers until Max started squirming. But he played nice and didn't yank his hand away.

"I've spent thirteen years watching people for signs of trouble. To me, you're like a window. I can see right through you, Max. So don't even *try* to lie to me."

Tara stopped twisting on his finger and brought it to her lips. She kissed it and kept hold of his hand. "There. All better. Now give."

Max said, nonchalantly, "It might have crossed my mind."

"Is that right?"

Tara raised an eyebrow. When she was little she'd practiced facial expressions in the mirror and thought that the raised eyebrow was particularly effective. She felt like the cat that ate the canary—victorious. She leaned forward with a predatory expression and pantomimed reeling a fish in.

"Amazing," Tara said. "We haven't even known each other twenty-four hours and I've got you hooked already."

Max rolled his eyes. "Come on, wait a second. You won't catch me saying that you're not the most interesting thing to come my way. Because you are, no doubt in my mind. But if you think I'm gonna go find your pop and ask for his daughter's hand in marriage, you've got another thing coming."

Tara narrowed her eyes, letting Max know right away he'd messed up talking about her dad. She knew he was joking around but still figured that it was Max's turn to show a little more consideration. She socked him on the arm, a little too hard to be considered playful—a love tap. "You've got no idea what it was like growing up with him."

Max was quickly apologetic. "You're right, Tara. I shouldn't have mentioned him."

A waitress turned on the TV behind the counter. Tara tried to tune it out 'cause she wanted to straighten things with Max. "Just listen to me, Max. I know Wyatt's my father…and that you don't get to choose your parents. It's just…"

Tara heard the words "1st Farmers Bank" and a chill came over her. She shifted her attention to the TV. A news reporter was talking about the robbery. "That's right, Diane. Both attempts to capture the fugitives ended in failure."

Tara glanced at Max, who shrugged. Why had there been two attempts to capture Wyatt?

The news reporter, whose disheveled and ultra-tanned appearance implied that he was out there in the war torn trenches of Arizona, continued with his report. "They did arrest a Billie Gates, although our inside sources tell me that Gates is not a suspect at this time and has no personal connection to the robbery whatsoever. But it may have been his vehicle that was used in the crime."

Tara giggled, "That's *Rule #3: Never use your own wheels.*"

Max nodded. "Makes sense."

He pulled out his tape recorder and repeated the rule, word for word, saving the useful item so he could digest it at a later time.

The camera zoomed back artfully, revealing the reporter, Brett Saberhagen, standing in a dumpster.

"Diane, I am standing in a dumpster at the Hideaway Motel, where the second attempt at apprehension took place," the reporter said. "Where the FBI's most wanted criminal had rented a room for the night. Room 999—also known as the sign of the devil. And with what occurred here late last night, the devil may very well have been in that room."

Diane, the perfectly coifed anchor whose pale beauty implied that she lived life in the war-torn trenches of expensive beauty salons and nowhere near an actual news story, proved that she wasn't just another dumb blonde when she interrupted. "Brett, I believe you're thinking of 666."

"What's that Diane?"

"The sign of the devil is 666, not 999."

Brett grimaced, having been corrected and shown up on live television during sweeps week. He kept it civil, even spitting out a, "Thank you, Diane, for your timely correction," before continuing. "The devil...I mean, the criminal mastermind, burst out of that room and brutally murdered one police officer and captured another before escaping. The captured officer was reportedly tortured for information in this very dumpster—while officers searched the surrounding areas to no avail. Why did the FBI let this devil escape? Why did they arrest an innocent man? Why indeed?"

"I guess you don't have to be bright to be on television," Max said. "I mean, why'd he say *brutally* murdered? Is there any other way to murder someone?"

Tara tuned out Max and the television. It was time to leave. *Now!*

The only reason Wyatt would torture information from the cop was to find her. So he was on his way. And their head start had vanished.

She grabbed her purse and started to rise, when she noticed a stunned expression on Max's face. She followed his gaze to the man walking up to their table.

"Speak of the devil," Wyatt said.

"And the devil appears," she replied.

CHAPTER 18

The first time you meet a girl's parents can be an uncomfortable situation. Now imagine the father has a gun pointed at your privates. Even worse, right? But that's not all. What if you knew that her father wouldn't hesitate to shoot your family jewels clean off?

Now multiply that feeling times ten.

Wyatt said, "Pumpkin, that's a shameful way to talk about your old man. I'm no more a devil than anyone else in this fine dining establishment."

Max cursed himself. He hadn't been paying attention to anything outside.

He'd been watching the newscast, snorting at the reporter's over-dramatization of every detail, eager for news telling which cop had been shot at the motel. His concerns were all well and good, and he'd been only a little surprised at the depth of relief he'd felt when they'd shown a shot of his pop walking the crime scene, uninjured.

But he should have been paying attention. Relief had been too fleeting and now he felt he had to atone for his lapse in concentration.

Wyatt pulled the gun he'd lifted from Officer Johnson at the motel and sat down next to Tara. He smoothly slid the gun under the table and trained it on Max, keeping it out of sight from the rest of the customers. Grinning like he was enjoying himself.

Max looked at the name tag on Wyatt's chest and cursed again. Had the bastard killed Dilbert? The officer was slow in the head and no harm to anyone—one of the pitiful things that needed protecting from the bad creatures in the world.

For that reason, and for what Wyatt had done to Tara, Max made a hard decision. The crazy son of a bitch would have to die.

Since Max had never killed anyone, or even thought about it, he wondered what the best way would be to go about this.

He thought that it would probably help if he had the gun instead of the psycho.

Wyatt turned on the charm and held out his hand, which was encrusted with dried blood. "We haven't been formally introduced. The name's Wyatt."

Max reached out with his right hand and shook Wyatt's hand awkwardly. "Max." He gave a nod toward Wyatt's bloody hand. "That looks nasty."

"Naw. Just a scratch, Max. Cut it on some glass while escaping from some police officers. It's why I love these small towns and their home-like atmospheres. A flesh wound is about the worst that can happen. By point of fact, I've dealt with things that were a whole lot worse than this," Wyatt said. "Why, just raising this girl here is more than this schizo can handle."

Max watched Tara, whose expression had changed from horror to cool and controlled. Did nothing faze her?

"Not the multiple personality crap again," Tara said. "That pig won't fly here, Wyatt."

Wyatt leaned over toward Tara, his charming expression gone, having been replaced by his more customary expression, the menacing scowl. "I'm still your daddy, so none of that lip from you, missy."

Wyatt turned to Max with his charming expression and said, "Multiple Personality Disorder wouldn't be so bad if a couple of my personalities were a little bit nicer. But what the fuck can you do, huh? You play the hand that's dealt you. Ain't that right, Max?"

"You must use that 'Cliché of the Day' toilet paper," Max said. "I gave my pop some for a Father's Day present—and it only took two days to regret buying that gift. You know, I think you and my pop would get along famously."

Max felt excruciating pain in his knee when Wyatt smashed the butt of the gun into his kneecap. He made a mental note—*do not antagonize people with guns.*

Wyatt said, "This is a civilized conversation, Max, but let's not forget what the situation is—or who's in charge."

Max clenched his teeth and fists in agony. He held back from responding and kept reminding himself of the gun aimed at his midsection.

Tara reached out and put her hand over Max's. He had about one second to appreciate the gesture before Wyatt's expression changed instantly to one of outrage. If he wasn't schizophrenic, it wasn't readily apparent to the untrained eye.

"You fucking little tramp. Did you really think I'd let you go? With this douche bag?"

Wyatt whipped the gun out from under the table and waved it in Max's direction. Wyatt whispered, "You haven't fucked my little girl, have you?"

Max didn't answer—thinking it wasn't any of Wyatt's business. But Wyatt grimaced, coming up with his own answer. One he didn't like. He turned the force of his gaze onto Tara.

"I can't believe it. You've only been out of my sight for ten hours," Wyatt said. "You need help, girl. A lesson...in right and wrong...like blowing your boyfriend's brains all over this nice place. You think that would keep you from screwing around?"

Drawn by the raised voice, the redheaded and shapely owner—EZ Edie—decided to bring coffee over to the noisy table. The fresh brewed aroma of her coffee always calmed people down. She noticed the gun and screamed, dropping her coffeepot onto the floor. The aroma's calming effect was overpowered by the scalding liquid that had scattered in a ten-foot radius. Edie's scream didn't help either. Everyone in the place was now agitated, focusing on Wyatt and his gun. Like a beehive that's been whacked with a stick by a bunch of school kids.

Max smiled at the attention, hoping this might be a way out.

Wyatt hesitated before whipping out the badge he'd commandeered the night before. He stood up and waved it around so everyone could see it, stepping carefully around the spilled coffee. He spoke out in his best red-necked cop impersonation.

"All right. All right," Wyatt said. "Don't get your panties in a bunch. This is PO-lice business."

Edie and her patrons relaxed a little, but even to them something didn't seem quite right. Wyatt grabbed Tara roughly by the arm and yanked her to her feet.

"You two are hereby and forthwith under arrest. Habeas Corpus, Ipso Facto, and all that."

Max stared at the patrons in disbelief—they seemed to be buying it.

Wyatt gestured the gun at Max and said, "You have the right to remain silent." And quieter, so only Max could hear, he said, "Come on, you piece of shit."

Max reluctantly rose and headed for the door with Tara and Wyatt. By the time they were to the door, Max noticed that most of the customers seemed nervous and energized. Hardly scared at all. Their eyes were fastened on the most exciting thing to happen to them all year. Better than the highest rated reality show. *Real* reality. So Max figured gunplay had its good points, too.

Outside, Wyatt pushed them toward his Cougar. As they passed Max's Bronco, Wyatt said, "New tires, huh? Must've set you back a bit."

Max kept his expression neutral and said, "You're a regular laugh riot, aren't you, Wyatt?"

Max opened the passenger door as Wyatt tossed him the keys. "You drive." Wyatt pushed him roughly into the front, where Max crawled over to the driver's seat, and pushed Tara into the back. The car roared as Max turned the ignition.

Max and Wyatt saw the police car at the same time. Wyatt lowered his gun out of sight and said, "If you honk, you're dead. Right here, right now. And so's the cop, and so is Tara."

Max looked into the police car as it went past and saw his pop and his bloodhound, Duke. Williams' attention was completely focused on Max's Bronco, and Max saw no way of catching his interest without it getting sticky.

He shifted into drive and pulled out quickly, causing Wyatt's door to swing shut from the force of the acceleration. The door was heavy, made of Detroit steel, so it only swung partially shut.

Max thought, *Thank you Detroit*, as they pulled onto the highway. It could be the edge they needed to survive this encounter.

BULL AND PETE WALKED AWAY FROM BILLY BOB'S SHACK OF A house—the second of four likely stashes in Arizona. It had been hard to hold their enthusiasm inside the house, picking up another of Wyatt's beloved packages. This one had taken longer than Chester's—Billy Bob had buried the treasure in the back yard. To fight off temptation, he'd said.

Bull couldn't believe that they hadn't even pulled a weapon and yet were still forty thousand richer. This was good country. Rich country. But Billy Bob had said something that worried Bull.

"Pete, why did he smile and say that no one was dumb enough to rip off Wyatt? That's about the same thing Chester said. What do they mean by that?"

"Well...I guess they mean that Wyatt is the craziest bastard they've ever known. And they don't think anyone in their right mind would mess with him."

"And us?" Bull said. "Are *we* in our right minds?"

"You have to ask?" Pete said. "Shit, Bull, you heard it on TV. Wyatt's in jail. What do we have to worry about?"

They opened their car doors and piled into the Caddy. Bull's lack of conviction must've showed because Pete turned to Bull and said, "Look, I've kept us out of any serious trouble over the years, right? That's 'cause I know what I'm doing. I'm smart enough to figure this stuff out."

Bull squinted. "I guess so."

"You guess? What the hell does that mean? Do we, or do we not, have possession of forty large without breaking a sweat?"

They'd taken turns digging the ten-foot hole for the buried loot—and Bull had gotten plenty sweaty. But he agreed anyway. "We do."

"That's right. Because I'm smart. And I'm so God-damned intelligent, I got a plan to take care of Wyatt." Pete tapped his forehead, indicating the location of the plan.

Oh. Well, that's all right then. As long as he had a plan, Bull thought. But how do you plan against crazy?

MAX PEEKED TO THE SIDE AND FOUND WYATT STARING GRIMLY at Tara. Max checked in his rearview mirror and noticed that her cool demeanor was cracking. In fact, he could see a bitter rage brewing.

"Turn off the highway," Wyatt said.

Max turned down the next road and looked around the car for a weapon. Anything. On the floor next to him were the remains of Dilbert's uniform. Sticking out of the socks and flak jacket was his baton. Max chuckled to himself, thinking it just might work.

Wyatt noticed the amusement. "What are you laughing at, you maggot? This is your last fucking day on this earth—kind of a serious type of situation."

"When you're right, you're right, Wyatt," he said. "Hey... do you guys have a rule about not antagonizing people with guns?"

Wyatt said, "The rules are for the people *with* the guns, not for the morons on the wrong end of them."

Wyatt waggled his gun, emphasizing which end Max was on, then threw a nasty look to Tara. "I can't believe she told you about the FUCKING RULES!"

"Why don't you just leave him out of this?" Tara said. "It's not his problem. This is a family thing."

"Well, since he fucked you, he's family. Since he tried to take you away from me, he's family. Since you sicced his daddy on me—who, by the way, has got all the damn bank money—he's family."

Wyatt put the gun to Max's temple and cocked it. "Welcome to the family, Max."

Max tensed, knowing Wyatt was about to pull the trigger. Tara cut in.

"You pathetic piece of white trash. This is *your* problem," she said. "You want Max to know why I left you? He doesn't even know the half of it. You want him to know what's going on in your mind—your little fantasy?"

Wyatt whipped the gun around and pointed it at her. He spluttered, practically frothing at the mouth.

"Shut up, missy! You keep your perverted mind out of the gutter and don't talk till I tell you to talk."

"Fuck you, Wyatt."

Max wondered what they were talking about. Somehow, this hadn't come up in their conversation last night and this morning. He looked at the baton, timing his move. But he wanted Wyatt even more distracted than he was.

Tara continued, "I'm through, Wyatt. Through taking your orders. In fact, I'm just through with you."

"You're never through with your daddy. With no help from your mama, I raised you, I fed you, I clothed you."

"You lusted after me."

Wyatt leaned over the seat and slapped her. Max turned to Wyatt, more than a little disgusted. But Wyatt wasn't even paying attention to him anymore. He was pointing the gun at her, his hand shaking with rage.

"I own your ass," Wyatt said. "And if you think you're gonna run away from me...WITH SOME OTHER MAN..."

Max took a deep breath. Wyatt and Tara had both worked themselves over the edge, and Max felt like the uncomfortable young man, brought home to meet the parents, with a private family squabble rearing its ugly head.

"You think you can do it?" Tara said. "Come on. Do it!"

Wyatt trembled and said, "You better get down on your knees and pray for forgiveness, baby."

Tara egged him on. "Come on! The only way you'll keep me with you is with a bullet in my brain, so come on! Do it!"

Wyatt raised the gun to shoot her and said, "I love you. God help me, I love you, baby."

Jesus. What a family. Max hoped insanity wasn't a genetic trait.

With Wyatt fully distracted, Max grabbed the baton and bashed it across the back of Wyatt's head.

The gun fired, missing Tara and breaking the back window, causing Tara to duck behind the seat.

Wyatt was woozy, but still awake—so Max hit him again until Wyatt's head lolled against the window. Max checked behind him to see if Tara was all right and found her sitting there, amazed and happy.

At a groan from Wyatt, Max took his feet from the pedals and put them on the seat beside him. He braced his back against the door and kicked out at Wyatt. The door flew open, and Wyatt was ejected like so much garbage.

PERCHED ON A ROCK IN THE SUN NEXT TO THE ARIZONA HIGH-way, the lizard tensed. It licked its eyeball with its long tongue, ready to make a dash across the asphalt—one that had claimed so many of his brothers and sisters before him.

The lizard took a few tentative steps onto the pavement before it felt the heavy vibration that meant a rolling metal monstrosity was headed his way and he skittered back to the safety of the sand. The lizard looked up and saw a smaller piece separate from the large car. Wyatt's body hit the ground at fifty miles an hour and rolled thirty feet, before coming to a stop on top of the unfortunate lizard. The highway hadn't claimed its life, but humanity's garbage had taken its rough toll on the ecosystem once again.

Tara couldn't believe it. Max was a bonafide stud.

She leaned over the front seat and wrapped her arms around him. She kissed him all over with an intensity that surprised her. Between kisses, she said, "That's the most romantic thing I've ever seen."

Max took his eyes off the road and kissed her back—getting into it. The car skidded, the wheels on the passenger side trailing in the dirt. Max stopped kissing her and regained enough self-control to bring the car back onto the highway—exactly the opposite of what she wanted.

What the hell! He still cared about driving?

She launched herself from the back seat and into the front seat, arms locked around Max's neck, kissing him the whole way. Pressing her body, and her breasts, up against him. Generating enough steam to power a freight train.

With all that was going on, there was a remote part of Max's brain that was still functioning—barely—the part containing logic and reason. And as he didn't want to die crashing the car, he used his last remaining logical thoughts to turn the wheel sharply to the right and slam on the brakes.

The car swerved off the road, did a three-sixty and came to a stop. Dust surrounded the vehicle like a miniature cyclone. The laws of physics demanded that Max and Tara be thrown against the driver's side door, lips still locked, with Tara on top.

In one swift motion, she ripped Max's shirt clean off and whispered, more to herself than anything, "That was the most manly..." She kissed him again, moving down his chest. "Powerful..."

This was so unlike her. She might have kept babbling, but

she lost her train of thought as Max grabbed her and pushed toward her—taking control. *Bonafide stud.*

They slammed into the other side with Max now on top, and she gave a little gasp on impact—not from ecstasy, but from the seat-belt mechanism digging into her back.

Then she kicked out with her bare foot—decorum lost somewhere along with the shoe. She struck the windshield with the curve of her foot. Then she did it again.

That part was from ecstasy. Bonafide ecstasy.

CHAPTER 19

EXCERPT FROM TAPE 3

*Great sex is a natural high. And like a powerful drug,
it's addictive as hell...and sometimes just as lethal.*

Wyatt's eyelids fluttered and then snapped open. He looked up at the blazing sun with deep suspicion—the fiery bastard looked so cocky staring down at him. Maybe he'd died and gone to hell.

He instinctively raised his gun, which he clutched like a bottle in a sleeping baby's unyielding grasp, and waved it wildly. He felt disoriented, and searched for something to shoot at. Anything.

Then he groaned, remembering what had happened. He wasn't dead, but maybe he wished he was.

He lowered the gun and sat up slowly, doing a body check. His brain wasn't working properly, 'cause he could hear a faint squeaking sound in the back of his head.

And blood was flowing freely down his face, yet again. He looked at the horrible mess on his chest, puzzled. For a moment, he feared the squishy mass was his entrails—that he'd hit something sharp when he'd landed—before figuring out it was the remains of a lizard.

Wyatt rose slowly and painfully to his feet. His left knee was in bad shape, making him wince when he put his weight on it.

"Damn it!" He felt bitter, angry, and unusually homicidal. He'd never been on the losing end before, and it sucked. He'd have to get creative when he got his hands on those kids—make life extremely painful and unpleasant for the both of 'em.

The high-pitched squeaking was getting to him. He grabbed his ears as the noise grew louder and faster. He whacked his skull a couple of times, but the racket continued. Then he heard the faint sound of a woman crying out. It was unmistakable—to anyone who's been there—the sound of a female in the throes of ecstasy.

Wyatt frowned, trying to place the sound. He shuffled, turning painfully around, and froze.

Off in the distance, his Cougar sat by the side of the road, rocking back and forth in a smooth rhythm. Squeaking. His eyes bulged and his heart constricted.

Incredulous, he lunged forward, his left leg dragging behind him. He stalked down the middle of the road, oblivious to his surroundings, a low growl in his throat.

"That tramp!"

Then things got worse. Wyatt heard one final cry and the car stopped rocking. He halted for a moment, stunned, and then picked up the pace, shuffling as fast as his leg would allow.

He peeled the lizard from his shirt and tossed it into the brush. He clicked open the revolver and checked the load. Plenty of bullets. *Good.*

He snapped it shut and stared murderously toward the car. Still shuffling along.

He had another hundred feet to go when a car came speeding down the highway—going about forty over the limit. It swerved around Wyatt as he hobbled down the middle of the road. The driver leaned on the horn and gave him the international gesture of goodwill on his way past. Wyatt barely restrained himself from shooting the driver, saving the few bullets he had for his beloved Tara.

Max and Tara were startled out of their blissful peace by the sound of the car horn. Max lifted his head off Tara's breast, and together they rose and stared down the highway.

Like a creature from *Night of the Living Dead*, Wyatt limped toward them, moving with the same spasmodic walk from which all zombies seemed to suffer.

Max turned to Tara, pausing half a second to appreciate her beautiful form, before turning the ignition. "Jesus, that was reckless. Even for my taste."

Tara smiled and tossed him his shirt as he shifted into drive and pulled away. "But worth every second."

Tara turned to her dad and blew him a kiss as they took off.

Wyatt let out a primal yell as the car disappeared down the highway. He shook his head, trying to wake from the bad dream, and then finally accepted his fate.

He'd heard somewhere that life was just one series of setbacks after another. It had sounded like a crock of shit at the time, though lately he wasn't so sure.

He reached behind his back and tucked his gun into his belt. His hand twitched a few times, then clenched into a fist.

He angrily stabbed his thumb toward the sky and thrust it toward the road—applying the international gesture once used by flower children in need of a good time, or a ride, or both. Now, the gesture symbolized easy pickings for hungry predators—for bad guys roaming the highways. But Wyatt never worried about being prey. He was the biggest, nastiest predator in the animal kingdom.

"I'm gonna sue their a**es," Billie Gates said, his swear words bleeped for TV. "They done probed me for the last time! My imported wife won't even touch me now the

Federales done that. Those mother f****ers haven't heard the last of Billie Gates. I know my God-d*****d rights."

Sheriff Williams turned away from Billie's angry face on the television screen. The idiot was stomping mad, and unintentionally interfering—from beyond the tube—with his interview of EZ Edie at her greasy diner.

EZ Edie talked about anything that flitted through her mind, which made for an incredibly long interview. She especially couldn't keep quiet when it came to television. She'd proudly told him she was a TV junkie and that she spent most of her free time with her rear plastered to the sofa, which wasn't hard to believe—she had a much larger rump than the average middle-aged woman.

Edie said, "Any show with cops whomping on bad guys is fine by me. But this particular show, *When Good Cops Go Bad*, is one of my all-time favorites. Don't you just feel sorry for that Billie Gates fellow. Bless his soul. His rights have been stomped on by that Agent Stratton guy. Heck, Billie should sue 'em for millions of dollars, don't you think?"

Williams squirmed—unhappily reminded that he'd withheld information from Stratton and the FBI. "Edie, would you mind turning that off?"

"That's a mighty large request, sugar. But for you, anything."

He showed her a police sketch of Wyatt.

"Yep, that's him all right. He took that nice young couple out of here at gun point," Edie said. "But I knew he weren't no cop."

Williams grimaced as his stomach growled. He was pretty sure he was developing an ulcer. He knew his wife would have approved of him hiding the information about Max and his girlfriend from the FBI. What mother wouldn't? But he still felt way out of his comfort zone. Protecting your son was one thing, but lying to the Feds went against his core belief system. The conflict was having an effect on his digestive system.

Edie continued, "Yeah, I could just *look* at him and know

he weren't no cop. Just like I know when my sonofabitch husband has been dipping his wick in that slut Darlene. Ya just get to know people. It comes from being a waitress twenty-four seven—all the people I run into on the job."

"Is that right?" Williams said.

Williams found Edie's talkative nature to be somewhat irritating. He wondered if she talked too much out of fear and a lack of self esteem—because her husband was fooling around—or if her husband had left because she'd talked too much. The chicken or the egg?

If it was the self-esteem, a compliment might grease the wheels a little bit—get her to pay a little better attention to the interview. He'd already noticed her affinity for her fresh-brewed, so he licked his lips and piped up. "This is mighty fine coffee, ma'am. In fact, the best I've ever had."

Edie blushed down to her toes and batted her eyelashes at Williams. She gave him a little shake of her ample behind and her best come hither look, causing Williams' eyes to widen. He sighed, thinking he'd overdone it and lubed the whole chassis instead of just the wheels.

He needed to get back on the road, back to looking for Max and his girlfriend. Keep 'em out of trouble by picking them up before the Feds or the cowboy from the bank robbery caught up with them.

According to Edie, he was already too late with the cowboy—and Williams silently cursed the mountain of paperwork he'd had to file before he could get away and on the trail. If Max's girl didn't know how to get around her ex-partner, Max's goose was cooked. And if Williams had any say in the matter, it was better to have Max incarcerated rather than killed.

He turned back to Edie, who was pouting at the lack of return interest. "Do you remember the license plate of the car they were driving?"

"Well, who remembers something like that?" she said, her lips pursed. "It was an older, faded black, American car. Isn't that enough?" She caught her breath. "Oh, wait. I've remembered something. It was a Cougar like my brother drove—a Mercury. That's pretty good, isn't it? That I could remember something like that?"

"Yes, ma'am." Williams nodded his assurance—that yes, she was indeed a moderately intelligent person. He hadn't intended it as a compliment, but Edie was back on board anyway, and smiling bashfully at Williams. He ignored it, feeling a bit of relief now that he knew the make of the car. With any luck at all, it would be enough for him to trace the kids.

There was a momentary pause as Williams digested this information, which freed Edie's mouth to run off again on yet another meaningless tangent.

"I think I saw him on an episode of *America's Most Wanted Men*. He impersonates cops all the time, don't he? Like my sonofabitch husband impersonating a loving and *faithful* husband."

"I don't know, ma'am," Williams sighed. "I don't watch much TV."

Edie stared at him, aghast at such a blasphemous statement. And Williams wondered why the people who so drastically needed self-help books—the very same books Williams enjoyed, but felt he didn't actually *need*—why those people were the ones who used them the least.

He looked out the window at Max's Bronco and decided not to tow the car back to Stoneybrook. Instead, he'd leave a note in it for Max, asking him to call him on his private cell number. With any luck, Max would come back to the car sooner or later.

In his Houston office, Stratton hung up the phone and tried to look at the insides of his eyelids. With no wisdom to be found there, he tried looking at his computer. But the incomprehensible thing just stared back at him, mocking him.

His bluster had evaporated after the half-hour verbal reaming by the Senator. He'd hung up the phone with a meek,

"Yes, sir—Senator, sir," as he hadn't called him dad since the fourth grade.

Senator Stratton had always been an unhappy man. But in the last two months he'd been caught leaving his mistress' house in an ambush by his soon to be ex-wife, he'd had his Texas highway bill unexpectedly killed by a rival Democrat, and now his imbecilic son was bringing him bad publicity with his errant arrest of Billie Gates.

In an election year.

Hell hath no fury like a Senator exposed to bad publicity. So after the metaphorical flaying of his son's hide, Senator Stratton had imposed the worst punishment known to man. To a rich man, anyway. He'd cut off his son's trust fund.

Agent Stratton needed an outlet for his wrath. *No trust fund!*

His left temple throbbing, he opened his office door and screamed out, "Dawkins. Get in here."

Dawkins removed himself from a group of agents that were watching, with great amusement, a tape of Stratton's recent television debut. To his credit, Dawkins maintained a straight face while approaching his boss.

Stratton found that his bluster had been merely hiding the last half-hour, not lost. And since he wasn't facing the fearsome Senator, he let loose a steady stream of invective on his subordinate, in the manner of one who's accustomed to yelling at servants.

When Dawkins merely smiled at his remarks, instead of responding in kind, Stratton realized something was up.

"What are you smiling at, Dawkins?"

"You still have access to the Senator's jet?"

"For the time being. Why?" *Damn. This must be good.*

"While you've been tap dancing with the Senator, we've caught a break," Dawkins said. "Fingerprints just came back. Our suspect is Wyatt Evans. Arrested once for second degree murder. Acquitted by...get this...reason of insanity. Must've had some lawyer."

Stratton knew it. The gods had finally smiled upon him. "Why the jet?"

"You'll want to be there for the bust, right? We tracked a call from the pay phone near the motel—to a Chester Mulroney. Long rap sheet, known associate of Wyatt Evans. Better than fifty percent chance he's hiding out there."

"Damn skippy," Stratton said. And in his casual southern drawl, he said. "You don't mess with Texas. Let's roll."

He'd always wanted to say that.

Tara gave Max a sideways glance as they drove down the highway, wondering how he was taking things. If the run-in with Wyatt had him thinking twice about his situation.

She sure as hell hoped not. As far as she was concerned, things were great. She already enjoyed his company more than anyone she'd ever met and she especially loved the times they spent just talking together.

And he'd held his own with Wyatt.

She gave Max a smile. She also had to admit that she was pretty happy with that whole multiple orgasm business. She'd read about them in the supermarket rags, and of course, *all* the women's magazines. But she'd struck out every time and had pretty much decided the whole thing was a myth, like Bigfoot or silent black helicopters.

That was before Max. Now, she couldn't believe she'd been missing out all these years.

She and Max had snuck back to his Bronco to grab her things. His pop wasn't there, so they'd picked up her suitcase and the note from his pop and taken off, heading north instead of west. Might as well take a roundabout way to California and make things harder for anyone who was looking for them. As she drove along, her thoughts had her floating on air.

Max broke into her reverie. "I thought my pop was bad."

The happy thoughts floated right out the window. Judge not, lest ye be judged. Tara threw him a sidelong glance. "Hell, Max. Everyone's got *someone* in his family who's nasty—who's been to jail. Or at the very least, *deserves* to be in prison. I bet it was someone in your family who taught you how to hot-wire cars."

"Uncle-Grandpa," Max said, shaking his head. "That was a good guess—and right on the money. But it's kind of a long story."

Tara did the eyebrow thing again. *Uncle-Grandpa?*

Max explained. "My grandma's eighth husband was kind of a strange guy. Or maybe it was the ninth—we lost track after a while. He was into tax fraud, had a marijuana farm, that kind of thing. And when my grandma died, this hillbilly married her daughter, trying to keep it in the family—so to speak. Anyway, long story short, I ended up staying with Uncle-Grandpa after school when my mama passed. Against Pop's better judgment, but you know how it is…kin is kin. And I learned all kinds of useful things from the dirtbag, not just how to steal cars."

If there were any more like that one, Tara thought Max's family might give hers a run for their money.

Max said, "Is your pop really a schizophrenic?"

Tara searched for the right words to describe her father. "Naw…he's more like…a psychotic asshole with an extremely short fuse. One of his defense lawyers made it up to keep him out of jail. They had him acting like a psycho on the witness stand. And he just had a grand old time with it."

"He got to frighten the jury and get off at the same time. A two-fer. I think he liked it so much that he pretty much acts that way all the time. Hell, he might even believe it now. I mean, he's pretty nuts anyway."

"He's made a believer out of me," Max said. "I gotta hope the psycho gene skipped your generation."

Tara laughed. "He's not really my daddy."

"Thank God for small favors."

Tara abruptly stopped laughing, and changed her tone. "Max…just 'cause he's not my daddy doesn't mean he'll leave us alone. It was bad enough when Wyatt thought I was leaving him. Then I sicced the cops on him, hoping to give us a nice head start. But it didn't work—and he lost the bank money. He was so ticked off he killed cops trying to get ahold of us. And now, add insult to injury—you threw him out of his own car. That's the ultimate humiliation for Wyatt. He's gonna hunt us down till both of us are dead and gone."

A SHINY NEW LINCOLN, BIG AS A BOAT, PULLED TO A STOP ON the highway. The car was a black beauty—and to Wyatt, fit for a king.

He lowered his thumb and thanked the Lord for the bounty bestowed upon him, then approached the passenger window. The stream of dried blood on his face marred his efforts toward a friendly expression.

"Are you all right?" the man asked.

Wyatt smirked. He had a knack for assessing people and their personalities. Right away he knew that there was something wrong with this particular driver. His years of studying criminal behavior had been well spent.

It wasn't that the guy was large, because he was big in a pudgy, soft-looking way. It wasn't the way his hair had abandoned his head like rats from a sinking ship, leaving his dome shiny and wrinkled with just a few hairy stragglers.

It was the eyes. They belied the inviting smile on his face. They were a predator's eyes.

To Wyatt it was like looking into a mirror. The guy also had tiny spasms coursing throughout his body, which Wyatt found a little unnatural.

But he returned the man's smile and said, "I'm fine. Thanks for asking. Headed through Sedona?"

"Sure. Hop in."

Wyatt sat down heavily on the seat, angling his body so he could draw his gun in a hurry, if necessary. It was amazing how often it proved necessary, even when he wasn't on the job. It actually seemed that mankind went out of its way to validate his deepest, darkest suspicions about the lack of quality in the human race.

"The name's Wyatt."

"I'm Jim," he said, as he pressed the gas pedal to the floor, quickly accelerating to highway speed. "You sure don't look like a cop, Wyatt."

"I'm not."

Wyatt looked down at his tattered uniform and back to Jim. The man's clothes might fit him, but the guy's body was convulsing regularly now—like he was receiving minute electrical shocks at three-second intervals.

Twitch. "Then why you dressed like one?" Twitch.

"It's a long story, Jim. And I'm not feeling real talkative."

Wyatt figured Jim would stop the car and try to kick him out—as any rational person would. But the man just sat there, twitching like a freak.

Damn. There were lots of freaks out in the world.

Wyatt had the uncomfortable feeling that he might just be the sanest person in the car. A first for him. And kind of a scary thought.

Jim twitched again and brought out what looked to be a butter knife and held it to Wyatt's thigh. "This is a scalpel, Wyatt. It'll cut through your femoral artery like a hot knife through butter. If I cut you, you'll be dead in thirty seconds."

"Is that right?"

Wyatt pulled the gun out from behind his back and put it to Jim's temple. "This is a .44 Magnum. It'll cut through your skull bone like a...well...like a hot knife through butter, to borrow the expression. And when I shoot you, you'll be dead before your brains hit the windshield."

Jim twitched again, but didn't say a word.

What a freak. "I guess this is what you'd call a Mexican Standoff, Jim."

Jim quivered. "I guess so."

Wyatt started to calm down. If the freak pulled a butter knife while driving a car, he couldn't be too bright. How could you concentrate on holding a man hostage while you were driving? It was *Rule #35*, plain as day.

So, even with the scalpel at his vein, Wyatt knew he already had the upper hand. He could tell that Jim knew it, too.

Wyatt spied a medallion hanging from the rearview mirror. He read it with growing distaste and malevolence. *Employee of the Month, Desert Mutual Insurance.*

The man was lower on the totem pole than a freak. Much lower.

Wyatt gritted his teeth. "You know what I do, Jim? I rob banks...among other things. And I'll admit it—I've also been known to kill people if they get in my way," he said. "But there's more honor in my little pinky than in your whole body."

Jim jerked, but wisely kept any response to himself.

Wyatt continued, "Tell me, Jim. What do *you* do?"

"What do you mean?" Jim twitched. "I don't kill people."

"What do you do for a living?"

Jim relaxed and followed Wyatt's gaze to the medallion.

"Oh, that. I'm an insurance investigator." Jim seemed relieved, so he obviously wasn't paying attention. "I check out people's claims all over the state. Make sure they're legitimate."

Now Wyatt was feeling a little twitchy. He said, "You know, when you stopped to pick me up, I'd decided not to kill you. On account of how nice you were going to be, giving me your car and all."

"Good idea," Jim piped in. "It's yours. Take it."

"I know it's mine. So shut up, Jim. That was before I found out what you do."

Jim jumped in his seat. "I don't do anything!"

"Really? What about the claim you're out investigating right now. You're a smart guy. I bet you found something useful for your company?"

Jim frowned. "What are you talking about?"

"Come on, Jim. I used to be in the insurance biz," Wyatt said. "You know what I'm talking about. Did you, or did you not, find anything to help Desert Mutual Insurance deny the claim?"

"Well, yeah. I can usually find something."

Wyatt squinted, then grabbed Jim's wrist and slammed it into the dashboard, holding the scalpel away from his body. He then shot Jim in the head.

As promised, the bullet traveled through the skull like it was butter, shattering the window, before escaping into the desert. The bullet had enough explosive force that it also went through a snake that was sunning itself on a rock over a hundred feet away.

Another two-fer.

Wyatt reached out with his left foot, tapping the brakes, then took hold of the wheel and eased the car to the side of the road. After stripping the man of his clothes, Wyatt gladly changed out of the uniform of Stoneybrook's finest. Then he dragged the body through the hot sand, with his knee still killing him, and around to the back of the car where he popped open the trunk.

Inside the trunk was a sight that made Wyatt's skin crawl. The remains of at least one body had been placed inside the roomy trunk of the Lincoln.

No, there were two bodies. It was hard to tell because they'd been cut up into pieces—but Wyatt counted four feet. He figured the weapon had to be that handy-dandy scalpel that had made Jim so proud. And that Jim must have been one of those serial killers or something.

Probably why the man was so twitchy. What a scumbag.

Wyatt dropped Jim into the trunk along with the other two, admiring the vehicle's spaciousness. He'd always wanted to drive a new Lincoln.

When he closed the trunk, he left a bloody handprint on the car, which he wiped off with the tail of his shirt. He tucked the bloody stain out of sight, hopped behind the wheel and drove away.

Insurance investigator. Not a court in the world would convict him. It was justifiable homicide. Plain and simple.

CHAPTER 20

When I came of legal age, my pop took me to Joe's Tavern for my first drink. Well…first drink he knew about, anyway. It was one of those man-to-man things, so of course he gave me some advice. He wouldn't have been Pop if he hadn't. He told me, "Son, if you're gonna do something…and I don't care what it is…if you do it, then you put everything you've got into doing it right. Right, damn it! Never half-assed. Or you're no better than the rest of these barflies hanging 'round here."

Max paused and took a drag of his cigarette.

And with that, he proceeded to get thoroughly shitfaced drunk—I guess to drive the lesson home. Anyway, I got the point loud and clear.

Bull gave a grunting, heaving laugh, amused by the sight before him.

On their quest for the third package of Wyatt's scattered stashes, a dishwater gray poodle had backed Pete up against the wall of Aunt May's farmhouse. It was a standard, not one of those toy-sized football poodles. It wasn't even growling or anything. But since the dog scam, Pete pretty much wet himself at the sight of a loose dog.

About two scams back, Pete had come up with the idea for a dog-semen heist. The Caddy had broken down in Bumblefuck, Nevada, and they'd stumbled upon a national dog-pulling contest—where dogs of all makes and models pulled weighted sleds across the ground for fifty dollars in prize money and a special trophy.

The money for the pulls wasn't impressive, but when Pete had seen what the top dog took in as a stud—eight hundred bucks a pop—he'd whipped out his tape recorder and come up with a plan for the studly pooch.

It was far beyond Bull's comprehension why dog prostitutes were legal, yet his favorite human ones were not. Then again, he'd always found white men to be incomprehensible bastards, at best. So whatever.

With contacts they'd made at the show, Pete and Bull lined up a few customers in advance, and then planned the job with their usual lack of precision. The buyers didn't mind if the semen fell off the back of a truck, so long as it came from a number one, champion dog. And Pete and Bull felt they were more than man enough to get it.

They dognapped the studly pooch and its girlfriend by slipping them a porterhouse chock full of horse tranquilizers they'd picked up from their old pal Crispin, the Vietnam Vet. Then they hid out at an abandoned farmhouse and tried every method they could think of to get the dog in a randy state.

First they put the female, Queen Latifah, in one pen. Then they put the stud, Eminem, into the next pen—with only a thin chain link fence between them. They'd put a tarp down on the ground beneath the chain barrier, hoping that Eminem would press up against the fence in a vain attempt, releasing his bounty where the two of them could easily get it.

Pete and Bull stood by for eight solid hours, with sterile cups and lids, to no avail.

They tried a Barry White CD for three more hours. And while Pete and Bull had felt a little uncomfortable and carefully edged away from each other, there was nothing from the dogs.

They tried shoving Latifah's rear end up against the fence, closer to Eminem. But again, nothing. Mostly the dogs just slept.

The next day, Pete called Crispin for some veterinary advice. He gave them a few ideas to try, some of which sounded downright disgusting, but Crispin thought the most likely scenario was that Eminem had sampled the goods once too often and that it might take a different bitch to get him going again. Preferably one in heat.

Since their theft of the heavyweight champion, all dogs in the area were now under maximum security, so no canines were to be found. Bull had unhappily driven to a porn shop at three in the morning in order to pick up the next best thing. A quasi-realistic, inflatable, blow-up dog.

Amazingly, the inflatable toy did the trick. Right up until the blow-up dog deflated, punctured by the teeth of an overly excited Eminem. The next try involved another trip to the city, this time to a hunting shop where they picked up essence of deer, essence of moose, and essence of buffalo—there was no essence of dog, or that would have been their first choice.

First, they sprinkled the deer oil onto Latifah. And when that didn't work they followed up with the moose, and then the buffalo. At the combination of the three, Eminem lost it. He had indeed become horny, but he was also foaming at the mouth and in a vicious mood. Latifah would have been dog chow if they'd let her near Eminem.

After three days of pain and turmoil, Pete and Bull finally gave up and decided to return the dogs to their owners. And that was when the incident occurred.

Their rental van, with Pete, Bull, and the two dogs, hit a pothole. Two things happened: A seemingly harmless bump caused the animal essences to spill onto Pete. And at the same time, the bump managed to knock open the pen containing Eminem.

It had taken Bull only thirty seconds to stop the van and remove the dog from the frozen form of Pete—a record time for the lumbering giant. But in those thirty seconds, Pete had suffered a fate that would prove to be the most horrible experience of his entire life. Extremely potent material for a psychiatrist to work with, if Pete were ever to give one a chance.

Pete looked in terror at the poodle before him. *No amount of money is worth this!* He wanted to grab the twenty grand as quickly as possible and get out of there.

Bull seemed to be laughing it up—no help at all—and Pete couldn't remember the damn dog's name! *Where was May?* The creature came up to Pete and licked his hand, then sniffed his crotch. Sure, it seemed friendly now. But that's how it always started.

Relief washed over him as he remembered the canine's name. Pete said, "Down, Cornelius!"

The dog knew him and obeyed. It just sat there, excited at having company, thumping its tail against the porch—and not attacking him or anything. Pete stood in triumph till he caught sight of Bull smirking by the front door. He opened his mouth to chastise his friend, but May opened the screen door first.

"It's great to see you, Pete. It's been years."

My God, she's more beautiful than ever.

He'd forgotten how much he liked her. May was a good, old-fashioned, country woman. And strong, too. Heck, she'd raised four girls on her own.

Her only misfortune in life was having a flaky older sister who had married a bum like Wyatt. And when she'd lost her sister, she'd been saddled with Wyatt and his low-life buddies on more occasions than she cared to remember.

But Pete remembered those times fondly. Typically they'd come unannounced, immediately following a heist. But since May had been brought up with uncommonly good manners— out of place in today's world, Pete thought—she'd treated all the criminals like family.

"Shoo, Cornelius. Can't you see that Pete's not feeling friendly today?" As the dog wandered away, May gave Pete a big squeeze and said, "I don't remember you being so afraid of dogs."

Pete watched the dog out of the corner of his eye, even though the animal was walking away. Just in case. "It's a long, unpleasant story, May. And one that's inappropriate for a beautiful lady such as yourself. Can Bull and I come inside for a minute?"

"Beautiful, huh?" May blushed. "You sweet talker. Why don't you and your friend come on inside and I'll get you some lemonade."

Pete found himself wishing he could stay with May a little longer than he'd originally planned. He got the feeling she might appreciate a little bit of male companionship.

Unfortunately, Pete's profoundly intelligent brain kept interfering, reminding him that staying put would be bad for his health. That they had to get in and out as quick as possible, before Wyatt was any wiser.

They'd heard the horrible news on the radio—that Wyatt was still loose. But if their luck stayed with them, they could finish here and hit the last Arizona stash an hour from now— and get away scot-free. Since their haul was looking big enough, Pete and Bull had changed their plans, thinking it was probably safer to keep as far away from Wyatt as was humanly possible. Always a wise move, if you're attempting to steal from the devil himself.

"CHESTER MULRONEY. THIS IS THE FBI. OPEN THIS DOOR immediately or we'll break it down."

Chet flipped the patch down over his good eye. He knew his lazy eye made people uneasy. He also fancied the image, thinking the patch made him look like a pirate.

Chet walked over to the front door and decided not to use the shotgun that he kept beside it, as the FBI were known for their lack of humor. He opened the door and immediately recognized Agent Stratton from his infamous television appearances.

Tears streamed down his face as he fell to the floor in laughter. "From *Cops*."

"Are you Chester Mulroney?" Agent Stratton asked, through gritted teeth.

Between laughs Chet managed to squeak out, "Chet."

Agent Stratton's eyes squinted, getting smaller and smaller till they almost disappeared. "You're in deep shit, Chet."

Laugh. "Bad as Billie?" Squeak. Laugh.

"Shut your trap and listen up!" Agent Stratton used an expensive shoe to drive the point home, kicking Chet in the noggin.

Chet's giggle fit evaporated immediately.

It was the same shoe, he noticed, that he'd seen O.J. wearing on TV many years ago. Chet found it weird, what his mind chose to focus on when placed in stressful situations. When Pete and Bull had been there, giving him stress, he'd counted rat droppings on the floor. Sixty-three.

He said, meekly, "What you want?"

Agent Stratton pranced into the room like he owned the joint. "For starters, I want you to pay attention."

A black man flashed his identification and followed Stratton inside, shutting the door. When the black agent didn't kick him in the head, and even told the white agent to take it easy, Chet figured the black one must be playing the role of good cop. Just like on the tube.

"This is Agent Dawkins and I'm Special Agent Stratton." The bad cop. "I was already in a bad mood, Chet, since I've been made the star idiot on one of those reality TV shows. But now you've done made me pissed. So, if I don't like what I hear, I'm gonna be your worst nightmare come to life."

The bad cop had a Texas accent, a chip on his shoulder, and two-thousand-dollar shoes—a strange combination.

"Tell me, Chet. Where's Wyatt and his partner?" Agent Stratton said.

"Who?"

Chet made his acquaintance with the shoe two more times, in rapid succession.

"Wyatt Evans called here yesterday. At twelve-oh-four in the P.M." Stratton raised his shoe a little, grabbing Chet's undivided attention, and said, "Your memory getting any clearer?"

"Oh. Yeah."

"So where the hell is he?"

"Don't know. Never showed."

Four words. Four more than Stratton deserved.

Since Chet didn't have the answer that Stratton wanted, he braced for impact. While waiting for the other shoe to drop, Chet realized at last that Pete had snookered him. That Wyatt wasn't in jail and that Pete had stolen Wyatt's package.

His lazy eye moved back and forth like a metronome, dreading Wyatt's anger when he found out. Chet held out slim hope that Wyatt would take it out of Pete's hide and not his own. More likely, Chet figured, Wyatt would find him guilty by association.

Probably ventilate his body with some unwanted and unnecessary holes with his favorite Peacemaker.

"Son, that's the wrong answer," Stratton said. "You're making me look bad in front of my junior partner here. Now I've got no choice but to make an example out of you."

"Wait," Chet pleaded.

Stratton leaned in close and whispered in Chet's ear. "You've got to give me something, Chet. I'm not gonna play the fool."

"Don't know."

"How about his partner?" Stratton whispered. "Maybe a description of Wyatt's accomplice? Just give me the scrawny man's name and I'll leave you in peace."

Man? What on earth was he talking about? Chet knew full well that Tara was Wyatt's partner. A shapely, female partner at that.

But the bad cop didn't.

And with that missing piece in place, Chet saw the bigger picture. A pretty picture. Something that would get the Feds off his back, make Wyatt a happier and hopefully more forgiving man, while taking care of the sticky-fingered, idiot named Pete. A grand slam.

But for it to work, Chet needed Stratton to be convinced of his sincerity. That would require his good eye. So he flipped up his eye patch. It would also require words—and lots of them.

When he spoke, it was with unusual clarity and eloquence.

"Yes, I can do that, sir. Wyatt's partner is Pete Corelli. He drives a nineteen-eighties red Cadillac convertible with California plates. He's got brown hair—he's about five feet, eight inches tall..."

MAX SAT IN THE PASSENGER SEAT WITH TARA'S SUITCASE ON his lap. He was surprised a twenty-two year old could carry such a massive arsenal of weapons in her suitcase, along with all the regular stuff women carried like make-up and curling irons. But it just added to her appeal.

"You've got more guns than my pop."

"A girl's got to be careful, Max. It's a crazy world. Anything can happen."

A bug committed suicide by leaping onto the windshield, causing Max to glance up from the suitcase and pay more attention to his surroundings. The towering red rock formations were pretty impressive, even at eighty miles an hour. They were headed toward the sunset, and the sky was full of exotic colors.

Max pulled out an old photo of Tara as a little girl. She was sitting on her mother's shoulders, laughing, and covering her mom's eyes.

She was just an innocent little desert flower. It was impressive, her growing up with Wyatt and turning out as well as she had.

He glanced at Tara appraisingly. She looked a lot like her mom.

Tara turned to him and said, "That's the only picture of her I've got. In fact, everything I own is in that one suitcase. Pretty sad, huh?"

"Yeah, it is," Max said.

A lot about her life was sad and he was surprised at how strongly he wanted to protect her—to protect that little girl who'd been forced to rob banks. He shook his head—*like she needs protecting.*

Most of the time she seemed so strong. But once in a while there was something vulnerable about her. Something he was drawn to.

He pulled out a handful of fake, stick-on tattoos. He flipped through them and found they were all snakes. Every one. "You've got some strange stuff in here."

She laughed. "That's from one of Wyatt's rules. The one about changing your style, your M.O., every couple of years. That way, if you're ever caught, the law will have a harder time linking you to any of your past crimes. Just in case."

"And these?" Max held up a Barbie with a mask drawn onto her face and a toy gun in her hand. "I've never seen a Barbie with a gun before. Even your toys are tough. I'm pretty sure Barbie is supposed to be glamorous."

Tara smiled. "Glamour is for normal girls," she said. "Those were my only toys, growing up with Wyatt. Heck, I think the only reason he let me keep them was that he'd used 'em to train me. Probably had some sentimental value, even for him."

"So he's a sentimental lunatic."

"Who knows? He's kind of hard to read," Tara said. "Speaking of Wyatt, if we don't want him to catch us, we're gonna have to ditch the Cougar pretty soon. Driving a zig-zag pattern across the country is working for us, but I think we should buy a car when we reach Kingman. And if we buy it legit, no one will ever know what kind of wheels we've got."

"Yeah. I've been thinking about that, too," Max said. "And Wyatt's got me more than a little bit worried."

She turned toward him with a serious expression. He wished she'd keep her eyes on the road, instead of on him.

"Max, what do you think about holing up for a while—and letting the pressure ease up a bit? Just the two of us. Does that sound too boring to you?"

Max put one hand on her shoulder. "No. It sounds great."

He took the other hand, put it on the steering wheel, and gently guided them back into their lane. A car whizzed by, narrowly missing them.

"I can't think of anybody I'd rather hole up with. But to do that takes money," Max said. "And we don't have any."

He pulled two guns from the suitcase and twirled them in his hands, western style. "What do you think? You up for it?"

Tara caught her breath. "You mean it?"

When Max nodded his head, she grinned seductively at him. "You know just what a girl wants to hear."

She pulled him into her for a deep and sloppy kiss. Then she pushed him away before things got out of hand.

Max grinned. He liked how excited she was.

"Well, there are a couple of schools of thought on the best way to do this. Massive intimidation is the style that Wyatt went for. The more scared they were, the less likely they were to try anything stupid."

Tara paused. "Wait, I'm getting ahead of myself. The first thing is the rules…"

Max held out his hand to stop her. He dug around in his bag, through his clothes and micro-tapes, and got out his tape recorder and popped in a new tape. He hit record and handed it to Tara. She looked at it skeptically.

Max said, "I'll never remember forty-seven rules."

"Yeah, that took me a while, too. And you don't want to forget 'em," Tara said. She held the recorder up to her mouth. "All right. *Rule #1…*"

DAH, DAH, DAH, DOM.

Wyatt tapped on his skull, but the sound happened again. Dah, dah, dah, dom.

As the chiming continued, Wyatt recognized that the electronic sound was not coming from his skull, but was a piece of classical music. Beethoven's Fifth. The question was why? And where?

He drove along in the luxurious Towncar, scanning the front seat for the source of the musical interlude. The offending culprit was a cell phone. Wyatt had always found cell phones to be irritating, and the people that carried them even more irritating, if that was possible. He'd even considered killing people just because they were talking on the evil little devices in his presence.

He'd barely restrained himself.

He pushed the window button and grabbed the thing, intending to throw it out. But instead of killing the electronic creature, he hesitated. Flexibility and adaptability had been crucial to his previous successes. They were part of the rules. If he could make friends with the thing, he'd be in better shape.

He stared for a second, mistrusting, before punching the green button that looked like a phone. At least that damned music stopped. He held it close to his ear, carefully, having heard that you get radiated if you placed cell phones directly on your ear. "Hello? No, Jim's feeling kind of sick right now. Yeah, I'll be sure to tell him the good news."

Wyatt pushed the red phone button, which appeared to be the hang up button. He turned toward the trunk and yelled, "Hey, Jim. Artie says you got a triple bonus for the Lassiter job. And that you'll probably get employee of the month again for exempting them from their claim. You worthless piece of..."

He dialed up his buddy, Chester, muttering murderous imprecations under his breath about insurance guys and their special room in hell. But the news he got from Chet made him even more foul-tempered.

The one good part—that Chet had sicced the Feds on Pete— was only moderately good news. Pete and his new partner were still dead-men walking.

Wyatt then called Billy Bob, hoping and thinking it was impossible that Pete could be ripping him off all over Arizona. Only to find that they'd been there, too.

Wyatt thought he might vomit. Throwing Pete out of the

car had been too good for him—and not nearly permanent enough.

Wyatt called May next, who had some good news at least. Even though she'd cheerfully handed over Wyatt's package, Pete had only just left. Maybe ten minutes ago, and she was pretty sure they were headed north.

Which meant they were headed for Crispin's place. The vet was the only place left in Arizona that had one of Wyatt's packages. A phone call to Crispin confirmed that the thieving thugs hadn't got ahold of that money yet.

After a frustrating and difficult conversation with the shell-shocked ex-soldier—Crispin barely had the faculties to carry out his chosen veterinary profession, and his conversations often drifted back to his embattled war times—Wyatt was fairly confident that Crispin would keep Pete there till Wyatt could make it.

Wyatt slammed on the brakes and yanked the wheel, spinning the car around. He came to a stop in the middle of the highway.

On the one hand, Pete deserved a swift death. On the other hand, he really wanted to torture Max and Tara. And if he left their trail, it might be hard to pick up again.

Wyatt pulled a coin and flipped it into the air, letting fate decide. It was heads, and Wyatt peeled away. He had a date with Pete and his buddy tonight.

CHAPTER 21

EXCERPT FROM TAPE 1

I know what you're thinking—why would the son of a sheriff be interested in robbing places? Well, let me tell you, from a pure excitement standpoint, nothing beats it.

And you know what else? I get a kick out of bringing excitement to other people's lives and helping our country's sagging economy grow stronger. It gives cops someone to chase, the media something to write about, people something to read about, and the insurance companies a reason to exist. And the victims, hell, they get their fifteen minutes of fame.

It's a win-win situation.

Just off the main highway, in the unincorporated town of Hero, Arizona, was a mini-mart ripe for the plucking. It was the perfect size for a two-man crew—entrances and aisles easy to cover.

Tara and Max waited an hour or so for the traffic to die down and for the take to grow to the proper juiciness. At their motel, they went over weapons, disguises, their proper positions once they were inside, and the always important rules. They both sported fake tattoos on their forearms—coiled cobras.

It was harvest time.

Oh, yeah! Tara thought. *The rush is back.* Her blood raced through her arteries at an exhilarating rate. She felt intoxicated.

The Cougar skidded to a stop on the left side of the minimart—the side without cameras. Max and Tara got out, each pulling a bandana over their face and putting on black cowboy hats in the style of the Old West.

It was her first time robbing a place dressed as a girl. Her hair was down, flowing free as a bird, and the light bob in her step was evidence of her appreciation at going *au natural*. Max carried a tire iron in one hand and a handgun in the other. Tara had the sawed-off pump. They unconsciously fell into step as they approached the building.

Tara watched Max, holding her adrenaline in check. Barely. She couldn't remember the last time she'd felt this excited—maybe when she was a kid. When she and Max had gone over strategies on the way over, she'd about lost it. And if Max did a good job today...the possibilities were endless for the two of them.

Max held the door open for her, like a gentleman.

Tara grabbed his behind and squeezed it. She said, "I could just eat you up." Then she let go of his rear and got back to business.

She burst into the store, looking around quickly and efficiently.

At ten o'clock, there was a large, round man at the counter with an enormous armful of Twinkies. At nine, a spindly attendant with freckles and red hair was ringing him up. At two o'clock, another man, a biker type with a T-shirt that read *Sturgis*, was in the back of the shop pouring himself a cup of black coffee. And a lone security camera perched in the corner, watching all.

Max entered the store right behind Tara and blasted the camera to pieces. As he approached the counter, Twinkies dropped and scattered everywhere, as if trying to escape the large voracious man.

There was a curse in the back. Tara reached the biker, who'd scalded himself with the coffee when he'd heard the gun blast. She rounded up the leather-clad individual and brought him to the front, where she could keep an eye on her new partner. After all, Max was new to this. A "mini-marts and gunplay" virgin.

Max looked at the name tag on the attendant's chest, *Jack*, and then smashed the tire iron into the glass countertop, shattering it. He raised his gun, sticking it into Jack's face—the pressure and precise placement making his nostril bulge. Jack glanced down, getting a good look at Max's snake tattoo.

At the unnerving sound of a wicked chuckle, Tara glanced over to Max. He was looking kind of crazy. Maybe too crazy. And way too much like her father for Tara's taste. It was unsettling, and her attention wavered between Max's situation and the biker she was covering.

Max narrowed his eyes. "If you give me every fucking nickel, jerkoff, I might not kill you!"

Jack took a moment too long to obey and Max whacked him with the tire iron. He hooked the tool around Jack's neck and pulled him closer.

"Jack, did I stutter? If I have to ask again, someone's definitely going to die."

Tara frowned and turned to Jack, who looked terrified—and bordering on extreme bladder failure.

Across from him, the large man had his hands raised in the air. A Twinkie was clenched in his left hand, squished flat, with the cream filling oozing from the package. Making a mess everywhere. The man was trembling and beginning to cry pitifully, a mewling sound like a newborn puppy.

Tara cursed, blaming herself for this mess. She'd told Max to act like Wyatt but she hadn't told him that some people needed to be coaxed. That there was such a thing as *too* crazy.

Max waved his gun toward the large man. And at the sight of the gun pointing in his direction, the man began to plead for his life.

"Oh, God! Please don't kill me!"

Max said, "I wasn't even talking to you, Twinkie."

"Please! You can't. Oh, God! I've got a family…"

"SHUT UP!"

But Tara was pretty sure the man couldn't stop whining. Everyone was petrified, sure they were going to die. That's when things could get dangerous. Even the weakest of animals, when pushed into a no-win situation, would fight back to the death.

Max put his finger to his lips and shushed the large man, but with no effect. "Shhh. It's all right. Shhh."

Max noticed the crushed Twinkie in the man's hand. He calmly and smoothly pushed it into the large man's mouth until it was stuffed full of golden cake.

The large man's eyes widened. The cake had an effect similar to a baby's pacifier, and he quieted down.

Max shook his head, upset with the way things were going. He was definitely trying his hardest, and Tara felt for him, remembering how poorly her first job had gone. She and the biker stood to the side, watching and wondering. What happened next surprised her. And everyone else.

Max made a T with his hands.

"Okay, everyone. Time out," Max said. "Time out, all right?"

Tara exchanged puzzled looks with Max and the others as he began pacing back and forth.

"I'm sorry, everyone—I don't know *what* I was thinking. And Jack, I owe you an apology, too. I don't hit people unless they ask for it. And you didn't."

Max began muttering to himself. "This isn't working because it's not my style. That's the real problem…it's just not my style."

Tara looked around, getting worried.

Max began chuckling to himself. "I got it," he said. "I got it."

He stopped pacing and stared at the large man for a moment. The Twinkie had been sucked down, with just a few crumbs around his mouth. Max gestured to everyone and addressed his audience.

"If nobody here's got any objections, we'll just start over."

Tara glanced at their intended victims. No one said a word as they looked at each other, wild-eyed and panting heavily.

"We'll just start fresh," Max said. "A clean slate, ya know?"

Max started toward the door. He tossed the tire iron to Tara, who caught it with her left hand.

"The tire iron's just not me," he said.

Chimes went off as he walked out the door and out of sight. Tara kept her eyes on the motley crew. It was dead silent. There was a long, pregnant pause as nobody moved. The frozen tableau could have been named *Still Life with Guns and a Mini-Mart*.

Jack stared at Twinkie, wondering what the heck was going on. Together, they turned to look at Tara and the biker. But Tara just shrugged, in the dark as much as everyone else. A cricket chirped in a corner.

While waiting for Max, Tara was momentarily distracted by the story on the magazine rack in front of her. *Ten* New *Ways to Turn Your Man On*. She hadn't read that one yet so she grabbed it, and a couple others for good measure, and shoved them in her belt. She waved her gun toward the guys to keep them from getting antsy. They all waited for a few seconds more.

When the bells chimed and the door opened, Tara sighed with relief. Max sauntered into the store and pointed his gun at Jack. He cocked the weapon and then stopped abruptly.

"Nope. That's not it. Just one more time."

Max turned quickly and stormed out of the store again.

The bells chimed once more as Max re-entered the mini-mart. He calmly strolled into the store, twirling his gun cowboy style.

This time, Tara noticed, Max walked with purpose and

authority. In complete control. Yet he also seemed to exude a certain charm and friendliness. She could tell he was grinning under his bandana when he threw her a wink and a kiss before turning to the others.

Max said, "Hey, there. How ya all doing? This here's a robbery."

Max aimed the gun at Jack, but in a more nonchalant way. A much friendlier way. He walked this way and that, getting close to each of them in turn, and acting like they were all best buds.

"Now if you all pony up some cash, I'll just get on out of your hair." He winked at Jack and the Twinkie man. "If you're *good* boys, and do as you're told, you'll have a nice story to tell your grandkids one day."

Max stopped next to Tara and the biker.

Tara watched the other guys' expressions, and felt pretty good with the way things were going now. It was unorthodox, but hey, whatever worked.

And now that Max was in a groove, and controlling the situation, she was starting to get turned on again—like when he'd thrown Wyatt out of the car. And Max must've been feeling the same way, 'cause just then he leaned over and raised his bandana just enough to kiss Tara on the back of the neck.

He shouldn't have, at least, not while on the job. But Tara melted, enjoying every second of the feeling—while still keeping her gun squarely trained on the biker.

Max stopped kissing her and made a feint with the gun toward Jack, menacing for a moment. Then he waved his gun away, grinning.

"Just kidding, Jack. But listen up. If you try something stupid, *we'll* be the ones telling stories to our grandkids. And they'll go something like this: She'll say, 'Hey, sugarbear,' because that's what she calls me. 'Sugarbear, you remember that time at the mini-mart when we had to blow away that *stupid*, fucking idiot?'"

Max looked pointedly at Jack. He tapped his forehead with the gun.

Max continued, "And then I'll laugh and say: 'Yeah. I sure do, snookums.' That's what I call her. 'I do remember that, snookums. But luckily, it was no big loss. The world needs fewer idiots anyway.'"

Max laughed at his own peculiar brand of humor. When he reached Jack, he casually waved the gun back in his direction. Kind of a reminder.

"Now, what do you say, Jack? Everybody?" Max said. "Should we do this hard or easy?"

Jack immediately started filling a grocery bag with the money from the register, working as fast as he could. Eager to please.

Tara laughed at the new style—impressed—having never seen this "friendly" approach before. And now she was more than a little bit turned on. She was getting impatient, wanting Max to herself.

At the lack of movement by the others, Max turned, like a scolding teacher, toward Twinkie man and the biker.

Max said, "Come on now guys. I thought I explained this. Aren't you going to play friendly?"

The large man and the biker gulped for air and then dug deep, instantly pulling out their wallets and tossing them into the sack.

Tara backed up to the door, checking out the way Max's muscles moved beneath his shirt. This was getting ridiculous!

But then Max twirled his gun again and that was it. The way he handled his gun was pretty hot. She wondered if that kind of thing turned everyone on.

Or was it just her?

Max gestured for the guys to get on the floor. "Thank you right kindly for your generous hospitality. Now, get down on the floor and stay there till you count to five hundred."

Twinkie, Jack, and the biker got on the floor, face down. Max backed toward Tara, who couldn't take her eyes off him.

"Go on now. Count so I can hear you," Max said. "And we just might come back in a few minutes to make sure you're counting proper."

The guys began mumbling and counting incoherently.

"Oh, come on now! That's pathetic," Max said. "Count together. And shout it out!"

They started over and sounded off, military style.

Max backed into Tara's arms. She grabbed him and pushed him against the wall, raising both their bandanas enough to reach his mouth. She kissed him hungrily, like they'd been separated for weeks on end. She ran her hands up and down the length of his body.

He started to do the same and then stopped. Max raised his gun and pointed it toward the guys on the floor. She felt a little embarrassed when she turned around and found the large man watching their affections.

"Sorry," said Twinkie.

He quickly lowered his head and got back to counting.

Max gave her an intense, drop-to-the-floor kind of kiss, then broke it off.

"Later," he said.

Max grabbed Tara and led her out the door.

"Every time I see one of those signs," Pete said, "I picture the illegals grazing by the side of the road like a herd of buffalo."

The Caddy's headlights had illuminated the "running family" road sign as Pete and Bull raced by. Bull kept his eyes on the road and tried not to let Pete distract him with his alien talk. Pete was always talking about something, so Bull had been forced to learn ways of tuning him out. Keeping his mind focused on ancient tribal rituals or his elders usually did the trick.

But every time Pete brought up illegal aliens, Bull's mind

focused on *ALIENS*, and turned immediately to the extra-testicle creatures.

Arizona was just one state away from the alien breeding grounds of New Mexico—way too close to feel comfortable. Only a few hundred miles. And it wasn't like aliens couldn't travel across state lines. They had spaceships for crying out loud.

"Watch out. You're crossing the double yellow line," Pete said. He was even paler than usual. "You've got to stay on this side of the line."

"I know. Sorry."

Bull swerved back into the appropriate lane. He'd only driven a few times in his life. The last time was in 1989, so he was a bit rusty. Normally, he was a passenger in life, not a driver, and he felt comfortable with his niche in the universe.

But tonight he was in a good mood. Feeling spirited—happy about his circumstances. Sixty grand could do that to a man. So he'd decided to drive.

The expression on Pete's face when he'd slid behind the wheel of Pete's beloved Cadillac had almost been reward enough. But the peaceful feeling he enjoyed while driving the convertible at night was the icing on the cake. The night air was extraordinary. It made him dream of the spirit world.

Bull's harmony was ripped apart by a high-pitched, wailing sound from behind. In the rearview mirror, he saw colorful flashing lights approaching fast.

His last coherent thought was *ALIENS!* Bull yelled out the cursed word while Pete yelled *COPS* in an equally frantic tone.

A rusted, beige cargo van passed Bull on the wrong side of the double yellow, followed closely by two police cars with the word Immigration stamped on their doors.

Bull watched helplessly as the van darted back into the right lane, nearly clipping the front bumper of the Caddy, and barely avoiding an oncoming car—a slow moving Dodge Dart with smoke seeping from inside the vehicle.

A law of physics reared its ugly head, and the sharp turn forced the top-heavy van to roll many times, treating its occupants to a sensation similar to being inside of a spinning clothes dryer.

As the van came to a grinding stop, the occupants that *weren't* wearing their seat belts ran afoul of another law of physics—an object in motion tends to stay in motion. The rear doors of the cargo van burst open, ejecting the crowd of immigrants with the explosive force of kernels of popcorn.

Bull had no where to turn. He saw the oncoming Dart on his left, the wreckage of the van in the middle, and a ditch to the right. He chose the lesser of all evils and turned quickly to his right.

The Caddy's wheels skidded on the asphalt highway. Instead of turning with the skid to regain control of the car, Bull turned the wheel the other way. His amateur driving instincts had betrayed him—and sent them careening into the van.

Bull smashed his head into the steering wheel as the spinning car bounced off the van like a pinball and turned sideways into the ditch.

The car came to a halt facing the road. Pete, and a severely dazed Bull, had prime seats for the rest of the action.

The last thing Bull saw before he slipped into unconsciousness was the Dodge Dart, having missed both the van and the Caddy, coasting down the road. The two police cars split to either side of the Dart. One drove through the soft shoulder and into the ditch on the far side of the road, rolling once, and the other hit the van dead on.

The Dart didn't swerve or slow down the entire time as its smoke-filled interior kept most of the exciting events from view. Only the flashing police lights had been visible through the marijuana haze, and those just for a second, so the teenage occupants sailed away unscathed. And unsure what had even occurred.

There was a lot of moaning, some ragged breathing, and quite a bit of bleeding among the unconscious illegals. They littered the highway like so much garbage.

Bull woke with a bump on his forehead, amazed the seat belt had held his massive frame in check. His brain felt kind of funny. Foggy. He figured he probably had a concubine of the brain. Or…was the word coconut? Wait. It was probably concussion.

Yeah…he was pretty sure concussion was the right word. And if he could remember a tricky word like that, he probably didn't have one.

He looked at Pete, who seemed unharmed, though extremely alarmed. Pete sat gaping at the scattered mess on the road. Mangled, twisted hunks of metal that used to be cars. Bodies everywhere—some stirring and some not. And two wrecked police cars not fifty feet away. Bull couldn't think of a worse sight to see upon waking.

One of the police car's bubble gum lights shorted out with a shower of sparks and let loose with a chopped-up siren sound for about two seconds. The sound had the effect of an alarm clock going off, waking many of the slumbering aliens lying on the road. They jumped up, scattering in the desert like cockroaches when the lights are turned on.

A stunned policeman opened his door and fell to the ground. Pete sprang into action. He grabbed the bag full of money and abandoned his Caddy, hopping over the smashed door.

He waved to Bull and said, "Come on! This isn't our party. Let's hoof it to Crispin's place. It's real close!"

Bull took off his seat belt and leaped over the door. Dizzy, he fell straight to the ground. Definitely a concussion.

Pete grabbed him by the arm and helped him to his feet, and they lumbered into the desert.

"BELIEVE IN ME, AND YOU CAN DO IT! YOU CAN DO IT! IF YOU can *dream* your path, you can *follow* your path."

Sheriff Williams yawned as the guru's words were met

with thunderous applause. He switched off the CD. The guy sounded more like a back road preacher than a psychologist, like he'd claimed.

Williams' bloodhound had howled along with the applause, and now that it was quiet he barked for more.

"Quiet, Duke."

Since it was pretty late, he decided to look for a motel. He hoped he was still headed in the right direction—that Max had even taken Highway 60. He turned on the radio and caught an announcer in the middle of a news update.

"And although no one was injured, the young couple that robbed the Kings County Mini-Mart was fast with their guns— and even faster with their hands."

Williams glanced over at Duke in bewilderment.

The reporter continued, "According to reliable eyewitness reports, the young couple could barely keep their hands off each other. They were so passionate they only stopped kissing for one minute—just long enough to rob the place. We'll bring you more of these Kissing Bandits on *CRIME WATCH* tonight. When it happens. Where it happens. We'll be there. This is Brett Saberhagen for KPPC News, signing off."

Williams turned it off with a chuckle. The news always tried to make more out of a story than it really was, but this was a little worse than usual. It sounded like a small-time armed robbery, except now the news guys were hyping the kissing angle, probably because sex sells. Williams figured it must be sweeps week.

He heard a call for "Sheriff Williams" on his police radio and picked up the handset. "Williams here."

Officer Lorna said, "Hey, big boy. Where you at?"

Williams blushed, direly wishing he could train his new honey not to talk like that on the public airwaves.

"Well, *Officer* Lorna, I'm back on 60, just entering Kings County."

"When are you headed back?" Lorna said. "The Feds and

the mayor have both been riding me, wondering where you are."

"Come on, Lorna. We've been over this. It takes however long it takes. I've got to watch out for my boy. You know that." Williams sighed. "Tell you what, put me down for extended sick leave. Then, at least, the mayor won't be able to give you any crap. And if the Feds keep giving you problems, you can give 'em my cell number. But only if you have to."

"Good. That'll help," she said. "But there's worse news regarding Max. It hasn't been officially tied to him, but the description of the Kings County Kissing Bandits is a little too close for comfort."

Williams shook his head. "It must be that tramp's influence."

"Come on, now. I think Max is a great kid, but he's always been able to get into trouble by his lonesome, hasn't he?"

"Yeah, yeah, yeah. I know," Williams said. "You could at least allow me this one little fantasy, couldn't you?"

"Just one?" Lorna's voice was low and sultry. "What about the French Maid thing?"

Williams face turned scarlet. He spluttered into the radio. "Damn it, Lorna! How many times do I have to tell you not to say that kind of stuff over the radio? What if someone hears you? It's completely unprofessional."

"I'm sorry, Sheriff."

"Sorry? You want to talk like a naughty little school girl, you call me on the cell phone, damn it."

"Fine!" she said. "Out!"

Williams waited for her to say something, but nothing came over the radio but static. "Lorna? Lorna?"

He slammed the handset back on the hook, hit the dash with his fist, and muttered under his breath. It was always harder to live with women than without them—he knew that. But there was supposed to be a balance, damn it.

Williams heard his cell phone start to ring. Where's the good stuff? The reason for putting up with all the crap that goes along with relationships? He answered the phone in his surliest tone. "Yes."

As he listened to Lorna on the phone, his anger gradually melted away. And after listening for a full thirty seconds, a sly grin crept over his face.

"You *are* a naughty one," Williams said.

MAX PUSHED TARA UP AGAINST THE DOOR. HOW HAD HE GOTten his shirt off so quickly? He pressed up against her, and she stopped thinking about trivial things, dropping the key to their room at the Lazy 8 Motel.

The hour-long car ride to Werner had been excruciating. The only thing Max did after stopping the car was to change the license plates. He didn't jump her or anything. He kept throwing the rules back in her face—telling her they had to get to ground before they could fool around. Like *she* didn't know the rules. Hell, she'd written some of the rules.

And he kept saying "later." *Later!* As if that was a soothing response. He was annoying, but she knew he was right.

Now it *was* later, and she could barely remember arguing with Max.

She pushed him back and onto the bed. She'd lost her skirt somewhere by the door—and for that matter, most everything else. They landed hard, and she saw her skirt on the floor, her black lace panties on top. Lace was sexy as hell, but completely impractical and uncomfortable to wear.

They rolled together, with Max ending on top. Unfortunately, pressing her back into something hard and annoying—which turned out to be the television remote.

She accidentally hit the power button and brought the familiar Brett Saberhagen to the screen—in mid-interview with Twinkie man from the Mini-Mart. As Tara and Max worked toward their joyful conclusion, they heard a nasty story on the boob tube.

Brett said, "We're glad you've survived your harrowing

nightmare. But the world wants to know—if you are all right, sir? Did the Kissing Bandits *violate* you in any way?"

Brett leaned in, hanging on Twinkie's reply.

"What the hell kind of question is that?" Twinkie said. "Crap. Is this sweeps week or something?"

"It is, sir. And television depends on great stories like this during sweeps week. And your story, if it's a good one, might well be played across this entire great nation. Millions of viewers will be watching your story. Wouldn't that be something?"

Brett had an unholy gleam in his eye.

Twinkie appeared to be thinking it over. "Well...they didn't violate me. But these guys were as vicious as Jack the Ripper. Mean as a snake. In fact, they had matching snake tattoos on their arms. Cobras. And what the Snake Bandits did to poor Jack, behind the counter, well I'm not sure I could repeat it on television. But, suffice it to say, he squealed like a piggy."

Their heavy breathing drowned out a lot of Twinkie's speech. But Max heard the last few words and lifted his head in concern. He said, "What's Twinkie talking about? Who squealed like a piggy?"

WYATT PULLED THE LINCOLN TO THE SIDE OF THE ROAD, KILLED the headlights, and parked—across from the entrance to Crispin's ranch.

The main house was an unusual structure, nestled right up against a mountain, almost as if the building was sprouting straight from the earth. Stretching across the entrance to Crispin's was a big wooden sign—*Vietnam Veterinarian, Doctoring animals since before the war.*

Wyatt looked around, but there was no sign of Pete or his partner. Just loads of animals wandering everywhere.

They should have been here by now, and he wondered if he'd misjudged where the dirtbags were headed. Then he figured, no, the idiots were probably just lost or something.

He got out and propped the hood open, going for the appearance of a broken-down vehicle. An overheated car in this hellhole was certainly a believable excuse if a nosy policeman came poking around.

Wyatt checked to make sure there was nothing obvious about Jim's body or his victims from the outside of the car. Jim had obviously pulled that kind of crime before—the trunk had been sealed with plastic.

Jim was the first serial killer he'd ever come across, and Wyatt liked his style. The way he'd lined the trunk was a classy move—no blood leaked from it. Just a few flies buzzing around the thing, hoping to get inside for a tasty treat.

Wyatt sat back inside and rolled down the windows. He wanted to be sure he heard any car that turned down Crispin's road. He kicked back to a more comfortable position to wait and sleep, then folded his hands in prayer.

"Now I lay me down to sleep. I pray the Lord my soul to keep. If I should die before I wake, I pray the Lord my soul to take."

Wyatt thought about it for a moment, then added, "Oh yeah, Lord. One more thing. If you could see your way clear to putting Pete in my grasp—I'll do you a solid and send his soul straight to Heaven. Then you can do with him what you will. Anyway, sounds like a fair deal to me. Amen."

CHAPTER 22

EXCERPT FROM TAPE 2

My pop always gave plenty of advice on women. He'd only ever been with one or two, but he'd somehow become an expert. He said that women always needed to talk. And after you'd shared each other's company, so to speak...they needed to talk even more.

What can I say? Even a broken clock is right twice a day.

"It was the hardest part about growing up with Wyatt—knowing my mama's death was his fault," Tara said. "I mean, he didn't pull the trigger, but he definitely deserved some of the blame."

Tara rolled over and laid her head against Max's chest. He stubbed out his cigarette and looked at the Lazy 8 Motel matches next to the ashtray, finding the motel's name a perfect fit for their situation. After their aerobic workout the night before, he and Tara felt as tired as a couple of newlyweds.

A lone cloud moved out of the sun's path, letting a ray of light peek through the window and illuminate Tara's hair like an angel's. But the angelic effect was more than offset by the candid discussion of her mother's murder. The two images didn't sit well together.

And anytime Wyatt's name was brought up, Max got a little

uneasy—'cause nothing he'd ever experienced was as nerve-racking as having Wyatt's specter perched on his shoulder. As if violence waited just around the corner.

He said, "Either Wyatt killed her, or someone else did."

"But that's thinking everything is black and white when most things are really shades of gray," Tara said.

She turned over to face him, the covers slipping and exposing her body. A beautiful sight to behold, much more pleasant than the thought of Wyatt chasing them.

She continued, "When I was eight, my mama and I got back from doing the grocery shopping. There was blood all over the house. And daddy was dragging this guy, this *dead* guy, out the back door. It was some deal that had turned sour—and dad had killed him."

Max shook his head, wondering what it was like to see this kind of stuff your whole life. In his mind he tried to put himself there—as if, at age eight, he'd found his dad with a dead guy. With someone he'd murdered. But his pop was too straight and narrow and Max just couldn't picture it. "What'd you do?"

"I did what any good little girl would do if they lived in a screwed-up family. I helped. While daddy was dumping the body, mama and I cleaned up the blood."

Tara took a deep breath before continuing. "It wasn't the first time, but the worst part was when the dead guy's brother came looking for him. I saw my mom killed, right before being shot myself.

"Of course, what Wyatt did to the guy after that was ten times worse than what he'd done to his brother."

Jesus. Max marveled that Tara wasn't more messed up.

She pointed to her chest. "That scar under my breast...is where the bullet went in. There's one on my back where it came out."

Max traced his finger along the scar. "Makes my story of walking in and finding my mom dead...well...makes it look easy."

Tara shrugged. "It's never easy."

"No. It's not," Max said. "But it's no wonder you're tough as nails."

Tara was quiet. "You have to be. If you go through something rough like that, and it doesn't kill you—it just makes you stronger. Growing up with Wyatt was rough as hell, but it hasn't killed me yet."

Max looked her in the eye. "Yeah, well it's only Tuesday. We'll see what happens the rest of the week."

She rolled her eyes. "Now there's a morbid thought."

Max bowed his head. "Sorry. It's a little unsettling to think he wants us dead. *And* it's a depressing conversation we're having. I mean, I'm glad you told me, except now I'm completely bummed out."

Tara moved closer and gave him a luscious, lingering kiss. "I think we can fix that."

WYATT HEARD A GROWLING SOUND AND WOKE UP INSTANTLY, aiming his gun out the window of the Towncar and toward the sound.

Outside was the biggest dog he'd ever seen in his life. Or maybe a wolf? The creature was ready to attack, and as it tensed to spring, Wyatt cocked his gun—figuring to blow the creature straight back to hell. But the creature reacted to the sound like any human would have, and high-tailed it off into the desert.

Wyatt checked Crispin's, but there was still no sign of Pete. He reached into the back seat and grabbed a suitcase that had belonged to the insurance man in the trunk. He figured the recently deceased wouldn't mind if he borrowed his clothes, so he found a nice western-style shirt and pulled it on. He called out to the trunk.

"Hey, Jim. You've got nice taste in clothes. I'll give the shirt back tomorrow, if you'd like." Wyatt cocked his head as if listening. "What's that? Keep it? Why that's mighty kind of you."

Wyatt then sniffed his armpits and wrinkled his nose. "Whew. I hope you've got some deodorant in here, Jim."

PETE STUMBLED ACROSS THE BURNING SAND, CURSING THE ARIzona wasteland. It was only about six or seven a.m., but had to be over a hundred degrees already.

"You said the vegetarian's place was close," Bull said.

"What...Crispin's place? It was only an inch on the map. How was I supposed to know that meant an eight hour walk?" Pete said.

"Cause you're smart? At least, that's what you claim. After being stuck out here, I'm not so sure any more."

"This coming from the guy who smashed into a stationary van and totaled my Caddy. I bet you took out a few aliens while you were at it."

Pete saw the glint in Bull's eye and decided to drop it. Though Pete'd had his share of doubters over the years, he *knew* he was smart. He definitely had brains enough to keep from antagonizing Bull. He figured the concussion was probably affecting Bull more than he'd originally thought. A new topic was in order.

"After we pick up the package at Crispin's, we'll see if he'll sell us one of those junk cars that he had in his barn."

Pete looked around for eavesdroppers before continuing, but there were only a couple of vultures waiting around. "I've fleshed out my reality advertising idea. We're talking hundreds of thousands of dollars here."

A grin crept onto Bull's face. "Yeah?"

"I think it should be our next job," Pete said. "But I've been worried about the suckers we're going to videotape. If they're in it, maybe they'll have ownership rights of any video we make. So what I figure, we get them to sign some sort of release beforehand. Tell 'em we're shooting a music video or something. Maybe for that rapper the dog was named after—Snickers or M&M—or whatever his name was. Since everyone wants to be in a video, they'll sign the release."

Bull grunted his agreement.

Pete continued, "Then we give the guy a name-brand soda and send him into traffic. That's where you come in, Bull. You swerve and crash right behind the guy. And after I get a good shot of the accident, I 'accidentally' zoom in on the soda. It's a million dollar idea. And this way, the guy who's holding the soda doesn't get any of the money. It's our regular two-way split."

Bull crested a rise and stopped in astonishment. Crispin's place was only a mile or so down the hill.

Pete joined him. "See, I told you it was close. You've got to have a little faith, that's all."

DAWKINS TRIED TO REACH THE SHERIFF FOR WHAT SEEMED LIKE the hundredth time, but the man never returned his calls. Williams was definitely hiding something. The only bit of info he'd gotten from the dispatcher, Lorna, was that the Sheriff was taking some personal time to look for his son.

Dawkins started some routine computer work using a complex algorithmic program the FBI had spent twenty million developing, and something a hacker could've developed for about a grand. *Our tax dollars at work.* He checked for recent criminal activity in Arizona, cross-referencing the crimes with Wyatt Evans' multitude of jobs, hoping for a match. Now that Dawkins had a name for the perp, he no longer thought of him as Yogi.

The closest style match for a Wyatt endeavor was the recent Snake Bandit robbery, which had been perpetrated by a young man and woman. Neither one was heavyset like Wyatt, so there was no physical match. But the woman matched Dawkins' personal description of Wyatt's partner. *Boo-Boo.*

Dawkins added the Sheriff's missing son into the mix, hoping to put the pieces together. They all fit.

Dawkins tried to factor Pete Corelli into the picture, but the extra piece didn't work. And as he pondered a couple of other scenarios, an alert came over his computer. Pete Corelli's Cadillac had been involved in a traffic accident in Arizona.

Time to fire up Stratton's jet.

CRISPIN PULLED THE SUTURE TIGHT AND TIED IT OFF. HE SNIPPED the thread with shaky hands and marveled at his successful operation. The pooch would live.

The German Shepherd had been standing guard for The People's Liberation Army of Arizona. A typical anti-taxation, anti-government militia.

The defenses at the PLA industrial compound were second to none. Bunkers were twenty-four inches of solid concrete—to protect them from rogue governments or commies or what have you—and the unfortunate dog had strayed into the demilitarized zone surrounding the camp and stepped on a land mine, calling Crispin's veterinary skills into immediate service. He'd saved all but one of the dog's legs.

For the last few years, the PLA had begged Crispin, as a decorated war hero, to join their paramilitary outfit. He had declined. Though the group took him back to his glory days, he found the PLA a tad crazy for his taste. Shell-shocked was one thing, but psychos were a different ballgame.

Besides, Crispin already had his own plans in case of war with the commies. His first love had always been animals, which was why he'd put his wartime surgical training to use helping critters at his practice—though he'd always found it kind of ironic that the army had trained him both to kill people, as well as save them and sew 'em up.

In case of nuclear annihilation at the hands of the Red Menace, Crispin had painstakingly connected his tunnels to an old mine shaft that led to a giant underground chamber—big enough for hundreds to live in. Then, as resources allowed from his lucrative practice of helping injured criminals, he'd amassed a stockpile of food, water, and animal feed—as well as two of every kind of animal he could get his hands on over the last few years. To restock the earth after the fallout was gone.

So far, he'd picked up thirty-four species, and had housed them all over his property—wherever they fit. Crispin had decided not to reserve space in his cave for humans, as he had a sneaking suspicion that the world might actually be better off if most people disappeared.

A frenzied clucking caused Crispin to turn to his newly installed security system. On the video monitor, he saw the wolf-dog leap out of the pen with yet another chicken firmly clenched in his jaws. *Now, there's a species we could do without.* That damned Wolfy had loved up three more chickens earlier this week, before snacking on the hapless cluckers. That's why he'd installed the deluxe four-camera security system.

He grabbed his rifle and headed for the front door, but stopped after catching a glimpse of his other monitor. An even more vicious predator had stepped onto his front porch—Wyatt Evans. And he was without Tara.

Crispin squinted as Wyatt pounded on the door and then trained a gun on it. One problem at a time—Wolfy would have to wait.

Crispin put down the rifle and grabbed his favorite M-16, Emmy, and a couple of extra clips. He'd need heavier, and automatic, firepower to take down Wyatt if he tried anything.

He pushed the metallic pad under his desk and opened the secret door to his underground tunnel system. He scooted quickly through the dirt burrow.

A short trip placed him in a large doghouse, directly in front of the main house, and behind Wyatt. He pointed Emmy squarely at Wyatt's back.

"Drop it, Wyatt."

Wyatt turned around slowly. "Don't piss me off, Crispin. It's been a bad couple of days." He gestured toward his gun. "This ain't for you. We go way back, you and me. This is for the slime that stole my money."

Wyatt tucked the gun away and raised his hands, innocent as a baby.

"They haven't showed," Crispin said.

"I know. But it's too damn hot to wait in the car," Wyatt
said. "And I've got a couple calls to make, if you don't mind.
So either use that thing, or put it away."

He didn't care for Wyatt, but he had no reason to kill
him. Yet.

Resigned, Crispin lowered his gun and led Wyatt inside
and into his surgical room. When they passed the three-
legged dog, Wyatt gave a loud snort of surprise, followed by a
chuckle. He took a seat at the desk and checked out the array of
monitors.

"Impressive security."

Crispin nodded, but kept quiet—his sensibilities mortally
offended by Wyatt's laughter at the dog's expense. Maybe he
should have killed him. Anybody who could laugh at a hurt
animal probably deserved to die.

"Don't pout, Crispin. It's not like *I* shot the damn dog.
Stumpy got that way without any help from me."

Crispin squinted through his thick glasses. The only
good that had ever come from Wyatt was the little angel he'd
spawned. And as Tara was the only one who'd ever held Wyatt
in check, it made him nervous that she wasn't around.

"Where's Tara?"

Wyatt's brow furrowed. "None of your damn business."

Wyatt might have said more, but he saw Pete and Bull on
the monitors.

"Stay in here with Stumpy. I'll be right back," Wyatt said.
"Oh, yeah. You might get some surgical tools ready. In case
I've got to torture them to find out where my money's at."

He yanked Crispin's M-16 out of his hands and took off,
leaving Crispin feeling naked, unarmed, and powerless. Crispin
opened his desk and pulled out his favorite Magnum, Nummy.
With the weapon, he felt clothed again.

He wondered if Pete and Bull were armed—if they would

even survive the upcoming encounter. He had a fleeting thought about helping Pete and Bull, but figured the world would probably be better off if all three of them killed each other. Especially if Wyatt died.

He deliberated for a moment. His cemetery by the chicken coop probably couldn't hold three more. It was getting pretty full. But if Wyatt were one of the three, he just might have to dig a little deeper and make room.

Unfortunately for Pete and Bull, they were the type that brought knives to a gun fight.

PETE AND BULL APPROACHED THE SIDE DOOR OF CRISPIN'S RANCH. Pete lagged behind, glancing nervously over his shoulder for the wolf-dog that had menaced him on his previous visit.

Bull knocked on the door. As it opened, he said, "We need us some water, Crispin. That desert nearly killed us."

Pete caught sight of Wyatt as the door opened, and felt the blood drain from his face. Wyatt had a rifle pointed right at them.

Bull grimaced, then half turned to Pete and said, "You're dumber than a herd of buffalo."

Pete was offended, but magnanimously chose to overlook it. It was just ignorance on Bull's part. As if Pete should have known Wyatt would catch up to them.

"That makes two of you, Tonto," Wyatt said. He gestured toward the duffle bag on Pete's shoulder. "Is that my money?"

Pete was about to answer, when he glanced to his right and froze. The wolf-dog was there. Forty feet away and closing fast. The lustful animal obviously remembered him, and advanced with a purposeful gait. Pete squirmed.

"Hey! We can do this easy or hard, Pete," Wyatt said. "Is that my fucking money?"

Pete trembled and nodded an affirmative while watching the approaching beast out the corner of his eye.

The confirmation was apparently all that Wyatt was looking for, and he shifted his aim toward Pete.

But Pete, entranced by the approaching wolf-dog, hadn't noticed that "death by Wyatt" was now a statistical certainty.

Bull quickly chose to take an active role in things. He leapt onto Wyatt as the gun went off. The two large men landed with a thud, with Bull on top. The impact measured seven point three on the Richter scale, and Bull's back erupted as bullets from the M-16 coursed through his body.

The wolf-dog shied, halting its advance.

Pete shook it off and ran in the opposite direction. The barn was a few hundred yards away. He raced toward Crispin's car collection, desperately hoping they were still inside. With death right behind him, his speed matched that of a professional athlete—with an extra six-tenths of a second shaved off.

Wyatt rolled Bull's corpse onto the floor. He shot at the growling wolf-dog, emptying the clip of the M-16. But the creature had the luck of the devil and slunk off, unharmed.

Wyatt tossed the empty weapon aside and pulled out his service revolver, then limped after Pete. His previous highway dust-up, courtesy of Max, had left him with little speed for the chase.

Pete reached the barn and slid open the wide doors. He jumped into the nearest car, an abused and ratty Honda Civic, and flipped down the visor, dropping the key into his hand. On the third try, the car finally started, and he sped off. He grinned and flipped Wyatt the bird as he passed, feeling safe behind the steel.

Wyatt was pretty far away, so the sound of him firing his gun didn't alarm Pete until a single bullet made it to the car, pierced the thin steel, and rammed into his left thigh. He wrenched his hand back inside the vehicle, vowing he'd never flip anyone off again.

Mother of God! Pete grimaced and put his hand over the wound, applying pressure. He pushed the accelerator to the floor. The little engine whined under pressure, but still put space between him and Wyatt.

The hitch was that Crispin was the only doctor he knew that worked on bullet wounds without reporting it to the authorities. And Crispin was, for the moment, off limits.

Pete decided to address the crisis using his renowned smarts. His main dilemma, he figured, was getting his leg fixed before he bled to death. An important problem, to be sure. But, as he thought for a bit, it was his only problem.

He still had the money. In fact, he now had twice as much, due to the unfortunate demise of his friend. Thankfully, Bull had gone out the right way and left his sizable earnings for his partner in crime.

Pete felt a tear stream down his cheek—he'd never had a partner die and leave his share behind. It was probably the nicest thing anybody had ever done for him.

He sent a prayer to the Indian spirits for his buddy, Bull. "Hope you have better luck in the spirit world, my friend."

Tara woke to find Max gazing at her. Their bodies were intertwined, a sheet strewn haphazardly across them. *Unbelievable.* Had she actually gone back to sleep?

She closed her eyes and shrugged away the covers.

"I was just having the wildest dream about you," she said.

"Well, all right." Max raised up on elbow. "That's the kind of thing you should share with your new beau."

She shook her head. "Nah. It was a pretty *adventurous* dream. But maybe we'll try it out later." Tara rolled over, remembering. "I think I read about it in a magazine, but it probably doesn't work as well in real life."

She pulled him down to her and kissed him deeply before pulling away.

"We should probably try it out anyway," Max said. He pressed against her, apparently ready to try now. "I think *adventurous* describes us perfectly."

She smiled. "I think that's the most beautiful thing I've ever heard."

Then she pushed him back and jumped out of bed. "We've slept half the day away. And if we hit just one more place, we'll have enough to buy us a car. Then, with new wheels…who knows? Maybe we'll hit something bigger."

"Bigger, huh?" Max rolled over and put a pillow over his head.

Tara pulled the pillow off, spanked him, and said, "Come on, get dressed. We've got people to see, places to rob. Money for the taking. The world is our oyster, baby."

"My gimp leg is bugging the crap out of me," Wyatt said. "You got anything I could use to juice it up?"

He brushed past Crispin and pulled open a cabinet, then pawed through the medicines inside—without identifying a single recognizable drug. Why couldn't Crispin keep any human drugs around?

"Damn it, Doc. Give me anything. If I have to watch Pete drive off with my money again, I'll kill myself."

Crispin rummaged through a drawer and held up an interesting looking bottle. Of course, Wyatt found all drugs interesting. His favorites were the trippy ones.

Crispin wheezed, then said, "I've got some Benzomethodryl lying around. I don't really prescribe it much because I don't approve of the side effects it has on the horses."

"Oh, yeah?" Wyatt said. "What's it do?"

"Well…it was originally used for fertility in marine animals. So they could breed an extra dolphin or two at amusement parks. But now it's used during horse races to give the animals an extra boost. Highly illegal, of course. The horses are so energized they can run on a broken leg. And since it's incredibly hard to trace, it's a perennial favorite at the track." Crispin's thick glasses slowly eased down the slope of his nose. He absentmindedly pushed them back up. "Regrettably, it also makes the horses a bit crazy. The stuff has an intensely psychoactive effect on an animal's mind, I'm afraid."

"Like I'd notice," Wyatt said. "It sounds perfect. Fix me up some of that go-go juice—just for emergencies."

The vet loaded a couple of syringes with the drug, handed them over, and edged toward the door. He grabbed Wyatt by the elbow and tried to usher him out.

"There you go, Wyatt. No charge. Say hello to Tara for me."

Wyatt stopped and removed his elbow from Crispin's wispy grasp. "It's interesting you should mention Tara. 'Cause I haven't seen the girl in a couple of days. And I think you're just the man to help me find her."

Crispin sighed deeply and his glasses slipped down the bridge of his nose again. "I couldn't possibly."

Wyatt grabbed a scalpel off the steel tray and oh so casually held it near the sleeping Stumpy. "You can't help me?"

Crispin held out his hands. "Did I say that? I meant that I'd be glad to help."

Wyatt dropped the scalpel and grabbed Crispin's elbow, marching him back to his desk and shoving him into a chair. He pushed the phone and the yellow pages toward the vet, then removed his recently acquired cell phone from the pocket of his jeans.

"Open it up to the motel section," Wyatt said. "And if we have to call every stinking motel in every small town in Arizona, then that's just what we'll do."

Wyatt flipped through a phone book and sat down. "Let's you and I get comfy."

CHAPTER 23

I hate to admit it, but robbing those places with Tara was more fun than two people should be allowed to have. No wonder it's illegal.

Max pulled into the parking lot and killed the engine. Today's target was a liquor store attached to a gas station.

The combo made for an appealing objective because Max had always thought it was a bad idea to mix alcohol with drivers. But hey, what did he know. He found the combination about as brilliant as putting billboards with cigarette advertising right next to schools—and then wondering why there was a thirty percent increase in teen smoking. But there were probably as many bad ideas in the world as there were people.

Tara pushed up against him, kissing him with the hunger of an inmate on his first conjugal visit. When she reached between his legs, Max broke it off. "Hey. No groping. It's not professional. Save it till we get back to the car, all right?"

Tara smiled. "Yes, dear."

Max did a quick weapons check and ran over the rules in his head. There were a lot of them, but he thought he had them down now. The only rule they weren't following was the one about driving a different vehicle. But they'd changed the plates on the Cougar and would be ditching the car in the morning anyway.

He and Tara had applied the snake tattoos back at the motel. They'd put on their hats and covered their faces with kerchiefs.

They'd gone over the plan. And now they were ready.

They exited the car and headed for the liquor store. He pumped a round into the shotgun. "You want to lead this time?"

Tara said, "Unh, unh. No way. I like watching you work. I'll take it next time."

Max grinned. He'd been thinking all morning about a new tactic to use. One he figured would entertain their victims—give 'em a good story to tell at their favorite watering hole.

And since no one had gotten hurt, he found this line of work to be pretty enjoyable. No harm—no foul.

There was one thing Max hadn't been too happy with—the constant news reports implying he'd sodomized the clerk behind the counter. All the news that's fit to report, his ass. More like all the news that's fit to imagine. He'd have to remedy that this time. Maybe leave one of the security cameras intact.

The only thing that really worried Max was the size of the take. These jobs were rinky-dink. Bigger fish, like banks, were obviously the way to go if you wanted to make a living at something like this. But it was probably better to take baby steps and work his way up to a big job.

He stopped at the entrance. "You ready?"

"Born ready."

This door didn't have an automatic opener so Max kicked it wide. It was better to make a grand entrance anyway.

With one blast from the shotgun, he turned the security camera to scrap metal. Max groaned—he'd forgotten to leave the camera alone this time.

Tara separated from Max, moving away from the cash register and covering the right side of the store.

Max twisted around and saw a man with an extreme acne problem duck out of sight behind the counter. *Shit*. Was he reaching for something?

Max hurried to the edge of the counter, only to find the man immobile, cowering on the hard linoleum.

He glanced around the store. In one of the convex security

mirrors, he noticed a man crouched down in the back aisle—an ostrich with its head buried in the sand.

"Honey, can you get that gentleman in the last row. He looks like he could use some company."

Tara blew him a kiss on her way past. She scanned each aisle on the way back, but there was just the lone customer.

Max looked at the name-tag of the prone man and gestured with the gun. "Ron. Hey, Ron! Would you get up off the floor, please?"

Ron rose reluctantly.

Max decided it was time to get the party started—try out his new idea. He put the shotgun barrel to his own ear and cocked his head as if listening to the weapon speak.

"What's that?" Max said to the gun. "I know, I know. I was just about to introduce you."

Max watched Ron's eyes bulge—his attention riveted to Max's dialogue with the gun.

Max stroked the barrel. "Don't be that way. You're embarrassing me."

As Tara brought the other guy to the counter area, Max held out the shotgun and waved it around for everyone to see. "Everybody, this here's my little baby. Simon. And Simon, I want you to meet Ron, who's behind the counter. And this is…"

Max gestured with the gun toward the nameless customer, a salesman type with greased hair.

"My name?" the salesman asked. "Uh, Stan."

"Is it *uh* Stan, or just plain old Stan?"

The guy started to stammer, before catching himself. "Just Stan."

Max took pleasure in the moment. He was getting comfortable, hitting his stride. He put Simon to his ear again and listened. After a couple of seconds, he stopped and waved the gun around.

"Now for the record, Simon here is in charge of this operation," Max said. "So don't even try to plead your case with me. If you all do what Simon says, then we'll all get out of this with our butts intact. If you don't...well...I'm afraid Simon's got a bad temper."

Max glanced over when Stan laughed nervously. But Ron wasn't laughing. He was obviously terrified by Max's odd display.

Max didn't fret. He felt pretty sure Ron would enjoy it later. Once Simon wasn't around.

Tara used a fake cough to cover her laughter.

Max listened to the shotgun again. "Uh-huh. Right. Sure."

Max turned to the group. "All right. Simon says to put your hands on your head."

Stan and Ron complied with the gun's command. Max listened for further instructions while Tara pulled the empty duffel bag from her shoulder and tossed it on the counter. Max pointed toward the lonely sack.

"That bag can use some company, Ron. Simon says for you to fill that bag with some friends of his—Andrew Jackson, Benjamin Franklin, and the like. And Simon says for Stan to hop up and down on one foot."

Stan obediently hopped up and down while Ron loaded the cash. Stan fell once, but gamely popped up and tried it again. Ron tossed the filled bag back to Tara.

"You're good boys," Tara said. "You guys must have played this game before."

Max said, "You can stop hopping now, Stan."

He was puzzled when Stan kept hopping, but quickly figured it out. "*Simon* says you can stop hopping now."

Stan stopped, and Max continued, "All right, now Simon says to lie down next to each other with your hands on your heads."

Ron and Stan carefully lowered themselves to the ground, placing their hands as directed.

With a hungry look in her eyes, Tara approached Max and leaned in with an eager kiss. He enjoyed robbing places, but why it made Tara so hot was beyond his understanding.

Then again, he didn't have to understand it to appreciate it. He responded to her kiss with enthusiasm.

Tara broke off the kiss and whipped her gun toward Stan. Max followed with his gun a split-second later. They cocked their weapons simultaneously. Stan cringed and froze in place.

"Did Simon say you could look?" Tara asked.

"No ma'am." Stan turned to the shotgun. "I'm so sorry, Simon."

Tara said, "Well, all right then. See that it doesn't happen again."

Stan lowered his head. "Yes, ma'am."

Max broke in with a grin. "Now Simon says that you all better count to five hundred before you do anything stupid like calling the police. And Simon…well…he just might come back and check on you. Make sure you remember how to count that high."

Max and Tara ran to the car and slid into their seats. Tears of laughter streamed down her face. "That was a riot. If you don't mind, I'd like to use that sometime."

She moved over next to him as they drove off—hungry as ever.

Max said, "Be my guest."

Stratton removed his jacket and glanced at his pit stains. He was convinced there was a conspiracy in the FBI to make him look stupid. There was no way his bad luck was his own fault. "Damn it, Dawkins. This is a dead end."

Dawkins shrugged and walked away.

Stratton squinted, figuring Dawkins was part of the conspiracy. Maybe the ring leader. All black men resented his authority. The arrogant bastards always had.

The last of the immigrant's bodies had been photographed and removed, so there was nothing to see as far as Stratton was concerned. He bumped past Dawkins as he stalked the perimeter of the accident scene before stopping at the red Cadillac. Pete Corelli's footprints, along with those of an unidentified heavy-set man that might've been Wyatt, led off into the desert.

To Stratton, the footprints were of no use whatsoever. The tracks could have led straight to hell, for all he could tell. He knew his tracking skills left a lot to be desired, and what's more, he took great pride in his ignorance.

His father, Senator Stratton, had taken him hunting exactly one time, when he was a teenager. And after killing his dad's prized hunting dog with an errant shot from his rifle, Stratton had been unceremoniously dumped back at the cottage and removed from all future hunting endeavors.

The canine killing had accomplished three things. The first was keeping Stratton out of the bug-infested forests of his father's estate. The mere thought of blood-sucking insects nauseated him, so removing himself from the hostile bug environment was always a good thing.

The second was living out his darkest thoughts and dreams—the bloody ones. Killing the dog had provided a much bigger thrill than anything else in his life, and provided a glimpse of his future ambition—working around corpses in the FBI.

The third thing was allowing him to stay home with the attractive Russian nanny his dad had hired to look after him.

After scoring with the nanny—which cost him a pretty penny from one of his trust accounts, but was entirely worth it—Stratton figured he'd scored a trifecta. And the confidence boost he'd received from the nanny served as encouragement for the rest of his life. He was currently batting six out of a thousand with the opposite sex. Which in his mind wasn't half bad.

But now, watching Pete and Wyatt's prints disappear into the desert—and with no way to track them—he felt strangely… inadequate. He glanced over at Dawkins, who was talking with some teenager, enjoying himself.

"So now what, Dawkins? It's your ass if we can't find them."

Dawkins merely shrugged and said, "Running Bear just got here."

Arrogant scum. He was definitely behind the conspiracy. Out loud, Stratton said, "What's that supposed to mean?"

"I told you already." Dawkins shook his head. "He's a tracker from the Navajo Reservation."

Pompous prick. Stratton said, "How long will that take? For some primitive to find the bastards?"

The teenager beside Dawkins bristled, causing Stratton to notice his darker skin. A Navajo. "You've gotta be kidding me. What are you, fourteen?"

"Don't be a jerk, Stratton. Running Bear is an expert at this kind of thing. He can find them," Dawkins said. "And you can't."

"My price is a thousand dollars," Running Bear said.

"You said five hundred," Dawkins replied. "We had a deal."

"The deal still stands. Five hundred for you, Agent Dawkins. If this man comes," Running Bear pointed to Stratton, "it's a thousand."

A thousand for a kid! Stratton turned to Dawkins, who promptly agreed to the new deal. Stratton's jaw dropped. Running Bear headed toward the tracks and examined the ground.

Dawkins said, "Your dad can afford it, so don't make this worse than it is already. The kid's good—and fast. If we want to catch up to them, this is our ticket."

Stratton mutely agreed. The quicker they caught these guys, the sooner his dad would turn his trust funds back on. "The kid doesn't get squat if he doesn't find them."

Running Bear looked up. "That is acceptable."

He stood up and said, "There are two of them. One is a big man, and one is a wispy man. The big one has some head trauma, and his feet wander. The injury was probably caused by the accident. The smaller one carries a bag on his right shoulder, causing an unusual step pattern with a heavier indentation of his right foot. But the track is eight hours old, so we'll have to move fast."

And with that, Running Bear ran off into the desert.

Stratton marveled, thinking the kid's feat was pretty impressive. Hell, maybe the world wasn't against him after all. He whistled to round up the other agents, and they all followed the diminutive Indian.

"This is Brett Saberhagen for Reality News. Bringing you all the news that's *real*."

Tara lay on the bed, her hair wet and a towel wrapped around her body. This motel was a little swankier, and the pool actually had water in it. She grabbed the TV remote and turned the volume up.

She was fired up, enjoying the fact that she and Max were on all the news channels. Together. She saw Max by the sink, brushing his teeth, and called out to him.

"Here it is!"

The reporter continued, "Arizona has become a war zone, a melting pot if you will. Of criminals, lowlifes, and hop-heads. Led by the now infamous Snake Bandits. My inside sources tell me the Snake Bandits have killed dozens of people before. In fact, these alleged porno stars might have been involved in the biggest bank heist in Arizona history."

Max crossed in front of the TV and turned it off. Tara's "Cheshire" cat grin evaporated.

"What are you doing?" Tara said. "That was some pretty funny stuff."

"It's embarrassing. They're making up whatever shit they want to. Anyhow, I don't like thinking too much about it."

He didn't like thinking about what? About robbing places? Tara cooled at the thought. She couldn't be positive that's what he meant, but with men, the magazines said, you had to read between the lines—that it was the only way you could tell if they were going to up and leave you.

This can't be good. And she'd just about decided Max would be worth keeping 'round for years to come.

She looked up to Max. He'd been watching her closely, noticing something was up, and he approached her cautiously. "Hey, it's all right, Tara." He pressed his body up against her. "All I meant was I'd rather think about you."

She hesitated, wondering if he was feeding her a line. But he didn't seem to be. And she was pretty sure she could read him easily.

Then she realized it didn't matter anyway. She couldn't hold back even if she wanted to. With a sigh, she realized she didn't have the upper hand any more. Not that it mattered, 'cause when Max kissed her, she realized losing control didn't bother her as much as she'd thought it would.

NIGHT HAD FALLEN BY THE TIME WYATT PULLED INTO THE MOTEL parking lot and spotted the Cougar in front of a row of motel rooms. *Motel rooms!* He'd called eighty motels before finding the one where Tara and Max were, but the idea of the two of them sharing a room still galled him. *Slut.* "I can't believe it! They're shacking up again. Right under my fucking nose."

Wyatt slammed the steering wheel three or four times. Just to ease the tension.

One down, three to go. Pete's partner had just been the first. Wyatt snorted, realizing he didn't know what the guy's name was. It didn't seem right to shoot people you hardly knew. But somehow, he would learn to live with it.

He rummaged around in his pants pocket for a minute, then searched the car until he came up with a quarter.

"All right. Heads, I knock on every fucking door till I find them. Or tails, I do the intelligent thing and wait for them to come out."

He flipped the coin in the air. "Come on, heads, heads, heads."

The coin landed in his hand and he slapped it onto his wrist. "Shit. Tails."

Wyatt backed the Lincoln a few rows away from the Cougar and up against a wall, making sure he still had a clear view of the offending vehicle.

"You think they'd get rid of the car." Wyatt shook his head. "But you can only teach people the rules. You can't make them follow."

As he turned the motor off, a motel door opened up. Wyatt froze. His pulse quickened as he watched Tara walk toward her car. "That's my girl."

Tara grabbed a bag from the trunk and hurried back inside. Wyatt cackled and grabbed the door handle. "This is gonna be sweet."

A police car crawled past the Lincoln. Wyatt ducked down and peeked over the edge of the dash—he hoped they weren't looking for the joker in the trunk.

But the cop was looking in the opposite direction—checking out the Cougar. *The same cop I shot yesterday.* Wyatt remembered stuff like that because he kept a special compartment in the recesses of his mind for the faces of people he'd killed. Or thought he'd killed.

He overheard the sheriff talking on a cell phone. "This is Williams. I've got 'em."

Wyatt listened in, hoping for something useful. He hated to admit it, but when it came to cell phones, he was beginning to see their usefulness and not just their annoyance.

Sheriff Williams backed his patrol car up to the wall, parallel to Wyatt's with another car sandwiched between the two. Spitting distance.

Wyatt continued listening to the sheriff's phone conversation as he searched the seats around him. He pulled up the same quarter as before and whispered to himself. "Heads, I wait to see what the cop is up to. Or tails, I take him out of the equation."

He flipped the quarter in the air. "Come on, tails."

When the coin landed on heads, Wyatt flicked it off his hand in annoyance. "Overruled."

He pulled his gun and cocked it, then opened the door quietly and eased out, slipping toward the police car. He stopped as Williams' voice rose.

"Damn it, Lorna. I don't want you notifying the Feds just yet. I've got to give Max a chance to do the right thing and give himself up."

Wyatt snorted quietly, questioning the sheriff's sanity. *How could the right thing ever be giving yourself up?*

"I know they won't like it," Williams continued. "Just give me till morning and I'll see if I can talk some sense into my son. Get him away from the girl and that schizo, Wyatt."

Not good. The cops knew his name.

But it looked like Max's dad didn't approve of the kids' relationship, either. Wyatt smiled to himself and slipped back into his car. It wasn't like the kids would be going anywhere. Wyatt could wait a bit to see how this played out.

Williams continued his conversation. "I know. I'm sorry, Lorna. You did a great job tracking down the Cougar. A lot of good phone work."

Wyatt kicked back in his seat.

Williams got comfortable in his patrol car. He barked a laugh. "Now don't distract me with dirty talk like that. Hell, the way you talk, woman, you get me all fired up. And I've got to keep my mind on my work—figure out what the hell to say to Max…"

Wyatt dozed to the soothing blather of the sheriff two cars over.

CHAPTER 24

EXCERPT FROM TAPE 2

*If you knew you wouldn't get caught, who wouldn't
want to rob a bank?*

The next morning, Tara looked in the mirror as she slipped
into her favorite outfit and pulled the zipper tight. Sexy as all
get out. She put the gun in her thigh holster and smoothed
the short dress.

She turned and gazed at Max, who was sleeping soundly.
Even while he was sleeping, he looked different than the lowlifes she'd hung out with the last thirteen years. Tara climbed
into bed next to him.

She whispered, "You done good, Max."

And he had. He'd done great by her, personally, and he'd
done a fantastic job with the mini-marts. Though there wasn't
much cash in 'em.

Tara sighed, looking at the little wad of bills on the dresser.
The rewards weren't worth the risk in these small jobs, but
they were good training for Max. And now he was ready to
take things to the next level.

She smiled, thinking about how much fun they were
having, and how the jobs had actually brought them closer
together. The family that robs together, stays together, or at
least that's what Wyatt had always said. She'd thought that
he'd been full of it, but maybe he was on to something.

Family.

She gazed at him for a while before Max gradually stirred,

and then woke to find Tara staring at him. "Is everything all right? What is it?"

She hesitated before answering. "You look amazingly… innocent…when you're sleeping."

"Is that right?" Max said. "So do you."

Tara found that impossible to believe. It must have shown because Max spoke up.

"Don't look so shocked. Most people think about nice stuff when they sleep. That's what makes them look innocent."

"The things I've seen…and done," she said. "I'll never be innocent again, not even in my sleep."

Max rolled over onto his elbow and pressed toward Tara.

He said, "Sure you will. 'Cause deep down, and I mean *way* deep down, there's a decent, law-abiding citizen waiting to get out."

Tara burst out laughing.

Max laughed and said, "Oh, yeah. I can hear her little, teeny voice calling out to me."

Tara raised her eyebrow.

Max touched her belly as if to say the voice was coming from near her stomach. He went on, "The voice is saying help me, Max. Help me. *Rescue* me."

Tara snorted with amusement and pushed Max off the bed. He grabbed her by the arm and took her with him, rolling onto the floor. She hadn't laughed this hard since her mama was alive.

WYATT WOKE TO THE SOUND OF A CAR DOOR BEING SLAMMED. HE pointed his gun hand toward the offending sound, but found his palm empty. The gun was on the seat beside him.

He grabbed it and peeked over the dashboard with bloodshot eyes, but the sound hadn't come from the Cougar. An old tourist couple dressed in Hawaiian shirts and leis walked by—hundreds of miles from the nearest luau. Probably lost.

He'd had the wildest dreams during the night. The last

one was particularly interesting, involving a decapitated Max. Wyatt had made him that way, of course. But the best part of the dream was when Max's severed head had spoken, threatening Wyatt with bodily harm. He'd laughed and kicked the head past a goalie and into a net that had suddenly appeared. The crowd roared its appreciation and a sports announcer yelled *GO-OOOOOO-OAL*, for what seemed an eternity. He'd danced in victory, with a proud Tara draped on his arm, until he'd been rudely awakened by the old couple.

Damn tourists. He looked at the syringe with the go-go juice the doc had given him, but decided to hold off till later.

He glanced around, looking for the sheriff, before finding him tucked away in an alcove at the corner of the motel. The sheriff put some money in the vending machines inside the alcove and grabbed a cup of steaming coffee.

Lucky bastard. As groggy as Wyatt was, he thought he might kill for some hot coffee. He seriously considered it. With great difficulty, he held himself in check.

MAX RUBBED HIS EYES AND SLID OUT OF BED, A LITTLE GROGGY after their morning roll in the hay. Tara was already up, dancing around at eight in the morning, extremely excited about something. He shook his head and smiled. There was no way to know where things were going, but it was impossible not to enjoy the ride getting there.

"I think you're ready," Tara said. She put the last of the weapons in her sturdy suitcase and slipped on her black pumps.

At first, he wasn't sure what she was talking about. But then he understood—she was talking about a bank heist. The crème-de-la-crème. *Oh, yeah.*

"You got one in mind?"

Tara moved closer to Max. "I sure do. There's one about an hour from here. I hit it with Wyatt a couple of years ago, so I know the layout pretty well. I think it would be perfect for your first try. And then we'll have enough cash to get cozy somewhere—get out from under Wyatt's shadow for a while."

Tara moved into his arms and said, "So what do you think? You tired of these rinky-dink jobs?"

She gave him a kiss that felt like a promise. "You ready for something more?"

Max understood she meant a couple of things by that question, but it didn't change his answer. Because he *was* ready. "Oh, yeah, baby. When you're right—you're right."

Tara kissed him again, putting her whole body into it. "Maybe we'll stop and see my Aunt May on the way. And you can meet someone nice from my family. Someone who won't try to kill you."

"That'd be different."

"I tell you what," Tara said. "Take your shower, while I go grab us a car from that lot down the street."

"I've got a better idea." Max kissed her on the back of the neck. "We'd probably save us some time if we showered together."

She skipped out of his grasp and headed to the door. "Yeah, sure. That'd save us a lot of time."

Tara grabbed her purse, but then stopped with her hand on the doorknob. "Any kind in particular?"

"Well…if we can afford it, a convertible would be nice."

Tara waved a big wad of cash in front of her face. "I'll see what I can do."

She blew him a kiss on her way out the door. Max grabbed his tape recorder and spoke into it as he stripped off his clothes and headed for the shower. "Robbing a bank's got to be the ultimate adrenaline rush. If you knew you wouldn't get caught… who wouldn't want to rob a bank."

WYATT WATCHED THE SITUATION DEVELOP FROM HIS FRONT ROW seat in the Lincoln. Tara had walked out the door and stopped dead upon seeing the police car parked against the wall. Wyatt glanced over to the alcove and barked with laughter as

Williams ducked out of sight behind the vending machines and spilled coffee on his shirt.

Tara looked around. When she didn't notice anything else out of place, she turned and walked quickly in Williams' direction.

Wyatt tensed for action, and then groaned when she passed right by the sheriff and headed down the street—there'd be no matinee show today. If Wyatt wanted entertainment, he'd have to provide his own.

He wondered what the cop would do. "What's it gonna be, the lady or the tiger?"

He arched an eyebrow in surprise when Williams took off after Tara. "Interesting choice. I guess that leaves the little pus-ball for me."

Wyatt grabbed the handcuffs off the seat and got out of the car. He whistled a little mindless tune as he headed to the trunk, hoping there'd be something useful in there to use on Max. Something to play with.

He popped the lid, then wrinkled his nose at the disgusting smell. The dead bodies hadn't improved in the hot sun. Flies raced into the trunk, buzzing with delight.

"Man, that is ripe." He held his breath and leaned into the trunk and poked around.

"I think I'd better get me some new wheels." Wyatt turned and looked at the Cougar. "Or some old ones."

Wyatt pulled a handy-dandy toolbox from the trunk and slammed it closed, then stalked toward the motel room. Listening at the door, he heard a shower running inside. *Perfect.*

With little effort, he pried open the door using a hammer from the toolbox. A cursory glance of the room didn't reveal much, but he did find the keys to his Cougar. He scooped them up, then placed the toolbox on the dresser and rummaged around, looking for goodies, sure there would be something fun and attention-grabbing. The right tool for the right job. It was *Rule #24*, but it applied to most parts of life.

Damn, no power tools.

The shower turned off. Wyatt moved out of sight from the bathroom door.

Max came through the door wearing nothing but a towel. Wyatt withheld a snicker. It was always a good idea to grab people when they weren't fully dressed—it made them feel more vulnerable.

Wyatt let him take a couple of steps forward and notice the toolbox on the dresser—just to make it a little more interesting. He wanted to enjoy this, though he knew he didn't have enough time for a proper torture session. When Max had registered the toolbox, Wyatt smashed his face with an oversized fist. Probably felt like a hammer.

Max hit the floor like a stone.

"You should've followed the rules, pus-ball."

Max was dazed and confused, but not exactly unconscious.

Good. Wyatt lifted him from the floor and sat him on a chair, cuffing his hands behind his back.

The cut above Max's eye, where he'd clocked him, wasn't serious, but it still bled profusely. Wyatt grinned, then filled the ice bucket with water and threw it in Max's face to bring him around.

"Wake up, pretty boy. Dying time's here."

Wyatt punched him twice in the ribs to get the ball rolling. Max coughed and sputtered a bit before meeting his gaze. Wyatt grimaced, amused at Max's expression—if looks could kill, he would be dead meat.

"You'd like a piece of me, huh?" asked Wyatt.

Max stared for a few moments before answering. "It's crossed my mind...that a world without Wyatt...would probably be a better place."

Wyatt's smile lit up the room. It was always better if they had a little fight left in them. Made things more pleasurable.

"One of these is a handcuff key." Wyatt held up a ring of keys in one hand and the pliers from the goody box in the other. He crossed behind Max and dangled the keys so they made a jingling noise, then leaned over and whispered in Max's ear.

"Tara will be back soon. So let's say you've only got about five minutes left. That's three hundred seconds till you die in excruciating pain." Wyatt cackled. "And just to make it interesting—don't get me wrong, Max, there'll still be pain involved—but to make it more fun, you can try to unlock yourself with this little key here."

Wyatt saw some confusion on Max's face. The little turd was probably dumber than Pete.

So he explained, "Then it'd be a whole new game. You could try to kill *me* instead. And maybe, just maybe, you'd get to test that 'world without Wyatt' theory of yours."

Wyatt dropped the keys into Max's right hand, then grabbed hold of the pinkie of his left hand. He put the pliers around the base of the pinkie as Max tried to pull his fingers away.

Wyatt whispered, "This is to make it a little more challenging for you."

Wyatt yanked on the pliers, snapping the pinkie backward and breaking it. Max writhed in agony, but didn't scream—making Wyatt even more pissed off. It took all the fun out of it when they didn't react the right way.

But he'd suffered that kind of problem before and knew just what to do. He just needed to try a little harder, throw his weight into it.

Wyatt grabbed the ring finger with the pliers and tweaked harder this time, snapping it back with a sickening sound. Wyatt felt every bit the proud craftsman when Max let out a yell this time. *That's much better.*

SHERIFF WILLIAMS STOPPED A COUPLE BLOCKS FROM THE MOTEL and staked out the corner opposite a used car lot. From there he watched Tara search through the cars.

He knew he was stalling, but right now the idea of confronting Max didn't seem all that appealing.

As he waited, he glanced up at the early morning sun and shook his head. It was hotter than blazes already, and a typical Arizona morning. Not that he'd complain. *If you can't stand the heat, get the hell out of the kitchen.*

He craned his neck—it looked like Tara had decided on an old convertible, and that she was dickering with the salesman. He snorted 'cause the back and forth haggling seemed to be frustrating her.

He couldn't blame her—the only time he'd ever come close to killing another human being, even as a police officer, was when he'd tried to buy a new car. He hadn't killed him, of course, but wondered if a jury would have even convicted him. They might have called it "justifiable homicide." After all, everyone on the jury would've felt the exact same way at one time or another.

Williams jotted down Tara's new license plate in a little notepad he kept in his pocket for just such emergencies. It had come in handy more than once.

He sighed, glad of the diversion Tara had caused him, but figured he'd put off his decision about Max long enough. Williams turned around and headed toward the motel. He still felt conflicted about whether or not to arrest Max. He knew it was right from a legal standpoint.

But for the first time, he wondered if there might possibly be another side.

Max groaned, wondering what Wyatt would do next. The psychotic SOB seemed to be building to a crescendo of craziness.

He smashed the table lamp onto the dresser a couple of times until the wiring came loose, then used a scalpel to cut it off with one quick jerk.

Shit. A scalpel.

Max kept perfectly still, not wanting to attract the animal's attention. He eyed Wyatt warily, and painstakingly tried to unlock the cuffs. But his broken fingers stuck out at an odd angle, hampering his efforts to get free. Every time he bumped the busted digits with the key ring, he winced with pain.

If and when he got loose, he wasn't looking forward to tackling Wyatt. The psycho paced back and forth like a caged lion, ready to pounce.

Max almost had the key in the lock. As Wyatt stalked past him, muttering like a madman, he elbowed Max in the face, causing him to nearly drop the keys.

His fingertips clung to the smallest key, and he carefully worked them back into the palm of his hand.

Wyatt sat down on the bed across from Max, muttering under his breath. "Piece of shit! Thinks he can fuck with me... take Tara away...unbelievable."

Wyatt had the look of a homeless man talking to imaginary friends. He whittled at the lamp wire with the scalpel, stripping the insulation bit by bit.

Max kept trying with the keys, but still no luck. He decided his best bet was to stall for time—and hope Tara showed up soon. *With guns blazing.*

Wyatt mumbled, "No way some pretty-boy, fucking punk is gonna do that to me. What the hell's he thinking?"

"You think killing me is gonna get her back?" asked Max. "I think you've got a few screws loose, pal."

Wyatt kept working on stripping the wire. There were now two wires, one with bare copper showing. "You think so, huh? Well that just tears me up inside. Don't be naïve, kid. It's way past that, now. I don't even want her back."

Max winced as he bumped his fingers, but managed to get the keys in a better position.

Wyatt said, "You know something, dipshit? Because of you, I've got to kill the one person on this earth I love."

Max looked at the wires. Both were down to bare copper.

Wyatt scowled, then separated the bare parts of each wire. "Because of you, I lost two-hundred and fifty grand from my bank job."

He took the other end of the wire and plugged it into the electrical socket.

Max groaned. *Shit. That can't be good.*

"Because of you, I've lost the love of my daughter."

Wyatt pushed the two bare wires onto Max's bare chest. The electricity coursed through his muscles, causing him to clench the keys till they pierced his hand.

Max's skin felt like it was being scraped off with a cheese grater. He resolved never to grate cheese again. He writhed in agony, barely noticing the sparks, or listening to the sizzling sound, or smelling the heavy aroma that was reminiscent of a Fourth of July barbecue.

Wyatt pulled the wires off, leaving Max gasping for air. With the electricity gone, his muscles released and he dropped the keys to the floor. *That can't be good, either.*

"Because of you, my daughter is spoiled for this world."

Wyatt shocked him again, leaving burn marks on the skin this time. Max clenched his teeth, not wanting to give Wyatt any satisfaction. What's a hundred and ten volts amongst friends?

He groaned and thrashed about. It was time to go on the offensive. And since he was cuffed to a chair, that meant a verbal lashing was about all he could manage.

When Wyatt removed the wires, Max managed to spit out a few words between shocks. "You piece of shit! What kind of scumbag teaches a nine-year-old to rob banks and shoot people?"

Wyatt squinted. "That's my business." Another quick shock. "She needed a trade."

Max groaned again.

"And she wasn't my daughter, anyway. Her mama fooled around with a buddy of mine."

Wyatt juiced him again. "Of course, my buddy's now deceased."

"You're full of shit, Wyatt," Max said. "If you raised her, she's your daughter. And you didn't love her—you stole her life away. That's just sick."

Wyatt spat. "You have no idea what it's like trying to raise a little girl by yourself! You try that and then tell me what love is." He pulled the wires off and began shaping the cord into a noose, being careful not to touch the bare copper.

It was a small victory, but Max appreciated it anyway. At least he'd managed to piss him off a little.

Wyatt placed the electric noose around Max's neck, but held the copper ends just clear of his skin.

Max fought through the pain, knowing there were only seconds left. He tried to breathe in enough air to speak.

Max said, "If you loved her, you'd care more about her life than yours, because that's what love is..."

Max saw him acknowledge the truth, but it didn't have the effect he'd hoped—it didn't prolong things any. Wyatt pulled away from him and let go of the copper.

The wires sparked as they touched his skin. Max yelled uncontrollably.

Wyatt took a step back, distancing himself, a strange expression on his face.

Max heard a loud thump on the door. Wyatt ignored it. Then another thump and his pop burst into the room.

Williams froze at the sight of his son convulsing.

Wyatt snapped out of his daze and ran for the window. Williams raised his gun and fired as Wyatt broke through the window in a shower of glass.

Max was dimly aware of his pop rushing to his side. If his pop had been a bit more mechanically inclined, he probably wouldn't have grabbed his son and shocked himself silly. Williams sucked on his fingers, then noticed the electrical cord around Max's neck. He yanked the plug out of the socket and caught Max as he slumped forward.

Even though the current had stopped, Max felt like he was still twitching. They both watched the Cougar blaze past the open doorway. Max turned to his pop and said, "Good timing."

Williams enveloped his son in a big bear hug. "When I

heard you screaming in here...and saw you like that...well I'm just glad you're all right."

"You and me both..." Max stopped, holding back tears. "Thanks, Pop. You were awesome."

His dad gave him another bear hug.

Max groaned, "Would you mind getting these cuffs off me?"

Williams bent down for the key, and Max winced in agony as his pop brushed against his fingers. "Ahh! Watch it. Some of 'em are broken."

"Shoot. Sorry, son. What's with that guy, anyway, and his fascination with breaking fingers?"

"I think it's *Rule #14*," Max replied. "The one about pressure points."

Williams ignored him. "We'll stop by the hospital to make sure you're okay. Then we'll go to the nearest station and straighten this whole thing out."

The handcuffs dropped to the floor and Max stood up, rubbing his wrists and fingers. He couldn't believe the words that just dropped from his pop's mouth like an A-bomb. Just when he was appreciating the man more than ever before, he had to go and say something like that.

"Pop. You've got to be kidding me. There's no way I'm going to a police station."

Now Pop was giving him one of his patented "looks." The kind that said Max must be the biggest dumb-ass around. But its power had worn thin through frequent overuse.

"You've got to, son. It's what's right."

Max and his pop stood there in a stalemate. Not much had changed. Max gave a tiny shake of his head.

"Hell, Pop...thanks for coming for me. I mean it. But it's time to let go. I'm ready for my own life."

There was that look again. Williams gestured around the motel room. "You call this ready? When I came through that door you were being electrocuted."

Tara walked in, gun at the ready, and caught her breath. She gave one look to her beaten and disheveled boyfriend before leveling her gun at Williams. She slid the hammer back.

"Looks like you don't get along too well with your daddy, either."

Max shrugged. "Well, you might be right about that, Tara. But my pop didn't do this." He turned to her. "This handiwork is compliments of your pop."

Tara put her hand over her mouth, then rushed over to him and put her arms around him. "Oh, my God! I'm so sorry, baby."

She kissed him on the cheek and the forehead. She looked at the burn marks on his chest and touched them tenderly.

Max appreciated her affection, but actually felt a little embarrassed about her putting on a display in front of his pop.

She looked down at the towel around his waist. "You better get some clothes on. We've got an important day coming up."

Max gave her a little smile. "Yeah, we do."

Tara smiled back then changed to her cool demeanor and tossed the handcuffs to Williams. "Nothing personal, sir, but you'll have to put these on."

Williams hesitated, then quickly complied when Tara gestured with the gun and looked right at his bandaged hand. He focused his eyes on his son, but Max wouldn't meet his father's gaze as he gathered his things.

Tara said, "Through the bed frame."

Williams glared at her, then put the handcuffs through the frame and locked them onto his wrists. He looked at Max's splayed fingers.

"Don't worry," Tara said. "My aunt was a nurse once. She'll be able to take care of his fingers."

"You've gotta be kidding. What if Wyatt catches you there?"

Tara grimaced. "I appreciate your concern, Mr. Williams, but we need to get Max fixed up. We'll just have to be extra careful."

Williams stared at his son. "Like you were today?"

Tara took a deep breath. "Look, I understand you're upset. But this'll work. Even if Wyatt guesses where we're going and is the watching the place, I can get us in and out without him ever knowing.

"Look. No offense, missy, but that sounds crazy. Son, we need to talk about this," Williams said.

Max glanced at his pop for a moment, but said nothing.

Tara tossed the handcuff key onto the floor, just out of reach. She put her arm in Max's and the two left together.

WILLIAMS SIGHED AND REACHED FOR HIS CELL PHONE. SOMEONE would've already called the local cops when they heard his shots, so he tried to reach Agent Dawkins first. His secretary said he'd been unreachable for several hours. Next he called Lorna.

"Hey, Lorna. I need to get an All Points out on a red convertible, license number."

He listened for a moment and then said, "No! It's not related to this case at all. This is something new, if you get my meaning. And all I want is a locate, not an apprehend. *Nobody* is to approach the driver of the car. They're just to let our office know about it. All right? Thanks, hon."

Williams sat down to wait for the locals. And considering the extraordinary amount of unpleasant paperwork and questioning ahead of him, he found himself dreading the next few hours.

CHAPTER 25

Excerpt from tape 3

You know, I've always wondered…are you born with homicidal tendencies, or are they a product of your environment?

Running Bear arrived back at the makeshift camp a couple of hours after dawn. The previous night had been one of the worst in his whole fourteen years of life.

His elders had warned him not to do business with the white man. But since Running Bear was practically grown up, and figured he knew just about everything there was to know, he hadn't taken their advice. And his mistake had turned around and bit him in the ass.

The worst and most constantly annoying thing about the FBI agents, besides the fact that they were idiots, was the noise—comprised of yelling, complaining, and bickering.

When they'd started their journey, they'd whooped it up like the trek through the desert was a mission to save the planet. That had lasted about twenty minutes.

Then the whining began.

First, they'd complained he was going too fast. Then they'd complained it was too cold. Then it was too sandy, and too hard to walk in such horrible conditions. Then they'd complained about each other.

Only the last complaints were justified, as far as he was concerned. The only person that hadn't complained incessantly was the black one, Dawkins.

How white men had ever taken over the entire country was beyond Running Bear's understanding. He figured, somewhere, there must be white men around that were a heck of lot smarter than these guys. Not that he'd ever met one.

Then, after a couple of hours, the heavy drinking began. The three white dudes all had flasks of whiskey stashed in their jackets. And with the drunkenness came the game of Indian name-calling—as if Running Bear was too hard to remember. *Tonto, Dances with Turds,* and *Sleeps with a Sheep* were among the favorites.

Running Bear sincerely wondered if the thousand dollar payment was worth the aggravation and abuse. He doubted it, but he always honored his deals, even if the white man wasn't known to. Besides, with a thousand bucks his people could buy a couple more gaming tables for the casino—which would make him a bit of a hero with his elders.

After the agents had passed out, one of them in his own filth, Running Bear had a nice long chat with the sober Dawkins, who turned out to be a pretty good guy.

After a while, Running Bear suggested they go off and finish the trail on their own—that they'd make better time if they left the white guys to sleep it off. But Dawkins had elected to remain with his fellow agents, though he'd encouraged Running Bear to roam ahead and see what he could find.

Without the three stooges in tow, Running Bear followed the trail to the old doc's place. He didn't get too close, because the spooky white dude who worked on the animals was known to take potshots at trespassers.

The journey there and back again had taken all night and a couple hours of the next morning. When he arrived back at camp, the first thing he noticed was that the agents were wide awake, but not moving a muscle. They were all frozen in terror.

Running Bear looked all around, trying to figure out why they were frightened. *A pack of coyotes?*

But all he saw was a little black scorpion resting on Stratton's chest. He laughed. The big white men were afraid of a little thing like that? Yes, they were. In fact, Stratton's eyes were bugged out in primal fear.

He didn't want to embarrass the village idiot, so Running Bear made a big deal out of sneaking up on the scorpion and oh-so-carefully grabbing it and flinging it away. Which brought laughter from the rest of the agents, and embarrassment from Stratton.

Interesting. It looked like the others thoroughly enjoyed Stratton's discomfort. They probably couldn't stand the guy either.

Stratton, red-faced and blustery, said, "Thanks a lot. I *surely* appreciate help from a Native freaking American…ah…what was your name again?" He smiled at his buddies. "No, I got it. Thanks a lot *Bear Shits in the Woods.* Or was it *Shitting* Bear?"

Running Bear turned to find the other agents laughing too—except Dawkins, who shrugged an apology.

So he rescued the idiot from the scorpion and all the guy could do was poke fun at his name. *Screw these guys.* The tables for the casino would just have to wait.

Running Bear headed off into the desert, leaving the idiots to fend for themselves. In their black suits, in the middle of a super-heated dustbowl—they wouldn't last the day.

Their laughter stopped abruptly as they realized he was leaving them all alone. He heard footsteps running up behind him and turned to find Dawkins approaching.

"What do you want, Dawkins?"

Running Bear didn't slow his pace. If Dawkins wanted to talk, he'd have to keep up. "I'm not helping these guys with squat. They're a pox on the land."

"All right. I understand where you're coming from, Running Bear. I do. But I don't want to die out here with these morons."

Running Bear thought about it for a moment. "Head north till you find the interstate. You'll be back in cell phone range by the time you reach the blacktop."

"Thanks a lot," Dawkins said. He kept pace for a few more

steps. "You mind telling me where the suspects went?"

Running Bear snorted. "That's a good one. You gonna give me my thousand dollars?"

Dawkins stopped walking. There was nothing left to say.

"I'M SORRY, HON. THIS IS GONNA HURT A LITTLE BIT," AUNT MAY said. Max, Tara, and her aunt all sat around May's kitchen table with half-empty lemonade glasses in front of them.

When Max nodded his assent, Aunt May quickly snapped his fingers back into position. Max grimaced, but otherwise held back any emotion.

Tara winced along with Max as Aunt May went about splinting his fingers. It was horrible seeing Max like this, and what's worse, she felt personally responsible for his injuries. She mentally cursed Wyatt to hell and back.

Not for the first time, she wished her daddy was a little bit more like regular dads—like Max's dad. Well...except for the part where Max's dad had tried to take him to jail. *I guess all families have a few fatal flaws.*

Max winced again, causing Tara to cringe with guilt. *How could I have been so stupid? Ignoring the rules, behaving just as stupidly as Wyatt.* And Max had been the one to pay for it.

She figured she'd have to make it up to him when they finished with the bank. *If* he still wanted to do the bank.

She said, "I'm so sorry, baby. This is all my fault."

"Nah. Don't worry about it," Max said. Then he gave her a bit of a smirk. "Besides, you're looking at things in shades of gray. I see them as black and white."

Tara smiled. If he was joking around, he couldn't be that angry.

"Listen, I know you're different than your pop," Max said. "And *he's* the one who did these things, not you. So I don't blame you even the tiniest bit."

Damn. He's a keeper. Tara felt like she'd won first prize in a beauty contest. She looked at her Aunt May, who suddenly gave Max a big squeeze and said, "You are a welcome addition to the family, Max."

Tara popped her hand over her mouth in surprise. "Shit, Aunt May. You'll scare him off talking like that."

Aunt May waved away the suggestion. "If Wyatt can't scare him off, nothing will."

Max stood up and gave Aunt May a return hug. "Thanks for fixing me up, Aunt May, but we'd best be getting out of here. For all we know, Wyatt could show up here any minute. And we don't want to get you involved in our troubles."

Max turned to Tara. "Besides, we've got a job to do."

"You got that right," she said.

As Aunt May turned to put her medical kit away, Tara leaned in and whispered in his ear. "After the bank we'll do what we usually do. And with any luck, we'll spend a month or two doing just about nothing else."

Aunt May gave an unusually heavy sigh. Tara turned in embarrassment, thinking she'd been overheard. But Aunt May was over by the sink, lips pursed, and looking down at her feet. And whenever Aunt May struck that pose, it always meant she wanted to ask for something.

As a child, her aunt had been taught that women shouldn't ask for the things they wanted—one of those southern traits meant to keep women in their rightful place. Which was bullshit as far as Tara was concerned.

In fact, it was that Fifties-style attitude, so prevalent in the South, that made Tara enjoy robbing banks down there more than in other parts of the country. Her personal version of the feminist movement.

Tara coaxed her. "What is it, Aunt May?"

"Well, I don't really know how to say this," May said.

"Go ahead, you can ask us anything."

May blurted it out. "I need you to take somebody with you."

Max and Tara looked at each other in confusion. She said, "We're going on a job, Aunt May. It wouldn't really be appropriate to take one of your friends along for the ride."

"I know…and I hate to ask you kids. But if Wyatt follows you here and finds Pete hiding in my cellar…"

Tara said, "Pete Corelli?"

"Yeah…the poor man. He's been hiding here since this morning." She leaned in, as if to tell them a secret. "Wyatt shot him in the leg." She straightened and took a drink of her lemonade. "But it's nothing serious. He won't slow you down or anything. In fact, he'd be a good driver on your job. Just like the old days."

Tara turned to Max, who shrugged and said, "It's your call."

She turned back to her aunt. "Well…all right, I guess. Any enemy of Wyatt's a friend of ours, right?"

DAWKINS TRUDGED ALONG, TRYING IN VAIN TO BLOCK THE three stooges' complaints from his consciousness. It was bad enough they were probably going to die out here, without listening to their pathetic drivel.

Stratton said,"I'm gonna take extreme pleasure from having your ass fired when we get back, Dawkins. Running Bear was your call. And by God, that's the last call you're gonna make."

Idiot.

Dawkins was pretty sure they weren't headed north anymore, not that the other agents had noticed. All they noticed was the heat. The sun was straight overhead, frying their brains, and keeping the group from referencing north. Most likely, they were meandering all over the place. When the vultures started circling overhead, Dawkins feared the worst.

"Hey, Agent Shit for Brains," said a voice behind them. "You guys know you aren't headed north any more? Right now you're headed for the dry lake bed. And the bed is about ten miles across and about thirty degrees hotter than it is here."

Stratton turned to face his nemesis, the foul-mouthed

teenager. "What? You figure you're actually gonna help us this time, *Running* Bear?"

"That depends on you. I decided that, in good conscience, I probably shouldn't let you guys die out here. But I'm afraid you'll just say something stupid that'll change my mind. So I'm not sure where that leaves us."

Dawkins was relieved to see Running Bear, but Stratton glared as if the kid were an ex-wife clamping his nuts in a vice. Running Bear was right—Stratton was bound to say something offensive and idiotic.

Dawkins said, "I've got a suggestion, if you don't mind?"

Running Bear turned to him and said, "Speak your piece, Dawkins."

"As soon as you guide us into cell phone range, I'll make a call and arrange for the money and a van to meet us at the highway. When we get there, you tell us where our suspects went, and we give you the money."

"But what about the big problem? Mr. Motor-mouth?"

"Well, I think we should all take a vow of silence till we get there." When Stratton glared at him, Dawkins added, "If it meant we weren't going to *die* out here, I wouldn't mind at all if we had to stop talking for an hour or two."

Running Bear said, "I think that'll work." He turned to Stratton. "If that's agreeable to you, *Agent Asshole*, just give me a grunt and we'll be on our way."

Stratton smoldered, but grunted an affirmation.

Running Bear said, "All right then. Let's move out." He turned at a right angle from the path they'd been following and started out at a brisk pace. The group straggled along as best they could.

"Hey, Dawkins," Running Bear said. "*You* can talk if you want to. But none of these other idiots are allowed."

Stratton glared at Dawkins, but kept his mouth shut.

WYATT DROVE DOWN THE HIGHWAY AT A SPEED GREATLY exceeding the legal limit. *I was so close I could taste it!*

He knew damn well he should have taken the cop out when he had the chance. Now he was on a mission. He searched fruitlessly for the kids, scanning both sides of the highway, the very picture of grim determination. *Maybe I'm losing my touch.*

Off on one side he saw yet another immigrant family huddled by the side of the road, next to some cactus and a huge cairn of rocks. But Max and Tara weren't hiding among either the family or the rocks.

Wyatt found himself identifying with the aliens—that finding Max and Tara again was probably as big a pipe dream as the immigrants finding decent jobs. But if the illegals wouldn't give up, neither would he.

Wyatt turned back to the road in time to see another Mexican family of three sprinting across the road in front of him. Papa bear, mama bear and baby bear.

He slammed on the brakes, and the sound of the skid caused the immigrant family to freeze like deer caught in the mesmerizing glare of a car's headlights.

Wyatt swerved around the threesome and fishtailed into the dirt on the side of the road. He killed the engine and sat there for a bit, shaking off the excess adrenaline from the near miss. But with the adrenaline came clarity. And with clarity, an idea.

Damn. That'll work. All he'd had to do was start thinking smarter, not harder. He jumped out of the car and rummaged around in the trunk—glad there weren't any body parts in this one. In no time, Wyatt found what he was looking for—a police scanner. A "must have" for every criminal.

He punched the car in excitement. *I'm back in the game!*

Sooner or later a report about Max and Tara's latest heist would come across this little baby and he'd have them again.

Wyatt brought the scanner to the front seat and plugged it into the cigarette lighter. He tuned it in, getting lots of static before finally getting it right.

"...A 1968 black Cougar, last seen in the vicinity of

Interstate 40, exit 142. Subject is armed and extremely dangerous. Take all necessary precautions."

Wyatt smirked at the description, but figured he'd have to get off the main highway and hit some back roads till things died down a bit.

He caught something out of the corner of his eye. On the floor on the passenger side was a Barbie doll. The same one he'd drawn a mask on when Tara was little. Bank Robber Barbie.

Wyatt's eyes moistened, but he didn't let the tears escape. He'd certainly miss her after he finally killed her, but what else could he do? He ripped the head off the doll and tossed the parts out the window. *Damn.*

He turned the ignition and peeled away, taking extra care this time to watch for crossing immigrants.

PETE SAT IN THE BACK OF THE CONVERTIBLE, LIKE A REDHEADED step child, straining to overhear Max and Tara's conversation.

He was pretty sure their hushed talk was about him. But they kept their voices too low and they'd turned the radio up too loud—tuned to that crappy country drivel. Bull had loved that kind of music. But Pete, like every city-bred human, thought that practically *anything* was better than country music. Even that rapper, Snickerdoodle.

Pete had gotten completely amped when Max and Tara had told him about the upcoming bank job. Cowering in May's cellar and licking his wounds hadn't been his idea of a good time. Driving for Tara on a bank heist certainly was. He already had sixty grand, but when it got right down to it, who couldn't use a little bit more?

And Tara was always fun to work with. Pete even felt a bit of compassion toward the kids, since they were all running from the same psycho. He felt a little simpatico.

But now he was bored. Max and Tara kept to themselves, and Pete had no one to talk to since Bull had fled to the big peace pipe in the sky.

He spied Tara and Max's bags on the floor of the back seat, then slyly reached with his foot and lifted one of the bags to his lap.

Inside, he found some of Max's clothes, a couple of guns, and the best possible treasure he could imagine. Well…maybe second best, after money. A micro-cassette recorder.

Pete, though surprised Max had the chops to be an idea man like himself, was as happy as a crackhead who'd found a surprise $40 vial under his pillow. He mourned his lost collection of million-dollar idea tapes. He'd been forced to abandon them, as well as his tape recorder, when Bull had crashed the Cadillac next to those cops. And the loss had crushed him as much as losing Bull. Perhaps more.

Finding these tapes is like karma or something!

Pete figured there might be some interesting stuff on Max's tapes and stashed them in his own bag. But since he needed his own fix right away, he popped in a fresh tape and pushed the record button. Pete slunk way down in the seat, and out of Max and Tara's view, ready to record a snazzy idea. But his brain gave him the finger and kept silent.

Then there was a lull in the woeful music and he overheard a bit of Max and Tara's conversation.

Max said, "But are you sure we can trust him?"

Tara replied, "Well…he's a good wheel man. We used him on lots of jobs with no problems."

"But that was a while ago. How do you know what he's been doing lately, besides pissing Wyatt off?"

"I *don't* know. I just remember him saving my life one time. But I don't really trust anybody one hundred percent." She paused. "I'd say I trust him around ninety, maybe ninety-five percent."

Max was quiet for a moment. "All right. That's good enough for me. But on this job we're going strictly by the rules, all right? We don't deviate one single bit. I don't want anyone finding us by our wheels like Wyatt did. So we're going to have to boost a car for the getaway vehicle."

"Absolutely," Tara said. "And I know you like doing that

kind of thing. But if you want, that's something Pete can handle for us. Maybe prove his worth a little bit."

The country music cut out for a news bulletin.

"This is Brett Saberhagen with a late breaking update. For twenty-four hours, we've known that the infamous, sodomizing, porn-kings known as the Snake Bandits were connected to bank robberies in twelve states. But what we didn't know was the reason. Now we do. Money stolen here in the U.S. funds the terrorist organization known as..."

Max turned off the radio with a jerk. "I wish that bastard would quit making stuff up about us."

Pete's eyes widened. "You guys are the Snake Bandits?"

Max lit a cigarette and smoldered. "Yeah, but it's not like what you think."

Pete said, "I've been watching stories about you guys on TV for a couple days now. And I don't want any part of that sex stuff on this bank job. That business with the clerk behind the counter...no offense, but that's just sick."

Max squinted and turned to Tara. "This is unbelievable. You mind if I tell him?"

Tara nodded and Max turned back to Pete.

"All right. Look, Pete. This here's the story. The *real* story... not that bullshit you saw on the TV box. Now, don't get me wrong. I'm not saying we're innocent. But our hearts were in the right place."

Max paused and took a drag of his cigarette. Pete continued to hold the recorder in his hand, absentmindedly.

Max continued, "No...we're not innocent. But then hell... who is?"

Pete snorted and wheezed, but held his laughter, hoping Max would go on with his story. Max sure nailed that one. Pete couldn't think of a single soul he considered innocent.

"HEY, I'VE GOT A SIGNAL," DAWKINS SAID.

Finally. Stratton sat down heavily on the rock beside him. They'd only climbed the stinking hill in the hopes of getting cell phone reception, and it was about time something went his way.

While Dawkins arranged for some transportation to meet them on the highway in an hour, Stratton gave some serious thought toward retribution for the snot-nosed punk that was finally leading them from the desert. He wondered if his dad could put the squeeze on the Navajo Reservation, and maybe take their casino away from them. But he knew that senatorial power didn't usually apply when Indians were involved. *Excuse me…Native freaking Americans!*

A beeping sound interrupted his thoughts, then cut off in mid-beep. Stratton turned to Dawkins, who stared at his phone in dismay.

Since Stratton wasn't allowed to talk, he gesticulated wildly and repeatedly to Dawkins, mutely asking what was going on.

Dawkins said, "My phone battery died. Do any of you guys have one that's charged?"

Stratton and the other agents checked their phones, only to find that their power had likewise deserted them in their hour of need. Running Bear laughed quietly to himself. Stratton thought he heard Running Bear mutter the words *Agent Impotent* under his breath, but he couldn't be sure.

Dawkins said, "Well…I think Speedo got all the information about where to meet us and about bringing the money, but I can't be sure."

Morosely, they roused themselves and started on their journey once more. Stratton seethed. If a van didn't meet them at the highway in an hour, he couldn't be held responsible for his actions.

CHAPTER 26

EXCERPT FROM TAPE 3

Something my pop always told me was that people are the glue that holds this piece of shit world together. And every one of them is important. If you ever watch television, this can be hard to believe, but it's true.

This is one of the few things where my pop and I always see eye to eye. If a soul out there seems lost, it's just 'cause he hasn't found his way yet.

Max eyed the bank with a little nervousness. In a place that size he'd have to cover twice as many people as he was used to. And the incident with Wyatt had left him a little wary of the whole crime business.

Then again, with that kind of money they'd be able to hide out for a while. And the thought of scoring an extremely large haul, with an adrenaline rush the size of Mt. Everest to go with it, was enough to help him get over his nervousness—throw caution to the wind.

He took a couple of deep breaths as Pete stopped their newly stolen car in front of the intended target.

Pete spat out the window. He shifted into park, but left the car running. Slapping Max on the back, he said, "I'll be waiting right here for you when you get done. So don't get caught."

Max nodded. Don't get caught. Don't get caught. Words to live by.

He and Tara put on their bandanas and hats and double-checked their snake tattoos. Pete was sporting one as well—just in case.

Tara gave Max a kiss. "I think it's time to retire these tattoos when we finish this job. Change our M.O. next time."

"Wise move," Pete said. "The snakes are getting kind of a bad rap. In fact, I'm a bit worried people will think I'm a hole-puncher just 'cause I've got one of these things on my arm."

"The snakes are history," Max said. "But let's get us enough cash on this job to stay underground for a while. Hang out just the two of us, all right?"

Tara nodded her agreement. "You got it, baby. After this morning's excitement, I bet you're ready for a break."

Max held up his broken fingers and said, "Bad choice of words."

"Sorry," she said. She pumped her fist in the air. "Let's do it!"

Tara took a step inside and waited for Max to enter the bank. She gave a quick sweep with her eyes, and registered a single guard in the corner talking to a trucker, and two good-old-boys at the counter chatting up two female tellers. The manager sat at a desk behind the counter.

Tara took point, going straight for the counter, while Max headed for the guard and trucker. Her guys at the counter wore greasy mechanic's shirts with their names embroidered on the pockets. Charlie and Jimmy. Charlie chewed a mass of tobacco like it was a wad of gum, while Jimmy wore camouflage pants and tried to impress the lady tellers with tales of his mastery over women.

"So I told my wife to just shut the hell up, or I'd give her something to cry about," Jimmy said.

Tara watched Jimmy's mouth drop open when he caught sight of her sawed-off shotgun. *I always love that part.*

Behind her, Max said, "Drop your gun, now."

Tara heard the guard's piece hit the floor and stole a quick glimpse of Max. He seemed to have the guard and trucker under control. *Sweet.* She gestured for the bank manager to come join the party at the counter.

Tara used her most authoritative voice. "All right everybody, it's time for Simon Says." She pointed to her gun. "This here is Simon. And you all better do as he says, 'cause you won't like him if he gets angry."

Jimmy looked at Max and then back to Tara and her tattooed forearm, smiling. "Aw, sweet Jesus. Is this our lucky day, Charlie, or what? You're the Snake Bandits, right?"

Tara tipped her hat.

Max brought the guard and trucker over to join them. The trucker paled as he noticed the snake on Max's arm. "Oh my God. You *are* the Snake Bandits. I'm sure as heck not gonna be sodomized by the likes of you!"

Max laughed. "You'd rather someone else did it?"

When the trucker spluttered in rage, Max said, "I'm just joking with you. We don't do that kind of thing. That's just some bullshit made up on the news."

The trucker stared, befuddled by the very thought of phony news.

Tara noticed Jimmy and Charlie were looking at each other with a couple of shit-eating grins plastered on their faces.

"I know something about you guys that ain't made up," Jimmy said. "There's a *ree*-ward on you guys by the F–B–I."

Crap. A troublemaker. Tara cocked Simon and pointed it at Jimmy. "But since you won't ever live to collect it, you might as well put those thoughts right out of your head."

Jimmy raised his hands in mock surrender. "I give up, sweetness. But hey, I'm just joshing with you. Don't worry your pretty little head."

Jimmy had the all the charm of used car salesman. She didn't buy a word of it.

The trucker danced around in agitation—as if he had to go to the bathroom. "I will not be corn-holed!"

Things were getting out of hand. Tara fired a round into the ceiling to remind them who was boss. Plaster dropped onto the trucker and guard, causing the Teamster to tap-dance a bit harder. Tara tossed the duffel bag on the counter.

"Simon says, fill the bag."

Jimmy shared a laugh with Charlie while the tellers got to work. Tara put the gun right next to Jimmy's face. "Simon's had just about enough of you, Jimmy."

Jimmy laughed even harder. "But I know something you don't, kitten. In our little town, we take your kind seriously."

Jimmy slapped the counter, his laughter making him out of breath. "So we've got something *special* just for dealing with criminals like you."

He's gonna make a move. Tara glanced around. His arrogant attitude had her concerned, and wondering if someone was coming up behind her.

Jimmy continued, "What we've got is the most liberal conceal/carry laws in four counties."

Tara was just registering the words "conceal/carry" when everything turned to crap.

Charlie grabbed her gun, and in his fervor mistakenly shouted "THIRD AMENDMENT ROCKS" while Jimmy shouted "CHARLETON HESTON FOR PRESIDENT" and pulled his own pea-shooter from his boot.

Max turned around to help Tara, but with a rallying cry of "NO SODOMIZING" the trucker tackled him, his excess poundage easily bearing him to the ground.

Tara managed to yank free from Charlie and bash him with the butt of the shotgun. She turned to Jimmy and saw him fire a shot before she could train the gun on the bastard's face.

She felt her stomach explode, and fired back, blasting Jimmy in the chest. The shotgun trumped the pea-shooter and Jimmy fell dead to the floor, while Tara had a mere .22 slug in her gut.

Charlie lunged for Tara with a knife. She ducked under it and fired twice, hitting Charlie and propelling him up and over the counter. Both the bank manager and the tellers screamed bloody murder as Charlie's body knocked them over like so many bowling pins.

The trucker noticed an absence of guns pointed in his

direction and took advantage of the lull, breaking for the door in a rumble of bottom-heavy flesh. Max scrambled to his feet with his gun in hand—but trained it on the guard, who'd remained cemented in place for the duration of the gun battle.

Tara heard the running footsteps and whirled around, shooting at the trucker with her usual precision. He tumbled to the ground.

Tara turned painfully toward Max and froze. The enraged expression on his face stunned her.

"ARE YOU CRAZY? WHAT THE HELL ARE YOU DOING?"

Tara felt dazed from the loss of blood, and from Max's reaction, but she managed a feeble response. "He was getting away."

"So let him! What the hell did he do to you?"

Tara shook her head and stumbled back against the wall, her face pale. "I think I need a little help here."

She grabbed her stomach with one hand, the filled duffel bag with the other, and slid to the floor on the edge of consciousness.

Max, her angry hero, raced over to her side. He ripped off part of his shirt and placed it on the wound, then put her hand on top.

"Put pressure on it."

Max picked her up and carried her out the door. Halfway to the car, Tara noticed the trucker had crawled outside and into the bushes, relatively unharmed. She figured his Teamster bulk, and the distance from her scatter-gun, had kept the shotgun pellets from doing any serious damage. When he caught her eye, she said, "Sorry."

Max gave a little wave to the trucker on his way past. "I told you, no sodomizing."

Pete scurried around and opened the back door for Max and Tara. They all piled in and raced away like bats out of hell.

PETE PULLED THEIR STOLEN VEHICLE OFF THE ROAD ABOUT A MILE from the scene of the crime. Max shook his head and pulled Tara out of the car. *I can't believe our first and most important fight is over something like this.*

Max kicked the door, slamming it shut.

Pete wiped down the fingerprints in the get-away car while Max carried Tara over to their convertible. They were back on the road in ninety seconds. And Pete assured him they'd be at the doc's place inside of twenty minutes.

Max looked down at Tara's head in his lap. At least she had a little color back in her face. But her eyes were kind of tearful.

Tara said, "Your pop was right when he said you'd never harm a fly."

"Of course he was. But this isn't about me," Max said. "It's about what's right. How the hell could you do that?"

"You think I wanted to kill those people?" Tara said. *"Rule #22: If someone is killed, you don't leave any witnesses.* So, after the first one with the gun...I had no other choice."

"Wrong. You always have a choice. And *my* choice is to not take other people's lives."

A tear rolled down Tara's face. "They shot me first. What was I supposed to do?"

Max counted to ten, calming himself. "I know you were just defending yourself with the first two. But the guy running away was just an innocent bystander. At the wrong place at the wrong time. And you tried to kill him for that. It's not right."

A second tear from Tara made him look away. Crying women always made him uncomfortable—made him want to rescue them like little lost puppies. Which was not the way to feel when making a point. He ignored it and stared out the car window.

"I'm afraid you wanted to kill him, Tara. That you're too much like Wyatt. And homicidal tendencies aren't something I can live with."

She began sobbing in earnest. "I know I act like my daddy sometimes. But that's why I broke away from him. Because that's not what I am anymore."

Tara gave another heaving sob and winced at the pain in her stomach. "That's not who I want to be."

Max looked down at the puppy dog in his lap and sighed. His problem was that he believed her completely. He was pretty sure she didn't *really* want to kill people. It was just instinct—and the rules. And that could be unlearned.

At least the trucker had lived through the ordeal. Max thought about it for a couple more miles, then made his decision.

"All right. Just promise me one thing, would you?"

Tara looked up at him with puppy dog eyes.

"Promise me you won't kill anyone else, all right?"

Tara smiled. "I promise, Max."

WHERE THE HELL ARE THEY? IT WAS WORTH A SHOT THAT THEY'D head someplace familiar, but they weren't here. Wyatt watched May take her butt-ugly poodle for a walk. The damn thing had one of those French haircuts that turned his stomach, but he didn't let it stop him from enjoying his burger.

Finally, after hours of listening to cops bantering with each other, he heard something interesting on the police scanner. He turned the volume up and munched away while he listened to the chatter.

"...And at least one of the Snake Bandit suspects has a serious gunshot wound. Harry, you head down to County General in case they're dumb enough to show up for treatment. I'll call the FBI team that's working in the area..."

All right. YES! Back to the vet. Wyatt let out a big yell and threw his burger wrapper to the floor. "YEEEEEE-HAW. I got you now, pretty boy."

Wyatt pulled out the syringe of go-go juice Crispin had given him and jabbed it into his thigh. He felt a burning sensation where the stuff entered his system, before feeling a little jolt as it kicked in. *That's got a better kick than rat poison.*

He turned the engine over and sped down the highway.

PETE AND MAX LIFTED TARA OUT OF THE CAR AND SUPPORTED her on either side as they walked down the gravel drive. "We shouldn't be here," Pete said. "If Wyatt hears that Tara's been shot, Crispin's is the first place he's gonna look."

"Damn it, Pete. If we had a choice, we wouldn't be here," Max said. "Tara's going to die if we don't get her to a doc immediately. And you know we can't go to the hospital."

"Well...yeah...but prison's better than being killed by Wyatt."

"Let's make sure neither one happens, all right? Keep a sharp eye out while we're here. And with any luck, Wyatt won't hear about this until we're already gone."

Pete shook his head, then checked over his shoulder, sure Wyatt was sneaking up behind him. "And what about that cop we passed on the highway? I think he was eyeballing us."

Tara stumbled past some free-range chickens and ducks. "Quit being paranoid, Pete. I'm telling you, our car is clean. There's no reason for a cop to be eyeballing us."

Paranoid? What does she know? She's probably delirious.

Even if Wyatt and the cop weren't on their trail, the wolf-dog *had* to be around somewhere. And Pete wasn't sure which threat worried him most. He glanced around wildly on the walk to the door, and was relieved when they reached the front porch without incident.

Max stopped and looked at the Vietnam Vet sign. "You sure this guy can fix you up?"

"Well, he is a little nuts," Tara said. "But he's real sweet. And he's been patching me up since I was twelve."

Pete stepped forward and rang the bell. After a minute, the door opened and Crispin poked his beak outside. He gave Pete a stern glare.

"You've got a lot of nerve showing up here, I'll give you that," Crispin said. "I had to bury your Indian buddy in my cemetery. By myself. And there wasn't nearly enough room for someone that size. So you owe me three hours of manual labor to make up for it. And a thousand bucks for that junker you stole out of my barn."

Pete started to reply, but was shoved rudely out of the way by Crispin when he noticed Tara standing behind Pete.

"Tara, my dear." Crispin beamed. "It's good to see you."

Crispin's smile flipped upside down when he saw the blood on her stomach. He looked at Max with suspicion, then rushed forward and helped her inside. "Oh, dear. What happened?"

"It's a long story, Crispin. But I'm really glad to see you again."

Crispin lit up with pleasure and beckoned for Pete to follow. Pete smirked—the doc obviously had a thing for Tara. But then again, who didn't? He closed the door and trotted after the group.

The place smelled like the hundreds of animals that lived inside. Crispin's Ark. The window panes had been decorated with black spray paint, making the place incredibly dark. Max tripped over a cat and a chicken that were playing tag amongst the huge menagerie of animals that covered the floor space and furniture of Crispin's living room.

He received a stern glare and a warning from Crispin.

Pete had seen the spectacle before—chickens, ducks, cats, frogs, and other animals that he didn't even recognize. They all lived together, mostly in harmony, like they were close members of Crispin's family.

Pete gave Max a little shove to move him along, and they moved a tad faster, but Max still craned his head as he looked around. The walls were decorated with weapons of all kinds, including several types of guns and knives, as well as a couple of rocket launchers and some pictures of Crispin's deceased war buddies.

"I'm glad to see you're not with Wyatt anymore," said

Crispin. "You guys were always getting into one scrape or another."

A chicken clucked indignantly as the group shuffled past.

Crispin continued, "It is *so* good to see you again, Tara. I just wish it could be under better circumstances."

Pete rolled his eyes and moved ahead of the others.He opened the door to the examination room, making sure not to step on the animals. Pete didn't want to make things worse with Crispin—'cause with the stolen car and him having to bury Bull, he was already in Crispin's doghouse.

"Sheriff, they found the car," Officer Lorna said. "Highway Patrol spotted the convertible off Highway 51. I've got an address for you."

"All right," Williams said. "Now we're cooking."

Lorna continued, "The bad news is that the same trooper also spotted the missing black Cougar headed in the same direction."

Williams pounded the steering wheel in frustration and cursed for a bit.

He switched the phone to his other ear so he could hear and write at the same time. He pulled to the side of the road—safety first—and grabbed a pen. "Shoot."

"I will. But wait a minute, sugar. Have you thought this thing through?"

Williams stared out the window. "Yes, damn it, I have. And I'm not any happier with the answer than Max will be. But since I don't want him dying, there's not much choice. And if I'm there, then at least that bloodthirsty Stratton fellow won't be able to just fire away."

Running Bear stood to one side as the agents wept and shouted for joy at the arrival of the van. *You'd think they were lost for days on end, and in danger of starvation.*

When they'd reached the blacktop, the vow of silence had been quickly tossed aside and the idiots had started babbling at a feverish pace.

Dawkins put a new battery in his cell phone and grabbed Running Bear's wad of cash from one of the agents in the van.

Running Bear feared the long ride back, as the van was loaded with more stupid white guys than he cared to see. But it was better than a ten-mile hike through the desert.

Dawkins' phone beeped a few times and rang as soon as it was switched on, which Running Bear found extremely annoying, and was why he didn't ever want one of the bothersome things. Dawkins answered it, and after a moment got extremely excited. He snapped his fingers at an agent and demanded a map.

Running Bear found he didn't really care what the fuss was about. He just wanted to get away from these guys—to tell Dawkins where the bad guys had gone and collect his cash.

Stratton spread the map and the agents huddled together in excitement. Stratton said, "Holy cow. That hick sheriff came through in the clutch. They're only ten minutes away. Everyone, get in the van."

Stratton turned to Running Bear with a wicked gleam in his eye. That's when Running Bear began to suspect that another white man's atrocity was about to be perpetrated on the Indian people. Or at least on Running Bear.

"Looks like we didn't need your help, after all. We already know where the suspects are located." Stratton grabbed the cash from a stunned Dawkins and stuffed it in the inside pocket of his suit jacket. When Dawkins hesitated, Stratton shoved him toward the van. "Get in, Dawkins. That's an order."

It figures. Running Bear watched his money evaporate like smoke on the wind.

Stratton grinned. "And since we've got to leave immediately, we can't even give you a ride back to the Reservation. Sorry. But I'm sure you can find your way back through the desert to your teepee."

Stratton got in the van and slid the door shut. Dawkins leaned out the window. "Hey, Running Bear. I'm really sorry—I'll make it up to you later."

Running Bear sighed as the van peeled away. He should have listened to his elders.

CRISPIN AND MAX HOISTED TARA ONTO THE WHEELED METAL table in the center of the room. Max noticed a goat standing in the corner and briefly wondered if the doc had ever heard of the benefits of sterilization.

Maybe he had, since Crispin shooed the animal from the room and closed the door, leaving the place relatively vermin-free.

There was a security monitor on the desk that showed four separate images—including the front door and a camera angle of the car they'd arrived in.

Max said, "Hey, Pete. Why don't you watch that TV there and keep an eye out for Wyatt? If he shows, we don't want him catching us unawares."

Pete ran over and sat at the desk. "YEAH. Good idea, Max. I'm on it." His eyes roamed frantically, glued to the screen.

Crispin brought a tray of tools to the table. He grabbed the cloth on Tara's stomach and saw the dried blood had stuck to her wound. "Sorry, dear. This is gonna hurt a bit."

Max used his good hand to grab Tara's. Crispin ripped the cloth off in one quick motion, causing her to gasp in pain.

The doc paused, eyeing Max with suspicion. "Who the hell are you?" Crispin casually gestured toward Max with his scalpel. "Are you responsible for this mess?"

Tara groaned and said, "Jeez, Crispin. This is Max, my boyfriend." She waited for the pain to pass. "He takes care of me."

Crispin sighed, then smiled at her. "You deserve it, dear. I can't tell you how happy I am for you."

Crispin jabbed a hypodermic into Tara's stomach and gave

her a local anesthetic and a couple of other goodies. "You may feel a bit groggy, but it can't be helped."

Crispin dug deeper, into the wound, and Max cringed when blood started spurting out of Tara like Old Faithful. *This guy's a quack.*

But Crispin deftly clamped the gusher. "No wonder Wyatt's after you guys. You know, people call me crazy, but I'm not nearly as far gone as that bastard." Crispin chortled. "I bet Wyatt doesn't care much for Max."

Max held up his splinted fingers in agreement.

Crispin gave an "ah ha" and pulled a bullet out with a pair of tweezers. "There she is. A nasty little bugger. But luckily it didn't do much damage."

The tray of medical instruments came crashing to the floor as Pete jumped in alarm. "Oh, shit. This can't be happening."

Max spun around, checked out the monitor, and saw a familiar black Cougar stop next to their convertible.

Shit.

CHAPTER 27

EXCERPT FROM TAPE 3

You know…I think we all could use one of my pop's self-help books. The problem is that most of us think we're in pretty good shape.

But I beg to differ.

Crispin ran around like one of his chickens when Wolfy was near. "Pete, push that metal pad by your knee," he said. "It opens the passage behind that cabinet there. You guys hide inside. I'll tell Wyatt you jumped out the back window."

A wild-eyed Pete jabbed at the button, and a tall cabinet swung away from the wall, revealing an earthen tunnel behind it.

Crispin paused his gyrations long enough to watch their expressions with delight, as proud as a father with his newborn baby. Max, Tara, and Pete were the first outsiders allowed into his prized tunnels. They looked astonished at the well-stocked alcove behind the cabinet. Enough food for a year.

Crispin said, "Max, grab hold of this clamp here while I wheel Tara inside."

He rolled the gurney over to the opening. Pete had already dashed inside and headed down the tunnel. "Don't go too far down the passageway, Pete. It's easy to get lost."

Pete stopped short and jumped about a foot when the doorbell rang.

Max and Crispin turned in unison to the monitor on the desk. But the camera angle showing the front door was empty.

Crispin whispered, "Max, whatever you do, don't let go of the clamp. Unless you want to see her blood pumping out all over the place. I'll be back as soon as I can to stitch her up."

Max looked down at the clamp and swallowed. He gave Tara a sickly smile, attempting to reassure her, but probably not succeeding. Crispin flicked on the tunnel lights before closing them inside.

Crispin took a deep breath, then crept into the darkened living room, tiptoeing past the clucking chickens and quacking ducks. He grabbed a Bowie knife off the wall and walked slowly toward the front door.

It was ajar, and he reached it without incident. *Where's Waldo?*

He'd never really been good at hide-and-seek—except with the Vietnamese in their rabbit warrens—and that was thirty odd years ago. He tried to remember some of his old combat moves, but his brain wouldn't cooperate. He shut the door and turned back toward the room.

He heard the alarmed clucking of startled chickens a split-second before Wyatt brought him to the ground, scattering the flightless birds. What Crispin's brain didn't remember, his reflexes did, and his combat training came back with a vengeance.

Crispin rolled around with Wyatt and attempted to stab him with the knife, desperately hoping they wouldn't squash the chickens as they thrashed about.

SHERIFF WILLIAMS PULLED HIS PATROL CAR INTO CRISPIN'S driveway, blocking in the other two cars. He punched in Dawkins number on his cell phone.

"Wyatt's definitely here. How far away are you?"

Williams listened for a moment and shook his head.

"Five minutes is too long. Max could be dead by then."

Williams thought for a second. "I'm going in now. Make sure to tell Agent Blowhard there's an officer inside and that he should *not* come in firing. I don't know...tell him it's a probable hostage situation. I don't care. Just wait to hear from me, all right?"

Williams gave Duke a pat on the head and cracked a window for him. He went to the trunk to grab his flak jacket and extra ammo—better safe than sorry—and headed to the side of the house to look for a back door.

WYATT ROLLED ACROSS THE FLOOR WITH CRISPIN, TRYING TO GET the upper hand. The little guy was wiry and well trained in hand-to-hand combat. But since Wyatt had about a hundred pounds on the guy, and some extra strength from the super juice, he wasn't worried.

Wyatt landed a couple of solid punches and grinned as Crispin's eyes glazed over. But he stopped grinning when Crispin plunged the hunting knife into his thigh.

He pulled away from Crispin and turned his leg. The long knife had missed the bone, but the tip stuck out the other side of his leg. It had gone all the way through.

Damn. And that was the healthy leg.

Wyatt flexed his leg and frowned. It should have hurt, but instead it felt right as rain. *Must be the go-go juice. Good stuff.*

With a jerk, Wyatt yanked out the knife and advanced upon a stunned Crispin.

The doc was glassy-eyed, but Wyatt punched him again for good measure. A chicken pecked at Wyatt's ankle and he took a moment to push it away. Kneeling on Crispin's wrist, he pounded the blade through his hand, pinning it to the floor.

Wyatt grabbed a bayonet knife from the wall, then went to the exam room and peeked inside. No Tara. No Max. Nothing.

Returning to Crispin, he staked the other hand to the ground with the bayonet, then watched the doc writhe in agony.

He took a step back to admire his handiwork. *Kind of like a crucifix.*

MAX LISTENED TO THE THRASHING SOUNDS FROM THE OTHER side of the tunnel door. He wasn't sure what was happening, but if they were fighting it out, Crispin was in trouble.

"Come on, Pete. Grab this clamp so I can help Crispin."

Pete's eyes bulged. "Are you crazy? I'm not going out there. *Wyatt's* out there."

"You don't have to go out. Just hold onto this clamp."

Pete said, "Max, don't even think of touching that door. Or so help me, I'll scurry down this rat hole without a second thought."

WYATT WAS AWARE OF THE PECKING AT HIS ANKLE. BUT WITH the go-go juice, it didn't hurt—it just annoyed the heck out of him. Peck, peck, peck. For the second time, he thrust the annoying chicken away.

He pulled his gun and thought about shooting the chicken, but stuck the gun against Crispin's cheek instead.

"I don't want to hear that shit from you, Crispin. I *know* you're hiding them here somewhere. You've got rabbit holes all over this place. All you've got to do is tell me where."

"You're not getting anything from me so go ahead and kill me you Commie bastard."

Wyatt deliberated for a moment. Crispin had probably been tortured during the war, so normal stuff wouldn't work. The vet wasn't even whining about his pinned hands.

The chicken came at him again. The stupid hen must've thought his ankle was corn or something. He stood up and kicked the bird away with as much force as he could he muster. There was an explosion of feathers as the bird shot through the window.

Crispin cried out, "CHICKY."

Ah, there we go. Wyatt smirked. "You know something,

Crispin. We've known each other a long time. And the only things I've ever you seen you appreciate in life were your furry friends."

Wyatt looked Crispin in the eye and aimed his gun at the chickens. "Last chance."

Nothing. He cocked the gun, and felt a familiar satisfaction as Crispin yelled in terror.

He fired into the flock again and again.

At the sound of the shots, Max yelled to Pete, "Get over here!"

Pete shook his head and bolted down the dirt corridor and out of sight.

Max groaned. *Good riddance.*

He looked at Tara. "It wouldn't be right to let Crispin die for us."

Tara looked up at him and nodded her head in agreement.

Well there you go. Proof positive her heart was in the right place after all.

Wyatt fired one last shot, then choked on a feather that was floating around. *Better than shooting fish in a barrel.*

Crispin struggled, attempting to pull his hands free. "You bastard! You better kill me, too. Or I will rip your heart out with my bare hands."

Wyatt felt a sharp twinge where the hen had pecked at him, and an incredibly intense pain where he'd been stabbed by Crispin. Time to give himself another shot of the super juice.

After the slight burning sensation, he moaned in pleasure. *Oh, yeah. That's good stuff.*

But this time his head spun and his vision turned hazy. Had he taken too much?

The stuff also made him feel kind of different. Kind

of emotional. *Shit. That's the last thing I need right now.*

He even felt a little compassion for how Crispin must feel with knives through his hands and his feathered friends' corpses spread around the room.

"Fine, Crispin. If you want me to kill you, that's no problem at all."

He raised his gun, but got distracted when he heard his name shouted from the other room. Through a fog.

Max called out, "Hey. We're in here, Wyatt."

Wyatt felt woozy, but it didn't stop him from grinning.

WILLIAMS CREPT THROUGH THE HALLWAY. HE REACHED THE living room and paused when he heard Max's voice. *Thank God he's okay.*

He missed a shot at Wyatt as the cowboy left the living room, heading for the area where Max's voice had come from. Williams spotted Crispin's prone form in his crucifixion pose. *What the heck?*

Williams inched his way forward.

MAX WHEELED TARA SLOWLY OUT OF THE TUNNEL AND INTO the exam room, one hand on the gurney and the other holding the clamp. He gave a cursory glance at the monitor and noticed his pop's patrol car parked in the driveway.

Max tried not to show any relief as Wyatt walked through the doorway—which wasn't all that hard to hide after catching a glimpse of Wyatt's gruesome countenance. It was horrifying. The only thing hopeful about him was his gait. He seemed to be drunk.

Wyatt said, "I've been waiting for this since I first set eyes on you, punk."

He stopped when he saw Tara on the table, and his expression changed drastically. "Oh my God, baby. Are you all right?"

Tara managed a feeble reply. "Yeah."

Max glanced behind Wyatt and caught sight of his pop and Crispin peeking through the doorway together.

Wyatt took one look at Max and the bloody clamp that he held, and put his gun in his pants. He held up his hands as if surrendering.

He must be drunk.

"Tara…look…I'm sorry about all this. This is all my fault," Wyatt said. "But…I just want you back. No hard feelings."

Max found it kind of weird to see Wyatt acting concerned about his daughter—like he was a regular human being. 'Cause if it wasn't Wyatt that was acting that way, it would have been touching. It almost made Max look at him in a different light.

Almost.

Max said, "Not a chance in hell, Wyatt."

"No one's talking to you, punk. Look, Tara. I won't even kill loverboy, here. If you just come back with me."

When Tara didn't respond, Wyatt started to get riled up all over again.

"Damn it, missy! I still love you."

"And I still love you, Wyatt" Tara said. "But wherever I go it's gonna be with Max."

Max appreciated the sentiment, but when Wyatt became instantly enraged, he wished she'd been a bit more mollifying.

Wyatt lunged toward Max and reached for his gun—and Max was forced to drop the clamp and rush toward Wyatt.

Williams stepped into the room and fired a couple of rounds into Wyatt, hitting him in the arm and shoulder. The impact twirled him around like a ballerina, but otherwise had no effect, courtesy of the go-go juice.

Wyatt fired, striking Williams in the flak jacket as well as the flesh on his side that the jacket didn't cover.

Max and his pop crashed into Wyatt at the same time, knocking him to the ground. But the two of them could barely hold him down.

Wyatt flung them around like rag dolls, so that all Williams and Max could do was hang on to the bucking bronco.

With a primal scream, Wyatt heaved their bodies away. Williams hit the wall first, and Max followed a second later, both neatly shot-putted through the air.

Crispin ran in from the living room, blood dripping from his hands. As Wyatt rose to his feet, Crispin hopped onto his back and jabbed a hypodermic into Wyatt's neck.

He pushed the plunger with his injured paw and held on till Wyatt slumped to the floor a few seconds later. Sleepy juice, this time.

Crispin rushed over to Tara and looked at the thin stream of blood shooting from her wound. He wrapped his hands in gauze and grabbed a stitch kit, then proceeded to patch her up.

Max turned to his pop and found him on the floor, clutching his side, and dragged him to a sitting position. "You all right, Pop?"

Williams pulled his hand away from his side for a second, then put the pressure back on. "Yeah. It's nothing too serious."

Then his cell phone rang.

PETE GOT TO THE INTERSECTION OF THE TUNNEL AND CURSED. He'd been here before—three freaking times.

He snorted. *Max is definitely certifiable.* Intentionally putting himself in Wyatt's sights like that. It was unbelievable. Apparently Tara liked her guys crazy like her dad.

Pete had always known there were times to walk away. And that sometimes you *ran* away with your tail between your legs.

Pete checked his bag. He still had the sixty grand. And he still had Max's tape recorder. If he could just find his way through these tunnels to the damn barn, he'd steal another car from Crispin. Then it'd be easy street all the way.

THE VAN FLEW DOWN THE HIGHWAY. STRATTON LOOKED AT THE cell phone with distaste, but it just kept ringing. Williams wasn't answering.

At the ranch, they pulled to a stop behind the other cars. The agents piled out and took cover behind the other vehicles, pointing their guns toward the front door as they'd learned in FBI school. Stratton and Dawkins took position behind the doors of the van.

Oh, baby. This is the real shit now! Stratton turned to Dawkins. "I'm only giving him thirty more seconds to respond. Then we'll bust on in."

Dawkins reached in and hit a switch on the dash that turned on the speaker phone. He dialed Williams' number again. After a few more rings, he finally picked up.

"This is Sheriff Williams, go ahead."

Dawkins said, "What's the story?"

"I've got a Code Three. But I've just about got the situation in hand. Just give me another few minutes, okay?"

Stratton slammed the side of the van. "It's all done? We missed it?"

"Jeez, you're a piece of work, Stratton." There was a click as Williams hung up the phone.

"I can't believe it," Stratton said. *Heads are gonna roll.* "All this work…in the desert and shit…and we don't get to shoot anybody? And what the heck's a Code Three anyway?"

"Who cares?" Dawkins said. "Serves you right for screwing that Indian kid out of his money."

Stratton squinted. *He's first.* Dawkins' head on a platter. With a side of collard greens.

He sat down in the van and pouted.

AS CRISPIN MADE THE LAST STITCH, MAX RUSHED OVER AND kissed Tara with a fervor usually reserved for romance novels.

And she loved every second of it. But it wasn't long before his pop cleared his throat.

Max stopped, embarrassed, and turned to face him.

Williams said, "So how we gonna get you two out of here?"

Max's jaw dropped. "You mean it?"

Williams nodded.

With help from Crispin, Tara stood up from the operating table and put her arm around Max. *That is so sweet. His daddy's not arresting him or anything.*

Aloud, she said, "Getting out won't be a problem. There are passages all over this place."

"Well, you better hurry," Williams said. "Any second now, federal agents will be busting down that door."

"Whoa. Wait a minute," Crispin said.

He blinked a couple of times behind his thick glasses and reached into a drawer full of medical gear, then came up with a brown wrapped package. He handed it to Max and Tara. "It's not a present or anything. It's some money Wyatt and Tara left here years ago. And since Wyatt won't be needing it anymore..."

Tara gave Crispin a kiss on the cheek, then watched him blush. "Thank you."

With a tear for her dad, she knelt down next to Wyatt's unconscious form and kissed him goodbye. Maybe she'd visit him in prison. But then she considered it for a moment and thought, *Maybe not.*

Crispin put his hand on Max's shoulder. "In the tunnels you take the first left and then two rights in a row. Then follow that passage to the end and you'll find a trap door leading to my barn. I've got an old Jeep I can trade you for that convertible out front."

"Fair enough," Max said. "Thanks a bunch."

Crispin nodded and exchanged keys with Max.

Max turned to his pop and gave him a big hug. "Thanks, Pop."

His dad squeezed him tight and said, "Stay out of trouble, all right?"

"No problem," Max said, but his sincerity was spoiled by a grin.

Williams rolled his eyes. "And you make sure to read that book I gave you. And stay in touch once in a while."

"I will."

Max gave his pop a wave and Tara blew him a kiss as they headed down the tunnel. *We'll have to visit him after things die down.*

Williams called out after them. "And make sure you tell me when I'm gonna have some grandkids, all right?"

Tara actually felt herself blush as Crispin slammed the tunnel door closed.

PETE FINALLY FOUND THE CATCH THAT RELEASED THE TRAP door. When he climbed out of the tunnel he felt like he was climbing out of his own grave.

He squinted into the sun. *Shit.* He was in the chicken coop area. *But where's the barn?* He looked to his right. Pretty darn far.

Pete sat down and noticed the security camera next to him. When he saw an empty soda can as well, it brought to mind his million-dollar idea—reality advertising.

He played director and placed the soda can in front of the video camera. *Not quite right.* He turned the can on its side, to make it look more natural. *Perfect.*

He grinned. Now, if only a car would crash through the chicken coop and earn him a million bucks, he'd be set. Easy money.

His butt cheeks involuntarily clenched when he heard a familiar growl behind him. Pete turned around and practically wet himself.

The giant wolf-dog crouched there, with a tension that Pete had the misfortune of recognizing. The beast looked the same as Eminem had after the animal juices had got him revved up and raring to go. Pete knew with a grim certainty what the animal wanted.

Pete screamed and reached for his gun as the animal leapt.

STRATTON HEARD THE BONE-CHILLING SCREAM AND JERKED around. He quickly spied the source—a man wrestling with his dog. But if they were just playing around, why had the guy screamed?

Stratton used his massive intellect to come up with a new scenario. One of the bank robbers had escaped the house, but ran smack into a guard dog.

All right! This is gonna be fun after all. He looked around for an agent to take with him, and chose Agent Speedo. From his talks with the rookie, he thought Speedo might be into the gory stuff, too. Straight-laced Dawkins certainly wasn't.

"Dawkins, stay here and wait for word from Williams. Speedo, you come with me."

Stratton ran toward the fracas as fast as his legs could carry him.

WILLIAMS LOOKED AT THE MONITOR IN HORROR. *WHAT ON earth is that creature doing to that poor guy?*

Crispin came and looked over his shoulder. "That's Pete. He was hiding in the tunnel with your kid. I guess he must've skedaddled."

"Ooh!" Williams flinched at the scene before him. "That ain't right. We should probably go out there and help get that beast off him, don't you think?"

Crispin pointed to the monitor and said, "Nah. Pete's in good hands."

Williams spotted Agent Stratton and Speedo approaching. They were partially blocked by the soda can filling the left corner of the screen. "Oh…yeah. I didn't see Stratton back there."

But the agents weren't jumping in to help. They just stood around, whooping and hollering, encouraging the animal.

Just as Williams decided to go out there and help, the beast finished and lay down next to Pete.

A cackling Stratton finally approached the beast—and shot and killed it while it lay there.

Crispin and Williams gasped.

"Tell me you recorded that on video," Williams said.

"Sure did."

Williams looked at Wyatt on the ground, out cold. Figuring he'd given the kids enough time to get out, he grabbed his cell phone to give Dawkins the all clear, but stopped when Crispin interrupted him.

"Wait a second, Sheriff. I've gotta ask you something. You're one of those 'by the book' guys, aren't you?"

Williams grinned. "Yeah, you could definitely say that about me. You can tell, huh?"

In answer, Crispin jabbed him with a hypo and injected a blue liquid into him. Williams immediately began to feel cold and numb. He slid to the ground, still conscious, and ticked off, but unable to move a muscle.

"Sorry about that." Crispin bent down and pulled Williams' gun from his holster. "It's just something to paralyze you. Won't hurt a bit. And it's only temporary."

Crispin flipped the safety off and stared into space.

"But you see…well…the thing is…it's probably better that Wyatt doesn't serve a *short* jail sentence, if you know what I mean. And I hear bank robbers are getting out in seven to ten these days. Overcrowding in the prisons or some such thing."

With a deep breath, Crispin raised the gun and pointed it at Wyatt's head, then closed his eyes and fired.

Williams couldn't move, or even blink—just observe.

Crispin put the gun into Williams hand, then grabbed

Wyatt's gun off the ground and put it in the psycho's limp grasp. "There. nice and cozy."

Crispin reached over and closed Williams' eyes, then lay down on the ground and pretended to be unconscious as Dawkins and the Feds stormed in.

MAX AND TARA CLIMBED INTO THE JEEP. SHE GAVE HIM A NICE slow kiss, then said, "I don't want to scare you off or anything…but I think we should make our partnership something more permanent."

She waited, hoping he'd take it well.

Max said, "Well…we'd need rules of our own. *Different* rules."

When she nodded, Max smiled and turned the key. "Like Aunt May said, 'If Wyatt doesn't scare me off, nothing will.' And when she's right—she's right."

Tara grinned.

Yep. He's a keeper.

EPILOGUE

Max and Tara weren't quite ready to have kids yet, no matter what his pop had suggested. But they were extremely interested in the actual process of baby-making and tried out new techniques as often as they could. After leaving Crispin's place, they looked for a place to crash and heal, a Justice-of-the-Peace, and more banks. Though not necessarily in that order.

Stratton's actions in the bestiality video, and lack thereof, caused his immediate release from the FBI. And after a hard-core animal rights group got hold of the horrendous video, they used it to keep Senator Stratton from being re-elected. Ex-agent Stratton was then permanently cut off from his trust fund. He now lives with a secret militia group in North Dakota.

Sheriff Williams received a commendation for his part in the apprehension of Wyatt Evans. His fifteen minutes of fame enabled him to run for, and win, the office of Mayor of Stoneybrook. He married Officer Lorna and raised a line of purebred Bloodhound dogs that were renowned across the southern states.

Dawkins never received a promotion, but as a reward, was allowed his choice of prime assignments within the Federal Bureau of Investigation. To make things up to Running Bear, Dawkins dipped into his savings and mailed him a check for one thousand dollars, along with newspaper articles detailing Agent Stratton's downfall. Dawkins still hangs out, on occasion, with both Sheriff Williams and Running Bear.

Crispin's secret cemetery behind the chicken coop was never discovered by the authorities. But over time, enough criminals crossed him that the cemetery was filled beyond capacity and Crispin was forced to move his menagerie to a new location in California, where he took a vow that he'd never work on human patients again.

Pete Corelli's infamous star-making videotape was circulated throughout the underground sex world for years. Pete tried to sell the famous soda company featured in the video the rights to air it as a commercial, á la reality advertising, but the conglomerate politely declined. As it was, with repeated viewings, the soda company received millions of dollars worth of free publicity.

Pete was caught with stolen cash about his person and a fake snake tattoo on his forearm. He tried to rat out Max and Tara, using Max's own audiotapes as evidence. But since the two were impossible to find, and both Williams and Crispin proved uncooperative, the evidence was thrown out—and Pete had a hard time convincing anyone that *he* wasn't the one robbing banks with Wyatt for all these years. As a bonus, the authorities also fingered Pete for robbing the convenience stores with an unknown female accomplice. A jury agreed—Pete was found guilty of just about everything. Though convicted on several counts, he served only seven years in prison before being released due to serious overcrowding in the prison system.

While in the lock-up, he used his time wisely and transcribed Max's tapes, including a complete listing of the *47 Rules.* After his release from prison, he published a book under the title: *A Dumb-ass's Guide to Bank Robbery.* It was an international best-seller.

THE END

Troy Cook has worked on more than 80 feature films, writing and directing his first at age 24. Shooting films in exotic locations led to brushes with the Russian Mafia, money launderers, and murderers. After surviving an attempted coup, riots, and violent demonstrations, he's decided it's safer to write novels.

You can visit Troy at www.troycook.net